I Know This of Myself

LINA HOLLOWAY

LEAFLESS PRESS

DEDICATION

For my parents, who have always told me I can do anything I want in this life. I feel so blessed to have you as parents. I try to live my life in a way to make you both proud of me. I hope I have succeeded.

CONTENTS

ACKNOWLEDGMENTS

This first person I have to thank is my friend and college roommate, Stephanie, who has been involved in this journey every step of the way. She has spent endless hours reading drafts of this book (along with many others that haven't made it this far) and giving me constant, honest feedback and encouragement. This book would have never made it this far without her pushing me and supporting me.

Sasha, my editor and friend, who gave me a deadline and made sure I stuck to it. Without the deadline, this book might have ended up in the half finished book graveyard my computer houses. I also have to thank her for working on this book during her vacation to ensure my schedule was not affected. For your undying dedication to this book, I thank you.

I have to thank my husband who endured being ignored throughout the process of writing this book. He complained a lot, distracted me a lot, but understood when I needed to work on it the most.

A big thank you to my entire family (that includes you, Niki) who have always given me support and had the confidence that I could do anything – even write a book.

Look for the next book by Lina Holloway
Coming 2016

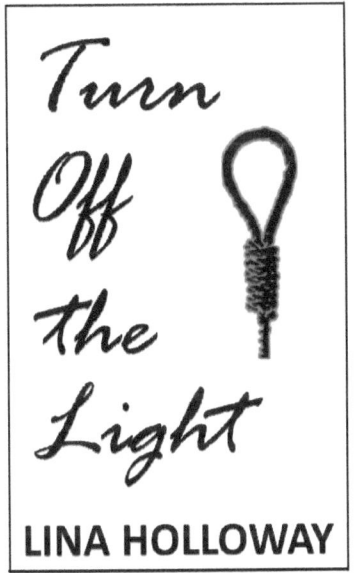

i

1 NIA NOW

I sit staring out the window at the rustling leaves of the willow tree in my back yard. The leaves have begun turning yellow with the dropping autumn temperatures. The long limbs sway in the wind having a hypnotic effect on me. I am not sure how long I have been sitting here when my sister loudly enters the house.

"Nia! Good morning. What a beautiful day today. Ahh, I am loving this weather. We should take a walk to the lake after you have your coffee. Here it is," she says in her cheerful morning voice as she sets it down next to my overflowing ashtray. I see her try to cover the look of disgust on her face when I glance in her direction. I always think about emptying it, but I know she will do it for me every morning so the effort seems unjustified.

"I had them put in two sugars. The raw kind. That's how you like it, right? Well if you need extra just let me know and I will grab some out of the kitchen."

At this point she is yelling from the kitchen. I take a

sip of my coffee. Perfect. It always is. Noie is nothing if not a perfectionist and she accepts nothing but perfection from the baristas when getting my coffee every morning. She knows it is one of the only things I look forward to each day and she would never allow it to be wrong.

I hear muted clanking. Right now she is probably straightening the silverware. It's one of her nervous ticks she actually enjoys indulging. I make a trip into the kitchen every day after she leaves and cause havoc in the silverware drawer. It's how I let her know I'm still here and I love her. I'm sure there are better ways, ways she would appreciate more but it's all I can give right now.

"Nia, what did you eat for dinner last night? There are no dishes in here. Did you order out? Have you tried the new Italian place on South 5th Street? Delicious. The eggplant parm is to die for." She makes an exaggerated moaning sound as if just the thought of breaded eggplant gives her a feeling of ecstasy.

I didn't eat last night. I usually don't. It's not on purpose, I just seem to lose track of time. When the sun sets, I look at the stars until I fall asleep in my chair most nights.

"Maybe we should go there for lunch. Or if you like the idea of going to the lake, I could get take out and we could have a picnic. It's not too cold yet. I am sure a heavy sweater would be all we need. We can buy a loaf of bread for the ducks. Do you remember when we would sit down there with a bottle of wine feeding the ducks until sunset?" She laughs and lets it trail off. Guilt takes a hold of me. I know she longs for the old version of me back. I know I do.

I don't know how she does it. She barely even takes a

breath when she has these morning conversations at me. Eventually she will settle down in the chair next to me in silence. I know she does it in hopes one day I will fill the void. I might…one day. I'm just not ready yet. I haven't learned the language needed to talk about what happened.

I grab my lighter and light another cigarette. The smoke swirls through the beams of light flooding the window. I watch the cigarette smoke like I watched clouds as a child, picking out familiar shapes as it moves towards the ceiling before dissipating.

I exhale and close my eyes as Noie sits down. Sixty minutes. The amount of time she sits is so precise, I have wondered if she sets a vibrating timer on her phone before sitting.

Her breaths have a calming steady rhythm. Mine are always staggered as I take long drags from my cigarette. Fifty-nine minutes. Counting down the minutes, I am thankful for the effort she puts in to creating some stability in my world which has completely fallen apart.

As the older sister, she has always felt some responsibility in taking care of me. We grew up in an upper middle class home with two loving parents who worked long hours at their corporate jobs to ensure we had everything they didn't have growing up. Their absence gave Noie a mom complex over me. As a teenager, I hated it. She was always there as my voice of reason when I wanted to run off with people she felt were a bad influence. She always checked in with my teachers to make sure my grades were on track. It was suffocating.

Now, at twenty-nine, I couldn't be more thankful for her care taking. She owns an early learning center which allows her to fulfill her need of looking after and guiding others. The last six months with me have just been a bonus for her, I guess. Forty-six minutes.

My eyes fly open when she clears her throat and begins fidgeting with her wedding ring, a tell-tell sign she is uncomfortable about something she is about to say. I brace myself knowing it must be important if she is going to interrupt our quiet hour.

"So, Thanksgiving will be here next month and Jett wants to go to Tennessee to visit his family. His father has been sick and we haven't been there for Thanksgiving in three years. I was thinking you might really enjoy coming with us. Remember last time you came and you fell in love with the little deli on Main Street?"

I jerk my head towards her, my eyes brimming with tears and she pauses. I wasn't alone when I discovered the deli and she realizes she is invoking memories I don't want to relive right now. I toss my cigarette, that has long since burned out, into the ashtray and grab another one. After a few drags I relax back in my chair and she continues.

"It will just be for a few days and the kids would love to have their Auntie Nia there."

Low blow using the kids. I hate disappointing them, but I also don't want them seeing this shell. They wouldn't understand. I hope they never understand how empty I feel.

"There is no pressure. You can use the car we rent to drive into town and explore during the day. You will have your own room to stay in and no one will bother you." She pauses and studies my profile. Looking for any sign I might answer. Twenty-nine minutes.

I know she is just afraid to not be able to check on me every day. Jett loves me, but I doubt he is very excited about bringing me to his family's house. He probably suggested they go there so he and the kids could get the full attention of Noie for a few days. I wasn't making her come here every day. I also know Noie wouldn't have it any other way, so it is my fault, I guess. He has every right to blame me.

One minute left. "Well just think about it," she says and stands.

"I am going to the school to check on things and answer emails. I should be back about eleven with lunch." Her voice sounds defeated and I hear a frustrated sigh as she closes the front door. Just then I spot a clown's hat in the smoke.

2 NIA THEN

I spread my soft hand-me-down quilt across the grass under my favorite tree on campus. As I lay down and close my eyes, I bask in the warmth of the sun on my face. This has become my pre-study ritual when the weather is nice. Trying to study in the freshman dorms is like trying to sleep at a rock concert. My roommate, Sarah, is nice and tries to be accommodating to my quieter than the average college freshman lifestyle. She joined a sorority and since freshman don't live in the house, our room has become the Delta Zeta freshman hangout. The girls are really nice and always try to include me, but wind, resettling leaves and the soft chirp of birds is where I find my focus. Spring midterms are next week and I am determined to maintain the A average I have in my classes this semester. That makes this tree of mine, Camp Nia for the next seven days.

I feel movement next to me and smile. Sam likes to sneak up on me when I am out here. Sam and I met during freshman orientation, kind of. Our eyes met multiple times where we seemed to have silent conversations about the people around us. Then on my first day, in my first college class, I see Sam drumming his pen against his notebook towards the back of the class and decided to take the seat next to him. We were instant friends after that.

"This is nice," a voice, not belonging to Sam, says next to me. I sit straight up and turn to the guy lying next to me with his hands behind his head, completely relaxed, as if this is Camp Stranger and I am the intruder.

"Excuse me, can I help you?" I ask in a tone filled with shock and disapproval.

"No, not at all. I am perfect," he says as he opens his pale green eyes and stares straight into mine. The corners of his mouth turn up. He is obviously amused by my shock at his invasion. Between his smirk, confidence, and the humor dancing in his eyes, I feel my body relax.

"Since I wasn't clear, let me restate my question. Excuse me, stranger, why the hell are you laying on my blanket and what can I help you with so you can be on your way before I phone campus police?" My tone has taken on an air of sarcasm, but phoning the police was still an option. I lift my phone, find the campus police number which is programed in my contacts and turn the phone towards him as a warning.

He chuckles as he rolls on his side and props his head up and says, "Relax and put the phone down. I don't mean you any harm" in a drawn out tone someone might use with a crazy person. I see the muscles flex in the arm propping up his head of shaggy brown hair. I am a little annoyed at how attractive he is.

With my finger hovering over the call button, I begin

counting down. When I get to three, he interrupts me.

"Ok, listen. I walk past here on my way to grab lunch most days. I have seen you out here a lot and you always look peaceful and lost on your own little quilted island. I, on the other hand, am usually rushing around and thinking about the five hundred things I have put off and need to get done. I decided to give your island a try. Maybe you have all the answers to the universe over here and are desperately looking for someone to share them with." His monolog ends and he looks at me questioningly.

I take a loud breath, roll my eyes and sit the phone down next to me. "Okay, you have my attention and yes, I do have all the answers to life's big questions, but those are not something I share with someone I just met and who hasn't even told me his name."

"Ian, my name is Ian," he says and formally sticks the hand not propping his head up towards me.

I take his hand and reply, "Well Ian, it is interesting to meet you. I am Nia."

"Well Nia, since we have that out of the way. I am going to lay back down. I was having a really good time before you started threatening me with the police. You can carry on with what you were doing and maybe I can get some answers over lunch when you are finished. That is as long as you can show me a little more civility than you have displayed so far." He doesn't wait for a response as he rolls onto his back, repositioning his hands behind his head and closing his eyes.

3 IAN THEN

I have been watching her since last semester sitting under the tree. At first, it was just a passing glance. Not knowing her name, I named her Snow White in my head. She has jet black hair and fair skin which looks almost unnatural together. I figure she dyes it. Her bangs always sweep her eyelids as if they are overdue for a cut, but they are always that length so I guess it is the look she is going for.

The last few weeks, I decided to bring my lunch and eat at a bench not far from her tree. I don't know why. I guess I just got more curious about her. A few times I have seen this guy, Sam, who I've played a few pick-up basketball games with around campus join her. They always seem to have a fun banter and I would find myself holding my breath when they would get too close. I realized I was afraid they were going to kiss, but they never did. I have also been privy to his interactions with some of the groupies who hang around the jock types and I don't think he is looking to be attached to any one person.

There is also a petite pixie-like girl with long wavy blond hair who bounces up to her now and then for a quick chat. I have seen her with some of the Delta Zetas at a few of the fraternity parties I have been dragged to this year. I've never caught her name.

I keep trying to figure out a way to run into her or be introduced through someone, but I just can't imagine asking around if anyone knew the girl who looked like Snow White. I can hear the endless supply of dwarf jokes from my friends. I think I'll pass.

I decided today is the day. Not only because I really want to meet her, but I am starting to feel like a stalker and don't want that to end up being her first impression of me.

I'm going to walk over and meet her with two goals in mind: don't chicken out and make her smile. At this point, I don't even care if I find out her name. I kind of like calling her Snow White.

4 NIA DIARY

Dear Diary,

I met a guy at school today. His introduction was strange but in a good way. Almost refreshing. He laid next to me for two hours while I studied without saying a word. It felt natural. I have never felt this at ease with someone I didn't know. I never really feel this at ease with people I do know.

I first came to the University of Louisville because my sister was here, but I never felt a connection to this school. Noie has her boyfriend, Jett, who she spends all of her time with and with them being ahead of me, they will be out of here two years before me. Today is the first time I have considered staying after she graduated. I had planned to transfer somewhere out east or west. Anywhere except Middle America. I know it seems premature and irrational, but I might have found the connection that makes me want to stay.

We went for lunch when I was finished studying. He kept the conversation going for the most part and I just sat across from him studying his face. The corners of his eyes crinkled when he laughed and a dimple on his right cheek would appear. In the moments of silence, he would look at me with his pale green eyes holding an intensity which almost took my breath away. I couldn't look away.

This is starting to feel like a gushing entry, bordering on too embarrassing to even tell you, but I tell you everything. I won't say it was love at first sight or any other cliché thing like that, but I will say I felt a spark in my chest. It feels almost like a craving. I crave the way it felt to just be with him and I crave the way he looks at me.

Maybe I go to sleep tonight and this entry will be the only thing left of him. We didn't exchange numbers or make plans to hang out again. We simply had an amazing few hours with each other and said we would see each other around. I am going to make sure we do.

5 NIA NOW

The cat is back again. He is scampering around the base of the willow tree swatting at leaves as they fall to the ground. His orange and brown fur seems fitting for the fall scenery. I wonder if he is a stray.

I know most of my neighbors and have been in almost all of their homes, but I have never seen this fall colored cat. This is the type of neighborhood which relishes in block parties and holiday gatherings. They even have an official greeting committee who welcomes new people to the neighborhood. There was constant pressure on me to join since I worked from home, but it felt too June Cleaver-ish for me.

When everything happened, a neighbor would come by every day with a casserole or some other obligatory thing neighbors are supposed to bring. It took them about three weeks to stop. I don't know if it was because I never answered the door or if Noie told them to give me time. I don't really care why they stopped, I am just glad the doorbell stopped ringing.

The cat loses interest in the tree and begins to slowly stalk his way toward my back window. I stub out my cigarette and lower myself to the floor. I match my movements to his hoping I will not scare him away. When I reach the window, I place my hand on the glass and flutter my fingers. I catch his attention. He walks towards me and swats playfully at my hand.

Up close, I can see the color of his eyes. They are a pale green. *His* green. I feel the urge to be closer and feel the texture of his fur. Without making any sudden movements, I rise and tip toe towards the back door. Quietly I unlock the dead bolt and slowly open the door. He pauses and appears to stiffen. I close the door and sit down with my legs folded hoping to spark his interest, hoping he will come to me. I stare at his eyes, silently pleading with him to come closer. I don't know how long this goes on when his head snaps up and he runs back towards the tree.

"Nia! Nia! Nia!" my sister shrieks from inside the house.

I stand and open the door. As soon as I step inside, Noie plows into me and wraps her arms around my neck. I stand there completely still feeling invaded. My skin is screaming for her to stop touching me, but the sound never escapes my mouth. When I don't return the embrace, she drops her arms and steps back wiping tears from her eyes.

"Where were you? What were you doing? You scared me half to death. When you were not in your chair, I checked the bedroom, bathroom and," she pauses before continuing, "the closet."

I turned from her and walked back to the window. I

scanned the backyard hoping he was still there. Beneath the tree he lays with his front paw to his mouth, meticulously cleaning it.

Noie comes up beside me to see what I am looking at. She spots him and sighs.

"Is that what you were doing outside, playing with the cat? Does he belong to a neighbor?" she asks softly.

I shrug my shoulders and sit back down in my chair to light a cigarette and take a drink of my coffee which always appears with my sister.

"Dr. Gillis will be here in a little bit. I will be heading to the school after he arrives. I brought you some leftovers from the dinner I made last night because I will not be able to make it back for lunch. I have appointments with a few families to see the school. I will try to stop by before I have to pick up the girls from school. I don't know if I will have time. You can always call or text if you need something," she says as she grabs my ashtray to empty it.

She seems on edge. I hope it is just from her over reaction when I wasn't in my normal spot and not something else going on she will surely keep from me. Too afraid it will upset me as if there is another level of sadness I could reach.

I am glad Dr. Gillis is coming today. I do talk to him. He never has pity in his eyes and he never tries to force me into talking about things I am not ready to talk about. I don't say much but I say enough. I mainly listen but I need the look he gives me. It's a look which says, "You are strong. You are worth it."

I always wonder how he knows I question if I am worth it. By all accounts, I am crazy now, so maybe I am just seeing what I want to see in his eyes. He could just be staring and counting the minutes, like I do with Noie.

"Gertie comes today too. I wrote out a check to her and left it on the counter. You need to sign it. Please remember to sign it as soon as you get the chance," she says with a slightly insulting tone I am not used to hearing from her.

"I wish you would take off that sweatshirt and put it in the laundry hamper before Gertie gets here so it gets cleaned. I know you have other sweatshirts so there is no reason for you to have the same one on for two weeks."

Her short tone confirms there is something wrong with her. I hope her and Jett are not fighting about the Thanksgiving trip. I should just tell her I am not going and put an end to it, but she would try to change my mind. I don't feel like listening to her beg me right now.

She sits down next to me and our quiet hour seems to fly by faster than normal. The distraction of the cat still exploring the backyard is probably why.

The doorbell chimes and Noie jumps up, kisses my hair and runs towards the door.

"Hello, Dr. Gillis," she sings as she opens the door for him. "Nia is at the back window. I put on a pot of coffee in case you want any. Sugar and cream is on the counter. I won't be back today, but Gertie will be here later. Look at me going on and on. I should get out of your way. Love you, Nia," she exclaims before rushing out the front door and closing it a little too loudly behind her.

"Good morning, Nia," Dr. Gillis says as he walks into the room. "I am going to make myself a cup of coffee. Can I get you anything?"

I grab a cigarette and light it as I shake my head.

"Very well. I will be back shortly."

I exhale my smoke making circles as I relax. His soft steady voice is a welcome change from the shortness Noie gave me all morning. I am poking my finger through a smoke ring when Dr. Gillis walks back in and sits down.

"I spoke with your sister yesterday. She told me she would like you to go with her to Tennessee this Thanksgiving. Do you want to talk about the possibility of going there?"

I shrug and look at him so he knows he has my attention.

"Have you thought about it?"

I nod my head yes.

"Have you made a decision about going?"

I shake my head no and look down. I am sure he is hoping, as much as Noie is, I decide to go. I don't want to see a look of disappointment if it is there.

"How does the idea of going make you feel?"

I look back out the window and take a few inhales of my cigarette before responding.

"Lonely, I guess."

"Lonely. Interesting. Most of your days are spent alone in this house, but spending the holiday with family feels lonely. Would you like to explore that feeling?" He asks and takes a sip of his coffee while waiting for my answer. He blows on the coffee and steam rises up, slightly fogging his glasses.

I stub out my cigarette and pull my legs up onto the chair. Grabbing the throw blanket from the back of my chair, I straighten it over my lap. Rubbing my hands over the plush brown fabric is comforting.

"I guess I can imagine everyone chatting happily and

then I see myself blank and quiet. The contrast is so harsh, it makes me feel out of place and alone because I don't fit into that picture."

He sits quietly for a minute until he is sure I have nothing more to add before speaking again.

"I understand and it is a valid feeling, but your sister told me you will have a private area in case you need to step away from everyone. Maybe you can stay in that room but still be close enough you could join in if you feel like you can do so without the feeling of being out of place. I want you to think on that. Think about the options available which do not include being in the middle of all of the festivities the entire time and we will discuss it again later in the week."

"Okay," I whisper.

"How about work? Have you given any thought to starting up a small class or taking on any private lessons?" He asks. This was always a question he asked.

I have a basement studio where I used to teach ballet classes but most of my time was spent doing private lessons for dancers at the local college. They attended classes at school but I would work with them one on one to help perfect their technique. I also worked with a lot of young girls whose mothers have dreams of them becoming prima ballerinas. I have always loved dancing and it never really felt like work. I would lose myself in a session with someone and frequently an hour session would turn into two hours before either of us realized it.

When I didn't respond, he continued, "Have you spoken to anyone at the practice? I am sure they would appreciate your help as well."

I was pre-law in college with a minor in dance. I

decided not to go to law school when the opportunity for teaching dance came up, but I did some part-time paralegal work for *his* and Jett's practice when it was needed. I haven't had contact with anyone in the office for months. I know Jett keeps them up to date on my status. *He* and Jett opened the practice together after law school.

I just shook my head no and looked back out the window to search for the cat.

6 NIA THEN

"Nia, you have to go with us," Sarah pleads excitedly. "It will be so much fun, I promise. This is the last big party before spring break because everyone will be leaving town after their exams are over this week. Please, please, please come with us." She gave me her best attempt at puppy dog eyes which was easy with her round brown eyes.

"Yes, Nia, you have to go," Sarah's Delta Zeta sister, Hadley, chimes in.

At this point they each have ahold of one of my hands, jumping up and down with excitement.

"Okay, okay," I concede. "Now let go before you pull my arms off."

Shrieks of excitement fill the room as they run to the closet to pick me out something to wear. That was the rule when going out with them. They always get to choose what I wear and pretend I am their life-size Barbie for the night. I don't really mind. They are fun and if I pick out my clothes, it would probably be a university sweatshirt and tennis shoes.

"So, where are we going exactly?" I ask cautiously.

"To one of the frat houses. I don't remember which one. We are meeting some of the other girls downstairs in thirty minutes, so hurry. They have all the details" Sarah says as she throws a black dress at me. "Hurry and put it on so we can do your make-up. Here take these," she says raising a pair of black strappy sandals.

I raise my hands and yell, "Don't throw those! It might ruin my look if you give me a black eye." She laughs and tosses them to the floor and grabs for my make-up bag.

I quickly strip down and pull on the dress, relieved. It is one of my favorites. It has a high collar in front with three quarter length sleeves and a hem which falls to my knees. Very simple except for one detail setting it apart, the back. It dips down into a dramatic V revealing my toned back.

In twenty-five minutes, Sarah is putting the finishing touches on my make-up. "Perfect," she exclaims, very happy with herself. "Now let's go so they don't leave without us."

We arrive in front of a house sporting letters from the Greek alphabet I can't place at the moment. The noise from the house can be easily heard from the street. I take a long calming breath and think to myself sarcastically, "Yay! Frat guys and beer pong."

Walking in, we are greeted with blaring music in a room full of tipsy girls and guys. Sam and Blake walk over to us and offer to get us a drink. Sam whistles and puts his arm around me before kissing me on the cheek.

"Looking good, Nia."

"Be careful, what are all of your groupies going to think if you are hanging all over me?"

"Please, everyone knows you're my number one," he says as he winks. "What can I get you to drink?" He throws his free hand up like a stop sign and says, "If you say water, I am going to pick you up and make you do a keg stand in that dress."

"Juice?" I say with an innocent smile.

"Fine, I will get you juice but it will be spiked!" he says as he walks to the make shift bar set up at the side of the room.

"Nia, we are going to go out back with Blake. Do you want to come?" Sarah asks.

"No, I'll wait for Sam. He is grabbing me a drink. We'll come find you in a bit."

"Okay," she smiles and Blake picks her up over his shoulder and makes his way to the back of the house. I can hear Sarah laughing and begging to be put down as they disappear.

"Here you go, love," Sam says as he hands me my drink. It looks like orange juice but I am guessing it also has vodka in it.

"Thanks. Who is Mrs. Lucky tonight?"

"I haven't found the right one yet, but I have a few candidates," he says and swings his head towards the corner of the room near the bar. I see two girls with their best come-hither looks staring at Sam. "After seeing you in this dress, I might just have to move you to the top of the list."

"Oh, stop it! I wouldn't want to ruin you for all other women."

"I guess you are right," he says with a grin. "Let's

head out back. We wouldn't want to miss the exciting beer pong game."

"I wouldn't miss it for the world." He wraps his arm back around my waist and leads me out back.

Hadley has just stepped up for her turn at beer pong against one of the frat guys. That doesn't look like a good idea. Luckily Sam and Blake always keep us in their sight at these parties. We have kind of become their de-facto little sisters, although I suspect Sarah and Blake will be dating before the year is out. They are just such good friends. I think they are both scared to make the first move. Out of the corner of my eye, I spot Ian talking to a few guys, but his gaze is not moving from me. I wave him over. He shakes his head and motions me to come to him. I shrug my shoulders and look back towards Hadley as she begins drinking a plastic cup of beer.

"Nia, do you know that guy?" Sam asks and tilts his head in Ian's direction.

"Yes, I met him the other day when I was studying at my tree. Why? Do you know him?"

"Yeah, I've seen him around. His name is Ian. He just hasn't taken his eyes off of you. Do you want me to tell him to back off?"

"No," I say a little too quickly to be nonchalant.

"Ooh, Nia and Ian sitting in a tree."

"Sam, don't be so juvenile. He is a nice guy."

"Ok, let me help," and before I can stop him, he yells, "Hey Ian, come over here."

He excuses himself from the guys he is talking to and slowly makes his way towards us. Sam has the biggest grin I have ever seen on his face and it is taking all my self-control not to punch him in it. I can feel the heat rising up my face and in this moment I wish I could disappear.

"Hey, Ian. How's it been, bro?" Sam asks as Ian nears us.

"Good, it's been good," he says without taking his eyes off of me.

"Well I need to go defend Hadley's honor over there. Can you keep Nia company while I am gone?"

"No problem."

Sam walks over towards Hadley and I hear him say, "Back away from the table and let me show you how it's done."

"So, you and Sam?" Ian asks.

"Me and Sam? No." I say emphatically. "He is like my best friend."

"I didn't realize you were the frat party type."

"Frat party type? You say it like an insult when you are at a frat party too." I don't like the implications he is making with his statement. I turn away from him and take a drink.

"I'm sorry. I didn't mean to suggest anything. I was just surprised to see you here. That was all. If I offended you, I'm sorry." He says quickly. His sincere backtracking is kind of cute.

I look at him and smile. "It's fine. This isn't really my scene but my roommate, Sarah, is hard to say no to when she really wants to get her way."

"I guess I owe Sarah a thank you." He looks at my half empty glass and asks, "Do you want to grab another drink and find a place out front to talk?"

I keep my eyes fixed on his for a minute without answering then look back to Sam. "Let me tell Sam where we are going. He will freak if I just disappear. Give me a minute."

I walk over to Sam, already regretting I am about to tell him I am stepping away with Ian. I can hear the constant ribbing I am going to endure for the next week.

I tap on his shoulder. "Hey, Sam."

He turns to me and puts on a frownie face. "Ah, did you already manage to send Ian running for the hills?"

"No! Actually we are going to grab a drink and find a place, a little quieter, out front to talk. I just wanted you to know where I will be."

"Do you need protection?" He asks with a laugh.

"Sam, stop. You know me better than that. Keep an eye on our girls." I say and kiss him on the cheek before turning back to Ian.

"Always, love." Sam calls out to me as I walk away.

Ian and I make our way to the bar and then out front. There is an empty tree swing in the yard of the next house over. I point at it and look at Ian questioningly. He nods.

As we walk in silence, I feel the butterflies fluttering around my stomach which lead to the heat rising up my face. Just perfect. Why is he having this effect on me?

When we reach the swing, he dusts off the double seat before I sit down. He sits down next to me and slowly reaches for my hand.

7 IAN THEN

My mouth almost fell open when I saw her walk through the door. She looked amazing. The black dress clung to her body perfectly. She nervously brushed her hair behind her ear and I caught a glimpse of her clear blue eyes that were accentuated by the black eye liner. As she turns, I see the cut of the back of her dress. It plunges down to the small of her back to put her toned back on perfect display. Every cell in my body wanted to run over to her, throw my arms around her and claim her as mine. Before I did anything stupid, Sam walked over to her and put his arm around her waist and kissed her on the cheek. I felt my stomach sink and decided I needed to head out back before I went and smacked his hand off of her.

I found a few of my friends out there and moved in on their conversation. I don't know what they are talking about. My mind is still inside with Nia. I am staring at the door when her roommate came out tossed over Blake's shoulder. The other blonde girl who came with them was close behind, but Sam and Nia didn't come out with them.

I was about to walk in and look for her when she came through the door with Sam. His arm still around her waist. I had no right to have a problem with the way he held on to her, but I didn't like seeing someone else touch her.

I couldn't look away from her. She was mesmerizing. I was mentally willing her to look my way. Finally she looked my way and waved for me to come over there, but my feet were planted firmly. I didn't want to walk over there until his hands were off of her. I motioned for her to come to me hoping to get her out of his grasp. When she just shrugged like it was my loss and then looked away, I felt my temperature rising.

I had to keep reminding myself to keep cool. I couldn't explain why I was having such a visceral reaction to seeing her with him.

I saw Sam look over at me and I could only imagine how creepy my staring was looking, but I couldn't stop it. Next thing I know, Sam is calling me over.

8 NIA DIARY

Dear Diary,

I saw Ian again last night. I have never been so thankful Sarah dragged me out. We sat on a swing for hours just talking and looking at the stars. I found out he is from Texas. Some small town outside of Austin. He talked about his home town in a way that made Texas seem enchanting. That was surprising.

He held my hand and traced the lines on my palm. I never wanted him to let go. We sat there as everyone began filtering out of the party. Sam, Blake and the girls came out around one a.m. and found us. Sam wanted to make sure we made it back to the dorm in one piece and my heart sank as I stood up to walk back with them. But Ian offered to walk with us! I was so happy I could have cried. Is that stupid? It probably is. Oh well, can't I get stupid over a boy?

Sam is such a good friend, even if he can be obnoxious at times. He must have read the dread all over my face as we approached the dorm. The girls wanted to go straight upstairs and crawl into bed. I think beer pong took its toll on them. Sam and Blake were going to grab something to eat and he whispered in my ear to hang out with Ian a little longer and he would come back after eating and make sure I got inside okay.

He is so funny how he always worries about me. When Noie worried about me, I always felt angry and annoyed, but on Sam, it was endearing. He made me promise to stay outside until he got back so he could see me walk in the door.

Then I did something I am really regretting right now. I invited Ian to my performance at the end of the semester. Why did I do that? I never ask anyone to come watch me. It feels too vulnerable. I just couldn't let him walk away without knowing I would see him again and it just spewed out of my mouth. He said he wouldn't miss it! Wouldn't miss it! It was such a sure answer. How am I going to get out of this?

9 NIA NOW

My eyes flutter open when I feel Noie brushing the hair away from the side of my face the way our mother did when we were little girls. I was still in bed. I look at the clock and see it is already eight in the morning. I usually can't sleep after the sun rises, so this surprises me.

"Your coffee is on the table next to your chair. Do you want me to bring it in here?" she asks in a whisper.

I shake my head no and pull the covers back to get out of bed and walk straight to the bathroom. Looking in the mirror, I feel panic rising in my chest. That isn't me. That isn't me. Who is that? I get closer to the mirror and look straight into the blue eyes. They are the right color, but nothing feels like me. I move and see the person making the same movements. What is happening? I begin to shake my head and tears fill my eyes.

The sobs grow louder and Noie runs to me asking, "What is wrong? What happened? Calm down Nia. It's ok. I'm here with you, just calm down."

I can't stop. I hear the screams escape my mouth.

They are piercing. Is that really me? What happened? Why is this happening? Who does that face belong to?

I feel Noie drop her arms from me and she disappears. Help me. Help me.

She's back. "Nia, calm down and take these pills. Please just stop shaking your head and take the pills. Please Nia, I don't want to have to give you a shot," Noie pleads.

I can still hear the screams. I cover my ears. Why won't the screaming stop? Please make it stop. Then I feel it. Noie pokes the needle into my arm. Within seconds everything is quiet.

"Ok, honey. It's ok. Let me get you to your chair. I brought you coffee with the two sugars the way you like it."

She guides me to my chair and sits me down. I try to pull my legs up, but I don't have the strength. She grabs the throw blanket off the back of the chair and places it around me and gently rubs my back until all of the shaking subsides. She quickly empties my ashtray and brings it back. She pulls a cigarette out of my pack and lights it for me. I reach for it and take a long drag.

"Can I get you anything else? Is there anything I can do for you? Nia, please talk to me. I don't know what to do for you if you don't talk to me."

The sadness in her voice is overwhelming. I just want her to be quiet. As if hearing my thoughts, she silently sits in the chair next to me.

I must have fallen asleep because I suddenly hear Dr. Gillis' voice coming from the kitchen along with Noie's voice and I don't remember hearing him come in. I sit up a little bit to hear what they are talking about. As I sit up, I spot the cat near the window and he is eating from a bowl. Did Noie put that out for him?

"I just don't know what to do anymore. I have been coming here every day for almost six months and she doesn't say a word to me. I barely ever see any sign of her eating other than lunch or a small breakfast if I take something to her after she finishes her coffee. She just stares out that damn window. I have seen her go two weeks at a time without changing clothes. I am trying so hard to be here for her, but she is just gone and I am at a loss. The other day I thought about not coming over here anymore because I was just so angry, but then she has this episode today and all I think about is what would have happened if I wasn't here. What do I do?" Noie asks Dr. Gillis exasperated.

"Noie, I know she is thankful you come here and in many ways she needs you, but you have to find some boundaries for yourself. You have a family at home who needs you too. Plus, you have to take care of yourself or you are no good to anyone. I agree Nia needs to talk about what happened, but she does not have to and trying to force her would be counterproductive in my opinion, but you could push for other things. Figure out a reasonable request you can ask of her and draw a line in the sand. Nia has the resources to pay for Gertie to come here every day, if necessary. Maybe you need to take a step back and schedule Gertie to be here more. I think you should have had her coming a few days a week when I first suggested it to you months ago," Dr. Gillis advises her and I hear him sigh.

"Okay, you are right. I will call Gertie and see how many days she is available to come here and I will take a step back and focus more on myself, my girls, and Jett. I know it would help our relationship a lot."

"It is settled then. Let's go see if we can wake her and I will stay while we discuss the new plan. She is going to be okay," he reassures Noie.

I hear them walking this way and close my eyes. I don't want them to know I was listening.

Noie places her hand on my shoulder. "Nia, honey, can you wake up?"

I open my eyes and look from her to Dr. Gillis.

"We need to talk about a few things," Noie says as she sits in the chair next to me. Dr. Gillis pulls a chair from the kitchen and puts it in front of the window before taking a seat. He has blocked my view of the cat. I wish he would move.

Dr. Gillis starts talking. "Nia, how are you feeling?"

I shrug.

"Good. Noie and I were talking about boundaries. Noie is going to set some boundaries for herself to ensure she is taken care of. She has some things to say to you. We do not want you upset or to aggravate whatever caused your episode this morning, but we need you to listen. Go ahead Noie."

"Nia, I love you more than I could ever put into words, but I don't think I am doing you any justice by coming here every day. You have not said a word to me in six months. I am going to take a step back and have Gertie come more. I will still come by a few days a week, but I need something from you. I need you to leave the house with me. It can be lunch, the store, a walk or the park, anything, but I need that from you."

I shrug and look away. Noie puts her face into her

33

hands and I can tell she is trying to stifle her tears.

Dr. Gillis places his hand on Noie's shoulder to soothe her. She wipes her face and looks at him.

"I'm ok," Noie says.

"Nia, I am going to be on my way. Call me if you need anything. Try to relax and we will talk about what happened today during our session this week. Bye, now."

He gives a slight wave and heads out the door.

"Well, ok. I made a pot of coffee. I will make you a cup in just a minute, but I wanted to tell you some good news first. At least I think it is good news. I asked your neighbors about the cat. He doesn't belong to anyone. People have seen him around and they all think he is a stray. So I went and got a litter box, food, toys and a few other things. I put a bowl of food outside so he can get comfortable with the house. I just thought we could take care of him and maybe at some point you would want him in the house. I think you should give him a name. He seems very friendly. I made an appointment for him at the vet for later this week. I will get him all fixed up. I think he will be good for you and vice versa. You have to let someone or something in. I am going to go into work for a little bit. I will call Gertie and get her set up to come here more days. I will let you know the schedule. I should have lunch here around one or two. Sorry so late but I have a few things I need to take care of. Also, Sam called earlier. He said you haven't called in a while." She trails off and then gets up and kisses me on the forehead before taking the chair Dr. Gillis was using back to the dining room.

As she walks back past me, she places her hand on my shoulder. I grab her hand and she looks at me shocked. I look into her eyes and say, "Thank you."

"You're welcome," she replies with tears in her eyes.

10 NIA THEN

I didn't get to see Sarah before she left for spring break. Her last mid-term was earlier in the day and she had to rush off to catch her flight. She and Hadley are going to Florida for the week. They tried to get me to come, but I like the idea of having almost the entire campus to myself. Plus, Noie and my parents wanted me to come home for the break and they would feel shifted if I said no to them and then went to Florida.

As I am about to reach the step of my dorm, I hear Noie calling my name. I roll my eyes and turn in her direction. I see her and Jett walking towards me.

"Hey sis, what's up?" I question even though I am sure this is going to be a lecture or a final plea for me to go home with her.

"Are you sure you want to stay here for the break? This place will be a ghost town and you will miss out on all the road tripping games," she tries to entice me with as she clasps her hands together and starts whining, "Please, please, please come with us."

"You almost got me with road tripping games, but the answer is still no. I am looking forward to having some quiet time. Don't you remember living in the dorms during your freshman year? Was there ever peace and quiet?" I question.

"Well you need to be careful then. There will not be people everywhere who can look out for you. Don't walk around alone after dark. Make sure to always have your phone on you with the emergency number ready. Call me every day and let me know you are ok."

"Yes, mommy dearest."

"Call me names if you want, but I want you to promise me. Say it!"

"I promise I will be safe while you are gone, but no promises once you get back," I tease with a grin.

"Thanks for being a smartass. I guess I shouldn't expect anything less," she says as she reaches for a hug. I squeeze her tight. I will miss her even if she does overdo it.

"Bye Noie, bye Jett. Love you both," I say and blow a kiss before turning back to walk into my dorm.

"Bye little sis," Noie and Jett say in unison.

I just want to go upstairs and take a nap. This week has been rough, but I made it through and I don't think I flunked any of my mid-terms. Although I will most likely obsess over my grades all break, I am going to make my best attempt at letting it go. I want to spend this time reading, napping in the sun and practicing for my performance that's coming up.

I groan. My performance. Ian. What am I going to do? My self-loathing is interrupted by tapping noises on my window. I look out hesitantly and roll my eyes. Of course the first person to bug me during my week of solitude has to be Sam. I hold up my finger to signal I am coming right down.

I bounce down the stairs and out the door and then I pretend to run in slow motion towards his open arms until he wraps them around me and swings me in a circle. I know it is a little dorky, but slow motion greetings are our thing. We are both laughing by the time he sets me down.

"What are you doing here? Aren't you leaving today?" I ask.

"I am here because I wanted to see if my best friend would join me for lunch and I am not leaving today. I leave in the morning. Blake had to take care of something here tonight so we will head out tomorrow. What do you say? Are you hungry?" he asks while poking me in the stomach.

"Absolutely! Let me grab my wallet."

"No, my treat. I don't want to wait for you to go digging for your wallet."

"Two minutes."

"Nope," he says and links his arm through mine as he pulls me in the direction of his favorite deli. "How are you and Ian?" he asks.

"This already? You are cracked. There is not a 'me and Ian.' There is me and there is Ian. As far as I know, we are both doing well, thank you."

"Go ahead and keep your secrets, but I have done a little digging on our new pal Ian. Since you don't want to talk about him I will have to keep it to myself."

"What do you mean digging and why?" I ask as my entire skin flushes.

"Don't look so disturbed. I told you I have seen him

around and I knew we had some mutual friends. I just asked what he was like with girls, is he single, things like that."

"I could kill you," I growl at him.

"Kill me? What did I do wrong? I just wanted to be informed before I make my decision."

"Your decision about what?" I ask, confused.

"I am trying to decide if I should kick his ass and warn him away from you or if I should be supportive of a future 'Nia plus Ian equals love' scenario."

"Seriously Sam, the maturity level with which you approach my love life never ceases to amaze me," I say and roll my eyes. "Is the verdict in?"

"Yes, it is. Very interesting you said love life. I was under the impression you were not open to a love life freshman year," he replies as we walk through the deli door. When I don't respond he says, "Let's order and I will give you the facts of my case. Do you want your regular?"

"Yes, please. I am going to grab a table." I find a table in the corner near the front window open and take a seat. I love people watching and this is a perfect spot. I see a woman walking an adorable tan colored dog with curly hair. The dog is very energetic. He keeps jumping around and then pulling her down the street. I giggle as the woman tries to plant her feet to keep him in place and he continues to pull. It looks as if she is skiing on concrete.

Sam is walking towards me with two plates and says, "Lunch is served," as he sets my sandwich in front of me.

It smells so good. I hadn't realized how hungry I was until he sits my hot roast beef sandwich on the table. This place is the best. They also drizzle some of the gravy over my fries as well, which is my favorite part.

"Start spilling," I say to Sam between bites.

"Everyone I talked to said they like him and he is a good guy. No one really had anything bad to say at all. He has casually dated a few girls since he has been here, but no one felt they were anything serious. He doesn't seem to have the same women problems I have, if you know what I mean," he says with a wink.

"You do not have women problems. You have a problem, you like too many women at the same time."

"That's unfair and I am appalled by your accusations. I do not like too many women at the same time. The same day, yes, but never at the same time. And they all know you own my heart."

"Ha, ha. Whatever you say. Can we get serious for a minute?" I ask and he begrudgingly nods his head yes. "Why are you being so weird and looking into Ian?"

"Because of the way he was looking at you at the frat party. He was staring and not trying to be subtle about it. When I was speaking to him, he never made eye contact with me. He was just fixed on you. That is intense and weird. I got a little worried and wanted to see what people had to say about him. I'm glad I did because now I know he seems to be a good guy. I am still going to keep my eye on him as long as he is hanging around you but at least now I will give him a chance."

"I might give him a chance," I say and regret it immediately because I don't want to make something out of this when we haven't even exchanged numbers.

Sam eyes me thoughtfully for a minute then says, "Interesting. You have treated every guy who has been interested in you like they have the plague since the first day of school."

"I just didn't want the first year of my college experience to be consumed by a relationship and I never treated you like you had the plague."

"How could you? Look at me. I am irresistible."

I smile and take the last bite of my sandwich.

We make our way out of the deli and back towards campus. I can't stop smiling after our talk about Ian. I am happy Sam looks out for me and looked into Ian. It is nice to know he is not running around with multiple girls.

"Sam, did you want to hang out tonight and watch a movie or something?"

"Would love to babe, but I have a cute little thing I already made plans with when I stopped by the campus bookstore earlier."

"You never change and you don't have to walk me back if you need to go. I am thinking about hanging out by my tree for a little bit and enjoying the fresh air."

"Okay then I'm going to head out. You be safe and I will see you next week," he says before kissing my cheek and turning in the direction of his dorm.

The weather is really beautiful today. I hope it stays this way. I would hate to be stuck inside all week because of rain.

As my tree comes into view, I realize someone is sitting under it. I sigh to myself. I know I don't own the tree but it is still my tree. I might have to put a sign on it. It can't be a name sign because people would ignore that, but maybe if I posted a danger sign of some sort. That might just work. I smile as I plot my hostile takeover of the tree. Closer now I see it is Ian.

I stop to study him because he hasn't noticed me yet. He is staring down in his lap at a book. His brown hair keeps falling into his eyes and he whips his head to move it from his face. He is wearing a snug fitting black t-shirt and jeans with holes in the knees. His bare feet are stretched out in front of him. I imagine how the cool grass must feel beneath his feet and I suddenly get the urge to kick my sandals off and run my toes through the cool green blades.

Suddenly he lifts his head and closes his eyes as a breeze encases him. His eyes open and as if sensing me, he turns his head in my direction and smiles as our eyes meet. I walk to him and sit down. He reaches his arm around my back and I lean my head down to his shoulder. His fresh scent overwhelms me. I close my eyes and take a deep breath. I don't know what is going on between us, but it feels so natural and I don't want it to stop.

"What are you reading?" I ask him in a whisper.

"The Scarlet Letter. It's one of my favorites."

"Mine too."

We sit like this until dusk when he finally says, "Do you want to go somewhere with me?"

"Where?"

"I want to drive out to the airport."

"Are we going on a trip?" I ask jokingly.

"There is a field just outside of the airport near the runways. We can watch the planes take off. I'll stop for food on the way and we can eat dinner out there."

"Sounds like a date."

"It can be."

"Okay."

Ian stands and puts his hands out towards me. I

place my hands in his and he slowly lifts me up and pulls me to him until our faces are an inch apart. His green eyes are focused on mine. The desire to kiss him is irresistible. I can feel his mint scented breath on my face. His lips part and I close my eyes.

"Let's go."

Startled, I open my eyes as he releases one of my hands and begins walking towards the parking lot. I follow him to a black two door car. It is older but in good shape. He opens the door for me and I sit inside. I reach over and unlock the driver's side door as he walks around like I used to do for my dad when I was a little girl. The dimple is back when he smiles at me as he sits in the driver's seat. He shakes his head and laughs as he puts the key in the ignition and starts the car. It roars to life with a sound louder and deeper than I would have expected.

"What's so funny?" I ask.

"You. Me. This situation."

I don't respond. I don't know what to think about what he said. Instead I roll down the window and put my hand out to ride the wind as he drives.

Thirty minutes later we are pulling into a field. The sun has set now and the runways are aglow with lights. We went through a burger drive thru on our way. Ian gets out of the car as I gather up the food bags. As I reach for the door, it opens. Ian is standing there with his hand out to help me up. I let him and then follow him to the trunk of the car. He pops it open and pulls out a blanket. We walk quietly to the front of the car and he lays the blanket over the hood. I set down the food bags and slide on to the hood of the car. He follows. I hand him his burger and grab mine when we see a plane taxiing to the runway in front of us.

"Lay back and keep your eyes open."

I do as he instructs and next thing I know the plane is barreling towards us. It takes off just before it reaches the field we are in. The wind it generates blows my hair around my head and I find myself yelling, "Wooooohooooo," and laughing.

Ian turns on his side to face me. I turn towards him with a smile so big it hurts. His hand reaches up and he brushes hair out of my face and then trails his fingers gently down my cheek. My breath hitches and I will him to kiss me. Instead he pulls me close and wraps his arms around me for a few moments before he says, "Let's eat before the food gets cold."

We sit quietly to eat, breaking every time a plane comes down the runway. It feels amazing sitting here with Ian in this moment. I was looking forward to a spring break spent solo, but now I don't want to spend a minute alone.

When we finish eating, he picks up the trash and puts it in the car. When he joins me back on the hood, he pulls me towards him until my head is laying on his chest.

I finally get the nerve to ask, "What did you find so funny about our situation earlier?"

He takes a minute to answer and finally says, "I have seen you around for a while and wanted to meet you. I just couldn't figure out how. Everything I came up with seemed like it would be awkward. Then I finally get the nerve to introduce myself and every moment I have spent with you since then has felt so natural. Nothing about it has felt weird or awkward. I just found it funny I waited so long to act on something so perfect."

I couldn't even respond. I just lay on his chest and breathe his scent slowly in and out until I drift off to sleep.

The sun is just breaking the horizon when my eyes flutter open. I am still laying on Ian's chest. He is awake and his eyes are on me when I look up at him.

"Good morning," he says with a rasp left over from sleeping.

"Good morning.

"I should get you home."

Panic flares in my chest. I don't want to go back to my room. The skin between his eyes crease and he looks confused before his face relaxes and he smiles.

"After you get ready for the day, I will come pick you back up. What did you have planned for today?"

I relax. "I wanted to grab some coffee and then go to the studio to practice for my performance, but I could skip today. The practice, I mean, not the coffee."

"No, I don't want you to miss your practice. We could get coffee together and I could come watch, if that's okay."

"Well, umm, I don't know. I don't usually let anyone watch."

He places his hand under my chin, lifts my face up and says, "There is a first time for everything."

"Okay, I guess I can give it a try."

I can feel his eyes on me as I dance. Instead of feeling self-conscience, I feel free and more connected to my movements than I ever have. I want his eyes on me. I want him to drink in every move because in this moment I dance only for him.

After an hour of going through the movements over and over again, I collapse to the floor. I gave everything to my practice and I am spent. I feel Ian beside me on the floor. He pulls me to him. I open my eyes. Our faces are only inches apart. He brings his hand up to my face to brush the sweat drenched hair away and then places a kiss in the center of my forehead.

"You're beautiful," he whispers in my ear. "Let's get out of here."

Ian stands and pulls me to my feet.

We walk across campus towards my dorm. The chill of the evening air is raising goose bumps all over my arms. I listen as he talks excitedly about his favorite band and how one day he wants to be on stage, filling the room with music people can really connect to. He tells me my dancing does the same thing and how as he watched me, he felt like he was on an emotional ride with me as I physically expressed the music.

He quiets as we reach the door of my dorm.

"You can come in and watch a movie," I offer.

"I have something I need to do tonight, but maybe tomorrow."

"Okay, I guess I'll see you tomorrow night."

"If I can help it, you will see much earlier than tomorrow night," he says with a grin and I flash him a smile.

I make a move towards the door but he doesn't let go

of my hand. I look back towards him and he leans in to kiss me. His lips are soft against mine. He doesn't pry, he just savors the feeling of our lips pressed together.

Eventually he backs away and watches me as I walk inside.

I must have forgotten to turn my alarm off last night and it starts blaring at six, zapping me from sleep. I throw my hand at the alarm in an attempt to hit the snooze button and I feel a piece of paper stuck to the top of the clock. I turn on the lamp to take the paper off and quiet the alarm.

The paper has writing on it. I struggle to focus before reading it.

Yesterday, with you, made me feel what it really means to be alive.

There is an arrow pointing towards my dresser where I see another note.

Get dressed. I can't wait to see your beautiful face.

I grab a pair of jeans and a light sweater and dress as fast as I can. I look under my bed to locate my sandals. Thankfully they are not playing the hiding game this morning and I find them quickly. Then I look in the mirror and run the brush through my hair to remove the knots that have taken over during the night.

Now I just have to brush my teeth and get out of

here. I go to open the door and see another note.

Meet me at the coffee shop just off campus.

I walk as fast as I can to the coffee shop and only slow when I am about twenty feet away. I open the door but I don't see him inside and my face drops. He didn't say a time and I was too excited to think about that. I am about to turn and head back to my dorm when I notice a note on an outside table.

Sit here. I missed you.

I sit and a moment later I see Ian walk out of the coffee shop holding two cups of coffee.

"I didn't see you when I looked inside."

"That was by design. I was worried this would be too early for you but I couldn't wait to see you," he says as he pulls a cigarette pack from his pocket.

"Can I have one?"

"I didn't realize dancers smoke."

"On occasion and six a.m. coffee during spring break is one of those occasions."

"You say that like you aren't thrilled about being here this early," he says in mock offense.

"Maybe, maybe not," I say and put the cigarette to my mouth for him to light. I take a drag and then say, "I have a question for you. How did you manage to get into my room?"

"I have my ways."

"Should I be worried? Maybe add extra security to my room."

"Why would you want to keep me out?"

"Good point."

We finish our coffee and then he takes me on a tour of our campus through his eyes. He shows me all of his favorite places. Some are hidden places where he can hide away when he doesn't want to be bothered. Then there are his favorite buildings and places to study. Finally he takes me to his favorite place to people watch which leads us to the bench which sits not far from my tree.

"When I told you I had seen you around, this is where I saw you from. I would sit here and watch you. I've been not much more than forty feet from you for months and it felt like another planet," he reveals.

He takes my hand in his and we sit in the eerie quiet of campus. With classes being out for the week it feels like a ghost town. I wish I had my quilt with me. I would love to lay under my tree with him.

Ian begins stroking the back of my hand with his thumb and then looks me in the eyes and says, "I'm never letting you go."

"Do you want to come to my place and watch a movie?" Ian asks as we sit near the river and watch the sun set.

"Sure, which dorm do you live in?"

"I don't live in a dorm. I have an apartment I share with my best friend, Jimmy. It is right next to campus."

"Okay," I say a little hesitantly. "Is your roommate there?" Something about being in his apartment feels more intimate than my nerves are ready to deal with.

"No, but he should be back tomorrow. He was only leaving town for a few days."

Not only will we be at his apartment but we are going to be alone.

As if sensing my nervousness, Ian says, "Just a movie, okay?"

I swallow down the lump in my throat and nod my head yes.

He jumps down from the cement barrier we are sitting on and then reaches up to help me. On the way to his apartment, we stop at the store for some popcorn and other various junk food items to binge on during the movie. My body is going to hate me for this later.

Ian opens the door to his apartment and I am surprised by the décor. I would have expected a futon and beer posters with scantily clad women on the walls in an apartment shared by two college guys. Instead, there are mix matched pieces of furniture which come together in a way that almost look like a designer did it. All of the colors are warm and inviting. The scent of tobacco and patchouli hang in the air. The walls have framed maps of different countries hanging on them. What college guy frames things?

He notices me taking everything in and says, "I like flea markets and garage sales. Most of this stuff was practically being given away."

"You did this?"

"Yes, everything except the framed maps. I had them on the wall with tacks and Jimmy's girlfriend thought it was tacky. She bought us the frames."

That makes more sense. I notice the set of drums and guitars set up in what was meant to be a dining room.

"I'm sure your neighbors love that," I say pointing to the drums.

"The neighbors are cool. Nothing but college students live here and we make sure not to play too late during the week. The movies are under the television. Pick out something while I make the popcorn."

I choose a movie starring an actress I like and we curl up on the couch together and hit play.

I wake up to the sound of cabinet doors opening and closing in the kitchen of Ian's apartment. Ian's arms are still wrapped around me so I don't know who is in the kitchen.

"Ian," I whisper and nudge him. "Ian."

"What?" He asks a little confused from sleep.

"Someone's in the kitchen."

He kisses my forehead and sits up.

"Hey Jimmy, is that you?"

"Yep, Sleepy. Did I wake you and Snow White?"

"Snow White?" I ask Ian.

"I should have never told him that," he says annoyed.

"Told him what?"

"I confided in him that I called you Snow White in my head before I met you," he says embarrassed.

Heat rises on my face from embarrassment too.

"He was probably being loud on purpose to wake us up so he could call us Sleepy and Snow White to embarrass me."

Jimmy walks out of the kitchen and says, "It's nice to meet the girl who has my boy all twisted up," he says with a laugh.

"The name's Nia. Only Ian can call me Snow White. Is that okay with you, Dopey?"

"I like this girl, Ian."

"She has her moments," he says playfully.

11 IAN THEN

When I found out Nia wasn't going anywhere for spring break, I bailed on my plans to go out of town with Jimmy for a few days. I have never felt as alive as I have since I met her and I couldn't walk away from that feeling.

I have to find a way to make this spring break so amazing that she won't vanish from my life. I also need to make sure there is nothing going on with her and Sam. I know she says they are just friends, but I don't wrap my arms around girls who are just friends. If they are friends, then I will have to summon the courage to deal with the brewing jealousy.

I wish I knew more about her to help me plan what to do this week. I should have asked her more questions at the party but I was so happy to be close to her, nothing else seemed to matter at the time.

I also need to find a way to run into her today. I don't want to show up at her dorm and scare her off. I grab my copy of *The Scarlet Letter* which I am reading for the fifth time and head towards campus. I will read under her tree. She is there so often that I hope she decides to go there today.

12 NIA DIARY

Dear Diary,

The last week of my life has been like a fairy tale. Ian is not what I wanted this early in college but there is no way I would walk away from it now. I know I am just falling head over heels without a net but I don't care. When he looks at me his eyes are so intense I forget to breathe at times.

We have spent so much time getting to know each other and he has taken me places around town I never knew existed. My favorite was when he took me canoeing. He brought a picnic and we ate on the water. Afterwards we fed bread to the ducks. It was so peaceful being out there with him.

I have to vent to you because I want to scream, "I love you" when I see him and that would be a crazy thing to do. I don't want to scare him off. I never want to spend a moment of my life without him.

I can hear Noie in my head as I write this. She would be telling me to take things slow and say I will date a hundred guys in college before I find someone worth saying I love you to. But maybe I don't have to date a hundred guys. What if Ian is THE guy?

I am going to keep all of these feelings between me and you for now if I can help it. Sam has already gotten too nosey and I am sure Sarah and Hadley would feel the need to overdo some attempt at match making.

13 NIA NOW

This week has been strange. Gertie has been here every day. The only time I have seen Noie was a few days ago when she dropped off coffee and left right away. I don't mind Gertie being here so much. She has long wavy blond hair like Sarah with a similar petite stature. Sometimes I pretend she is Sarah and it is comforting, but then she will speak and her German accent brings me back to reality.

I really do miss Noie, but I know things are better for her this way. I have been thinking a lot about what she said and I don't want her putting demands on me. It made me really angry at first. Is she just going to stop being my sister because I don't want to be out there yet? Then I got really afraid of losing her. I don't want to lose her and I am searching for the strength to meet her demand.

Noie may not be here but I know her heart still is. Gertie was here when a delivery of patio furniture came. It was two large wicker chairs with plush outdoor pillows a shade of orange that reminds me of the sunset. There is also a small matching round table. Gertie made sure they set it up out back where it wouldn't block my view. Later the same day a fire pit was delivered. Looking out the window at the gifts she sent, I feel some excitement about using it. I have always wanted a fire pit. We talked for years about getting one every fall, but it just never happened.

I haven't held the cat yet, but he does stay close to the back porch since he has a steady supply of food. Maybe if I sit out on the new furniture, he will come to me. Right now he is back under the tree swatting at the leaves. He crouches down in the grass and stills before he jumps up and pounces on another leaf. I have heard some cats will grab a bird right out of the air and kill them before bringing them to their owners as gifts. I really hope this cat never does that.

"Nia, would you like more coffee?" Gertie asks as she comes up behind me.

I shake my head no.

"Then I will bring you some toast for breakfast unless you want something else."

I shake my head no.

With that, she makes her way back to the kitchen and I can hear her press down the lever on the toaster.

I decide to call Sam back. I take my cell phone out from between the cushions of the chair and hold the power button to turn it on. I scroll through the contacts until I find his number and hit send.

"Hey, Nia." Sam says when he answers the phone. "I hope you are doing ok. You haven't called in a while. I was getting worried. If Noie wouldn't have answered when I called the house the other morning I probably would have been on a plane to come check on you. I probably should have done that anyway. It has been a month since I have been there, but work has been busy."

He pauses and lets the silence settle comfortably between us. I love hearing Sam's voice. He is always happy and positive. I have never met someone who could truly maintain that level of joy from day to day, except maybe Hadley.

He finally continues, "I got some good news from Sarah last week. She wanted to be the one to tell you, but she said I could tell you if you called. She is pregnant. Can you believe it? She is really excited, but Blake is scared to death. He wants Sarah to be able to stay home as long as possible after the baby is born but he worries about the change in income. I cannot wait to see her when she is about to pop. Do you think she will wear heels to the hospital when she goes into labor?" He chuckles a little at the thought of that and I smile as a tear flows over my lashes and down my cheek.

"Well she is due in March and I am planning to fly out to visit for a week. I would like to stay with you." When I don't respond he adds, "I'll talk to Noie about it. Maybe you can go with me to see the baby. You and Sarah really need to talk. I know you probably think she hates you, but we both know that is nonsense. We all know you have been through a lot and we can never know how we would respond to it, but that doesn't change that other people have gone through a lot too. It has been hard on everyone to watch you shut out the world. Sarah only said those things because she was angry and upset she has basically lost you in all of this. She was more pissed off at the world than anything else. I know she misses your calls because every time we talk she asks me if you still call. If you ever decide to dial her number, I am sure she would be excited to tell you all about the pregnancy."

The silence is back.

"Nia, I miss you. Every morning when I wake up I think about you and I want to call you so we can laugh about how much of an idiot I am or anything else. I could really use your advice right now. I met someone. Don't roll your eyes. I like this girl. I'm thirty years old and this is the first time I have ever considered dating someone longer than a few weeks. I need you in on this. I have told her about you. I was a little worried because a lot of women get jealous but she didn't. She seemed to understand our relationship and said our stories make her think about her and her brother. Her name is Maria and I want you to meet her. Nothing beats Christmas time in D.C. Please come stay with me for the holidays. I want you to come mid-December and stay through the New Year. Please think about it. I am going to call Noie and I will send you a plane ticket. I want you to use it."

He pauses again to let the idea sink in. I can't even process the idea of going there for the holidays with all of the other revelations.

"I'm going to go. I have a meeting in a little bit and I need to finish preparing. One last thing. Noie told me about the cat. I think you should name him Russell. Love you. Call me again soon."

I hear the beep in my ear signaling the call has ended and quickly turn the phone back off.

I am thinking about going into the kitchen for a cup of coffee when Gertie walks in with one for me even though I told her earlier I didn't want one. She sits it down next to my ashtray with a new pack of cigarettes. I open the cigarettes and light one thinking about everything Sam said. I am unable to hold back the tears. The thought of Sarah and Blake having a baby brings me so much joy and sadness. I don't know how to rectify those feelings.

I need *him*. I stub out my cigarette and walk to the bedroom. I open *his* dresser drawer and pull out *his* worn college sweatshirt. Raising it to my face, I breathe in *his* scent which still lingers in the fabric. It was the last thing I saw *him* wearing and I hope the smell of *his* skin never leaves it.

"Nia, are you in there," I hear Gertie say as she gently knocks on the door before opening it. "Oh, I am so sorry for interrupting," she says as I stuff the sweatshirt back in the drawer and turn to her. "I just wanted to let you know I will not be here until tomorrow evening. Noie called and said she will be by here in the morning."

I nod my head in acknowledgement of what she said. She turns to leave and shuts the door softly behind her.

I lay on my bed and think about *him* and start crying. I want to kick and scream and tell *him* how angry I am with *him* and that I hate *him*. Then I want *him* here to comfort me. The conflicting feelings are at war in my head and my heart.

14 NIA THEN

"Last party of the year. Is everyone in?" Sam asks the group.

"Sarah and I are in," Hadley says and then adds, "So is Nia." She looks at me with the most serious look she can muster.

"I don't know. Ian, do you want to go?"

"Yes, we should go and I will call Jimmy. He'll want to go too."

"What about you Blake?" Sarah asks.

"Do you even have to ask?" Blake replies and gives Sarah an adoring smile.

"Ian, you better look after Nia. Everyone gets crazy at these parties," Noie says. She and Jett joined us for lunch because they are heading to Cincinnati this afternoon. They both have internships there this summer.

"Noie, you and Jett could let your hair down and join us. Cincinnati is only a couple of hours away. You could leave tomorrow. Then you could keep an eye on me yourself."

"No we have dinner plans with some friends in Cinci. Plus I haven't seen Ian leave your side since spring break so I think he will keep you safe."

I'm so excited for the summer. These last couple of months with Ian have been amazing and he has fit in perfectly with my group of friends. Hadley, Sam, Jimmy, Ian and I are taking a road trip to California next week. Starting next summer we will all be taking internships so we want to make the most of our summer of freedom.

"Nia and Sarah, I need you to finish eating. Chop, chop. We need to get done up smoking hot for this party," Hadley says.

"My girl is always smoking hot," Blake says and kisses Sarah's cheek. They finally made things official last week and it is cute how they dote on each other.

"Okay, Hadley. I see the vein popping out of your forehead. We are coming with you to get all dolled up." I turn to Ian and kiss him before scooting out of the booth. "We'll see you all later. Noie and Jett, you two be safe. I'll miss you this summer." I give them both a hug and then grab Sarah's hand and try to pull her off Blake's lips. Hadley joins in and we finally wrestle her free.

"I'll get it," I say as I open our dorm room door.

"We might not be able to keep you out of trouble dressed like that," Sam says and spins me around.

"Shut-up, Sam," I say and jokingly punch his arm. "We are almost ready. Where are the guys?"

"Ian and Jimmy are outside smoking and Blake should be here any minute."

"Hey sexy," Hadley says when she comes out of the bathroom and sees Sam.

"Look who's talking. You might just get lucky with me tonight."

"I'm sure the slutty Sam fan club will be out in full force tonight."

"And I don't want to keep them waiting. Let's go."

We all head out and I jump into Ian's arms when I see him outside. He kisses my neck and sits me down. We make our way to the party.

"Bar!" Sam shouts and points across the room as we walk into the house. We all follow behind and almost lose him in a group of girls who are overly happy to see him.

When we get to the bar, Sam starts pouring shots for everyone and passes them out.

"Everyone raise your glass," Sam instructs and then says, "It has been an incredible first year of college and all of my favorite people are right here. Let's drink up and party our asses off."

Everyone clinks glasses and downs their shots. Hadley grabs Sam's arm to drag him to the beer pong table like always. I laugh and watch them walk out.

"Ian, let me steal Nia away from you for a minute," Sarah says.

"Just bring her back."

Sarah and I walk out onto the porch where we can hear each other a little better.

"What's up?" I ask Sarah when we sit down.

"Nothing really. I just wanted a few minutes with you. I'm leaving tomorrow and we won't see each other until August. I wish I could come on the road trip with you but my mom is making me come home. I think she is worried about me being on the road with Blake. She didn't believe me when I said he wasn't going."

"Does she not like Blake?"

"She doesn't like me having a boyfriend. It's nothing against Blake. How are things with Ian?"

"Great but it is going to suck after the road trip. He got a gig playing guitar with some small band. He will be gone for most of July."

"What will you be doing?"

"Sam and Hadley will be here so we are going to figure something out," I say before being interrupted.

"Hello beautiful, what's your name?" Some guy asks with a slight slur in his voice.

"We're busy here, do you mind," Sarah says in a voice that says back off.

"I wasn't talking to you," he says before turning his eyes back to me. He takes a step closer and stumbles. Next thing I know he is laying over me, trying to get his footing.

Suddenly the guy is off me and I see him tumbling down the porch steps. Ian is standing there with a crazed look in his eyes. The guy makes it to his feet and starts slurring profanities towards Ian. Ian is about to lay him out when Sam and Blake step in the middle. One of the drunk guy's friends comes to his aid.

"Okay, okay. Everyone needs to calm down. This is a party, not a boxing match," Sam says.

"Sam, back off and let me fucking go. He was all over Nia and…"

Before Ian could finish, Sam let Ian go and turned around punching drunk guy in the face. Then he yells at the guy's friend to get him out of there.

"Bro, what was all that about?" Ian asks Sam.

"You said he touched Nia."

"Yeah and that was my shit to take care of. You shouldn't have broken it up in the first place," Ian says and then turns back to me.

"I have to get out of here. Text me when you get back to your room."

"I'll go with you."

"No, I need to be alone," Ian says and starts walking off.

"Ian!" I yell after him.

"Nia, just stay and have fun. Let me take care of Ian. He'll be ok," Jimmy says and then runs to catch up with Ian.

"How has Ian been since the party?" Sam asks as we pack my bags in the back of the van he rented for the road trip. "I haven't heard from him."

"He's fine. He just needed some time alone. Jimmy said it's just how he works stuff out."

"Have you seen him?"

"No, but I will a lot sooner if you get in the van and drive," I say.

"Are you okay with him just walking away like he did and not coming to see you?"

"No, I'm not. I'm going to talk to him about it when we camp tonight and let him know he can't do that. I don't care if he needs to blow off steam but being a no-call no-show for days isn't cool."

"Seriously, hurry. I am sick of sitting in here,"

Hadley yells from the van.

"You do realize this is a road trip. We will be sitting in the van a lot while we are on the road."

"Yes, Sam. I am aware but this is not 'on the road' this is sitting outside the dorm while you two chat like busy bodies," she says and sticks her tongue out at him.

We pull up to get Ian and Jimmy. I get out of the car and wait for Ian to walk over. A huge smile is plastered across his face and his eyes are locked on me when he walks over. He drops his bags on the ground, wraps his arms around my waist and leans in to kiss me. I remember being angry with him but with his lips on mine, it doesn't feel important anymore.

When everyone starts clearing their throats, we pull away and heat finds its way to my face.

"We cool bro?" Sam asks Ian.

"Yeah man," Ian says and slaps him on the back.

"Then let's get on the road," Sam yells.

The trip has been amazing. We took two weeks to get the twenty-three hundred miles from Louisville to San Francisco. Everyone chose something they wanted to see along the way and we made sure to stop. Every night we slept at a different camp ground. Some were so isolated you could see more stars than I ever thought possible. It was the first time I saw the Rocky Mountains. They were so majestic.

Now we all stand on the Golden Gate Bridge looking out at the water. We are camping here tonight and then turning in the rental van tomorrow. I almost wish we would have planned to drive back instead of fly. I never want this to end.

"I thought about driving out here alone last summer but Jimmy wouldn't let me go alone," Ian says to me.

"Why didn't Jimmy just go with you?"

"I wanted to be alone. I have always seen pictures of this bridge and I thought it would be a good place to think."

He is looking off into the distance with a wistful look on his face and I wonder how we found each other. I never thought I would find someone like him. Someone who makes my heart ache to be near them. At night, when he is holding me, I feel the urge to share his skin. I just can't get close enough.

"I'm glad I didn't come because being here and seeing this with you is perfect," he says and turns to me. "Marry me. I know we haven't known each other for very long. We are young and still in school. There are so many reasons for which me asking you this is crazy, but I'm not saying we do it tomorrow. Just tell me you will marry me one day."

"Yes!"

He picks me up and kisses me long and hard.

"Okay guys, break it up," Sam says. "We need to start setting up camp."

"Don't be jealous, Sam," I say with a wink.

"Jealous? You think I am jealous? I feel bad for Ian being a one woman man. Watch out because I might corrupt him," Sam says jokingly.

"You wouldn't dare," I say with a scowl.

"He wouldn't be able to if he tried," Ian says to me.

I look at Sam with a satisfied grin and start heading

back to the van.

15 IAN THEN

I asked Nia if she would marry me and said it didn't need to be now, but secretly I want it to be now. I want to know she will be with me forever. I feel so anxious all the time thinking I will do something wrong and she will leave me or another guy will come along and take her away from me.

I have to do everything in my power to be the man she deserves. I have to make sure she is always happy. I know she is mad at me for disappearing for a couple of days. I want to promise her it will never happen again. I don't want it to happen again, but I know it would be a lie. There are times when I have to get away. I wish I could make her understand, but trying to explain it will just make her unhappy. I will need to be more careful about how I leave in the future so she doesn't get upset. Whatever I do in this life, I need to make sure she is happy.

Jimmy will understand. He will help me to do things so she will not be upset. I will have to talk to him about it. I hope he doesn't fight me on it because in the end, I know he will do what I ask. He is the only person in the world who knows everything about me.

16 NIA NOW

I wake up well before dawn to get ready. It has been so long since I have needed to leave the house so I don't know how long it will take me to get ready and I do need to leave the house, because I need Noie. I need her to not give up on me. I have to find the strength to face whatever is outside that door.

I bathe, brush my hair and find something Noie would approve of for me to wear. As I pull the jeans up, I realize how much weight I have lost. Noie has been saying I was losing weight, but I have not really paid attention. I thought she was just being overprotective. I take the jeans back off and search the back of the closet for an old pair which might be a smaller size. I find a pair one size smaller and put them on. They are still too big to fit correctly, but at least these will stay up.

After I finish dressing, it is almost eight o'clock and Noie should be here any minute. I go to my chair by the window to have a smoke and wait for her.

The cat is lounging on one of the new chairs on the

back porch. I stand up to go out back when I hear Noie's key opening the front door. When she comes around the corner and sees me, she stops with a look of shock on her face before continuing towards me and setting my coffee down. I just stare at her.

"Nia, you look very nice today. Why don't you sit down and drink your coffee while I get some food for the cat," she says as she walks past me to the kitchen.

When she emerges with the food and walks past me to the back door, I pick up my coffee and cigarettes to follow her. She opens the door and steps aside, letting me go out first, when she realizes I am behind her. The cat stands at attention from his resting place as we walk out. Jumping off the chair, he scampers towards the tree as I take a seat in the chair he wasn't sitting in.

Noie places the food in his bowl, which I now see has tiny paw prints painted on the side. She grabs the matching water bowl and goes back inside emerging a couple of minutes later with it full and places it back down. She gazes out over the yard to where the cat is crouched stalking some imaginary prey.

Sitting down next to me she says, "I was thinking we could go to the bookstore. Audrie and Audra need a book from their reading lists and I thought you might want to pick up a new book as well. How does that sound?"

I nod my head yes and she smiles and then leans back in the chair. I light a cigarette and focus my attention back on the cat. Now that we are not near the food, he starts cautiously walking towards it.

"Have you picked out a name for him yet?"

I nod my head yes and force the name from my lips, "Russell."

"Russell. I like it. You will have to tell me one day how you chose his name."

We sit in silence as Russell finishes his food and walks away to groom himself. A little bit of panic begins to set in as I think about going to the bookstore. I stub out my cigarette and stand up to signal to Noie I am ready to go before I lose my nerve.

She follows quietly behind me as I go back into the house and locate my wallet in the kitchen.

"Are you ready," she asks.

I nod and we head out the front door and get into her soccer mom minivan. She isn't really a soccer mom. Audrie and Audra are in gymnastics and used to take dance classes with me, but her van fits the soccer mom stereotype.

I open the door and get myself settled as she starts the ignition and pulls out of the driveway. It takes us twenty minutes to reach the local bookstore. It is a small place owned by a husband and wife who appear to still be living in their hippie glory days. I have spent many hours in this store. The smell of old and new books overwhelm your senses when you open the door. I see Rainbow, their calico cat, perched next to the register in his normal spot. I hear shuffling from the back of the store and Nora, the owner, appears between two rows of bookshelves.

"Well hello Nia! Ben, come see, Nia is here," she practically screams when she sees me.

I nod and smile at her and then Ben as he emerges from the back.

"Oh, sweet girl how have you been? We have been so worried about you. You poor thing, come here," Nora says and holds out her arms as she walks towards me.

Noie comes to my rescue before they continue my way. Stepping protectively in front of me, she says, "Hi. It is so good to see you both. Nia and I are in a bit of a hurry, but we need to pick up a few books for my girls."

I use her distraction to disappear down an aisle of books labeled New Fiction. I haven't had a new book in a while and don't want this to take longer than it has to, so I scan the shelves quickly. A book with a bright red cover catches my eye and I pick it up. Not even reading the title, I walk back to the register because I hear Noie thanking them for helping her locate the books she needs. I set my book on the counter and pull a twenty dollar bill from my wallet.

Nora steps behind the counter to ring me up and when she looks at me, I see the last thing I need at this moment. A look of pity directed straight at me. I hate how every person I know in this town is privy to the most horrible and private parts of my life.

"Nia, take my keys and go get the van started. I will get your change," Noie says, to rescue me for the second time today.

I wait less than five minutes before she is walking out of the store. She jumps in the driver's side and quickly pulls to the other side of the parking lot and parks. She rests her forehead on the steering wheel and says, "I'm sorry Nia. That did not go the way I wanted it to. It has been so long since you have been out and I figured most people wouldn't be thinking about it the moment they saw you."

I pull my cell phone from my pocket and power it on. I find the pin I have saved in the map app and start the navigation. Noie's head snaps up when the automated voice begins giving directions.

"Are we going somewhere else?" She asks a little puzzled.

I nod my head yes.

Thirty minutes later we are pulling up to the field behind the airport.

17 NIA THEN

"Nia, get over here," Noie calls to me. "I am so proud of you. I can't believe you graduated today. I need pictures of the whole group. Get everyone over here."

I gather up our gang and pull them over to where Noie and Jett are waiting.

"Okay, put your arms around each other and say cheese."

"Cheese!"

"Let me get a couple more," Noie pleads.

"Noie, can you get a picture of this first?" Ian asks and then gets down on one knee in front of me. "Nia, the summer after our freshman year, you stood on the Golden Gate Bridge and told me you would marry me one day. I'm ready for that day to be here. Will you marry me?"

I can't get myself to form the words so I just fall to my knees in front of him and nod my head yes. He takes the ring out of the little box and slides it on my finger. Suddenly Hadley and Sarah are screaming and telling me to show them the ring, but Ian and I are just staring into each other's eyes. In this moment, everyone else falls away and I say, "I love you."

"Have you set a date yet," Noie asks.

"Yes. The seventh of July."

"Good, that gives us a little over a year to plan. We have a lot to do. Start thinking of where you want to get married and we can go from there."

"This July," I say.

"What are you talking about? July seventh is only a few weeks away. How are we going to get everything planned by then?" Noie asks flustered.

"There isn't much to plan. He starts law school in the fall and things will be crazy for a while. We are only inviting a few people. We want to do it at the overlook in Covington. I think we can get someone to come out there to perform the ceremony. All we really need to do is find me a dress and a place to eat afterwards."

Noie sits quietly, twisting her ring around her finger. I think I am disappointing her.

"Can I at least come with you to pick out the dress?" she asks, still looking down at the table.

"Of course. Plus we have to pick out something for you to wear. I want my maid-of-honor to look stunning."

"Maid-of-honor?" She asks.

"Yes, if you accept."

"Yes, yes, yes," she exclaims and gives me a huge hug. "I'm so happy for you, but now I have to leave. Do you still need me to drop you off at the coffee shop?"

"Yep. I'm meeting Sam and Hadley. Sam leaves for

D.C. tomorrow and Hadley leaves for Chicago the day after."

"Are you sad the gang is breaking up?"

"Yes, but Sarah, Blake and Jimmy are staying in town. Hadley and Sam will come visit when they can."

We pull up to the coffee shop and I jump out quickly so Noie can get to her appointment.

"Hey, Sam, is Hadley running late?"

"She will be here soon, but I want to talk for a few minutes alone, so this worked out."

"What's up?"

"As one of your best friends, I want to make sure you are ready to get married."

"Yes, I am," I say confused. Why is he doing this? "Do you think I am making a mistake? I thought you liked Ian. You and he have gotten close over the years. I don't get why you are asking me this," I say with a little anger in my voice. This is a big step and it isn't made any easier when your best friend questions it.

"I like Ian a lot, but you are my best friend so you come first. I had to ask. I want to hear from you that you are sure."

"I'm sure. Don't worry that gorgeous head of yours," I say relaxing and rub his hair playfully. "Are you going to make it back for the wedding? I know it's soon, but I really want you there."

"I wouldn't miss it for the world," he says with a smile that doesn't reach his eyes.

"Do you Ian, take Nia to be your lawfully wedded

wife? To love and to cherish, in sickness and in health from this day forward, until death do you part?"

"I do."

"Do you Nia, take Ian to be your lawfully wedded husband? To love and to cherish, in sickness and in health from this day forward, until death do you part?"

"I do."

"Nia and Ian would like to say a few words to each other."

"Ian, I knew from the moment we met you were different. You were someone worth changing all my plans for and not for one day have I regretted jumping in with both feet. I look forward to everything life throws at us."

"Nia, my Snow White, before I met you I was wasting away in this world. You breathed new life into me and my music. With that, I want to play a song I wrote for you."

I watch him play the guitar and sing the beautiful lyrics to me and wish we could go on the road with his music. I could be happy having nothing except the passion that comes from his music. I don't need the house and picket fence he wants to give me as long as I have him.

He finishes singing and there isn't a person here without tears in their eyes. Ian sits his guitar down and comes back to hold my hands and mouths, "I love you."

"I love you too," I mouth back.

"By the power vested in me by the state of Kentucky, I now pronounce you husband and wife. You may kiss the bride."

He leans in and kisses me softly before pulling away. I want more and I can see the lust in his eyes, but that will have to wait until later.

After Noie takes about a thousand pictures, we drive to a restaurant where she has rented out a private room for us.

When we get our drinks, Hadley stands to make a toast.

"I was looking forward to chasing boys with my friends during college. You ruined that, Ian, but seeing how happy Nia is today, I have finally decided to forgive you. May you two have a long and happy life together," Hadley says and raises her glass. "Cheers."

We have the best group of friends. Everyone takes a turn toasting us.

When dinner is almost over, Noie says, "There is something me and Jett want to share with everyone," she pauses and looks at Jett before saying, "I'm pregnant."

"Noie! I thought you were going to say you were getting married. Pregnant! Congratulations, but this means you can't harp me about everything I do when you are having a baby out of wedlock. Shame, shame," I tease.

"Oh, stop it."

"You know I'm kidding. I can't wait to be an aunt!"

18 IAN THEN

She did it. She married me. She is officially Mrs. Erickson. After the wedding, she tried again to talk me out of going to law school and pursue my music instead. She thinks it will make both of us happy, but, the financial stress and stress of moving around all the time will get old for her. I know it.

I want her to stay here in Louisville, where she can be with Noie and her friends. Plus, she has an opportunity to teach dance here. I see how happy she is when she dances and I can't be the one who takes that away from her.

Also, Jimmy already landed a job in town. I know he would follow if I went after a music career, but everyone will be happier this way. I will start law school at Brandeis in the fall. Jett will be finishing before me, but we have already talked about setting up a practice together when I graduate.

Nia and I will start a family like Jett and Noie are and be able to raise our kids together. I will give her the life she has always dreamed of and if she is happy, I will be able to be happy too.

Everything will be okay and fall into place for me just like Jimmy has always promised me it would.

19 NIA DIARY

Dear Diary,

Life is moving at a rapid pace now that we have graduated. Our wedding was perfect and finding out Noie is having a baby made the day that much better. It makes me want to start trying for kids right away, but that won't be possible for a while. I don't think I should start a career teaching dance if I am pregnant. With Ian starting law school, we will not have the money for a while.

Noie's school got off to a good start last year. She has twice as many people trying to enroll their kids this year which has created a waiting list. I hope I get bumped to the top of the list when I do have kids.

The one thing that has been really hard to cope with is Hadley and Sam taking jobs so far away. They made it to the wedding, but I wonder how long it will be before I see them again. I feel like I am going through withdrawals. They have been by my side for the last four years. They both have been rays of sunshine in my life. I have to make sure we never lose touch.

This entry is starting to make me sad and this is supposed to be the beginning of a happy new chapter in my life, married to the man of my dreams.

20 NIA NOW

It has been two weeks since the first time Noie and I drove to the field behind the airport to watch the planes take off. We have been three more times since then. It has become our new routine. On the days Noie comes over, she brings me my coffee and we sit outside and watch Russell eat. He has stopped running from us, but he isn't quite ready to jump in my lap when Noie is here. It's just a matter of time. When he is finished we hop in the minivan and go. These trips have been in almost complete silence. Noie hasn't tried to have long winded conversations with herself. She seems content we are leaving the house.

Today, I stay in my sweatshirt and pajama pants instead of getting ready for our outing. I settle into my chair, light a cigarette and wait for Noie to arrive.

She walks in right at eight o'clock and instantly asks if something is wrong when she sees me. I shake my head no and reach for my coffee as she settles down in the chair next to me. She doesn't say anything and she doesn't have to. The look of defeat and disappointment is written all over her face.

"Noie." I say her name and she looks at me. "Do you mind if we stay here today and talk?"

"Yes, yes. Absolutely," she blurts. "Let me put some food out for Russell and then we can talk."

I take a drag off my cigarette, thankful she is giving me a few minutes to steady myself. It's not that I am about to tell her anything painful, but I am about to agree to something I am still unsure about.

I watch as Russell runs up to greet her. He is finally feeling at home here. I go outside every day and sit with him. He will crawl into my lap and purr for hours while I stroke his soft fur when I am alone. I have taken over the duties of feeding him from Gertie, but I still leave it for Noie to do on the days she is here in the morning. I can tell she enjoys her few minutes with him and I don't want to take that away.

Last week he was at the vet for four days to get neutered. Noie wanted him to be kenneled there for a few days to heal because she felt it was safer for him that way. I hadn't realized how attached I had gotten to him until he was gone. Every morning I would sit in my chair hoping he would show up even though I knew it was impossible.

Noie finally comes back inside and takes her seat. I clear my throat and stub out my cigarette.

"I am very thankful for everything you have done for me over the last six months. I don't know how I could have survived without you. I know I have been hurting you, but that has never been my intention. I am not ready to talk about what happened. I don't know when or if I ever will be. I need you to understand and not pressure me. I have enjoyed the time we spent at the airport lately, but sometimes I still do not want to leave the house. I will make myself sometimes for you and because I know it is what's best for me. I am glad you have stepped away over the last few weeks. Not because I don't want you here, but because I know that is what you and your family need. Please never feel guilty for taking care of your needs. I know how you are and I don't want you to think you are doing something wrong by not coming here every day."

I stop to gather my thoughts. I feel like I am rambling at this point. I take a sip of my coffee and light another cigarette. After two drags, I continue.

"I thought my life was perfect. I mean really perfect. The stuff books and fairy tales are written about. To find out that was all a lie did something to me I still don't fully understand."

"It wasn't all a lie," she interrupts.

I put my hand up to let her know I don't need to hear that right now.

"It was a lie. Maybe it was just a lie I made myself believe, but it was still a lie. I don't know how to carry on with my life. I don't know what a normal life is supposed to look like anymore, but I want to find out what my new normal can be. I haven't given up so please stop worrying about what I might do. I have made my decision about Thanksgiving. I will come with you. I know that will give you more peace of mind and I owe you at least that much."

She looks at me and smiles. I reach my cigarette over the ashtray and she rubs the back of my hand with tears in her eyes.

"Please let Jett and the girls know how sorry I am."

"Oh, Nia. They understand. It has been hard on them, but they understand."

"I need some time alone before Gertie gets here today if you don't mind. She has stocked the pantry with soup so I can get myself something for lunch."

"Okay, but I have something for you." She reaches for her purse and pulls out a stack of mail. "I checked it on my way in and noticed Jimmy and Hadley both sent you a letter. Do you want me to stay while you read them?"

I shake my head, no, hoping she will leave quickly so I can read Jimmy's letter alone.

"I'm going to go then. I love you and will see you in a few days."

I smile up at her and reach out for her hand. She places it in mine and I squeeze gently.

As soon as I hear the lock click on the front door, I open the letter from Jimmy.

Dear Nia,

I had a dream last night about you. We went to the carnival and bought tickets for the fun house. You know the kind that are full of mirrors? When we went inside, there were no mirrors. Just doors everywhere. I woke up in a panic and knew I needed to write you. I should have come by to see you like I have promised in all of my previous letters, but I can't. I hope you can understand that. Even if I could, Laura would never let me. She took the kids on a camping trip this weekend with some friends. I think sleeping alone is why I had the nightmare. I hope this letter finds you well and I hope we can get together in the future. Maybe we can meet somewhere for coffee.

Jimmy

I fold the letter back up and place it in the envelope. I wish he would have said more. I wish I could see him but I don't want to meet for coffee and have the inevitable conversation in public.

I decide to open Hadley's letter. She is always upbeat and I don't want to focus on thoughts of Jimmy right now.

Hey Nia!

Sorry it has been so long since I have written. Things have been crazy. Work keeps me on the road so often I barely get a moment of downtime.

I was in D.C. last week and saw our favorite boy. Dang he is looking good. Tell me again why I never hooked up with him? Anyways. I met his new girl, Maria, and she is a knock out. They met at some support group he has been going to. Weird, right? What kind of support group would he need? They were all hush hush about it.

He told me he is flying you in for the holidays. I hope you go. I will try to get out there too and visit for a few days. It will be a blast and maybe Sam has some cute friends hanging around for me!

I am going home to Nashville for Thanksgiving this year. I promised my parents. I am totally looking forward to hearing about my unavoidable old maid status since I am thirty and unmarried. I will find something really naughty to share when they ask me what I am thankful for at dinner. Maybe that will get them to back off.

Well, I love you girl and miss you bunches. I have to finish packing. Off to the airport in the morning.

Xoxo,
Hadley

I wonder why she didn't mention Sarah being pregnant. Hadley loves her no strings attached lifestyle so maybe baby talk is just completely off her radar.

Russell is at the back window again and I can hear the faint sound of his meow. I go to the hall closet and grab a comforter and pillow to take outside with me.

I lay the comforter on the patio folded in half. I lay down between the warm down alternative and position the pillow under my head. Russell comes over to me and curls up at my side. I don't have the energy to pet him but he presses his body into me and purrs anyways.

"Nia, wake up," Gertie's voice rings in my ears and I rub my eyes before opening them. "What are you doing out here? Should I call Dr. Gillis or Noie?"

I shake my head no and sit up stretching. The sun is directly overhead. It must be close to noon. Gertie is still standing over me with a look of concern on her face. I stand up and bend over to grab the comforter and pillow. Gertie grabs them from me and walks back into the house. I follow and close the door.

I settle down in my chair and light a cigarette. Gertie walks back in from the laundry room and asks, "Have you eaten anything for lunch?"

I shake my head no.

"I will make you some soup and crackers. You need to eat," she says as she storms towards the kitchen on a mission.

I can smell the tomato soup heating in the other room. My stomach begins to growl and I realize I haven't eaten since lunch yesterday.

While I wait for my soup, I grab my phone and turn it on. I scroll through the contacts until I find *his* name and hit send. It rings five times before the familiar voicemail picks up. I listen to *his* voice and my eyes fill with tears. It ends too quickly so I dial again. Then a third time and leave a message, "I miss you. Every day I wake up and wonder how this happened. I just want you back here with me and I can't understand why you are not here. I love you still."

I quickly hang up the phone as Gertie sets the bowl of soup down beside me. I hope she didn't hear that.

21 NIA THEN

"Jimmy, have you talked to Ian?"

"Not since yesterday. What's going on?" He asks.

"He didn't come home last night. He met with Jett about the practice they are opening after Ian passes the bar exam, but I haven't spoken to him since then. I have called all the hospitals. I don't know what to do," I say as tears come back to my eyes.

"I'm sure he's fine. Let me see what I can find out. Just take a deep breath and relax. I'll call you as soon as I know something," Jimmy says before hanging up.

I hope he is okay, but if he is, what does that mean? Where did he stay last night? Since he graduated from law school he has spent every free minute studying for his exam. He has been so distant. I don't want to believe he would be with another woman, but now that he hasn't come home, I can't help but consider it as a possibility.

I want to call Jett again, but I am too embarrassed. When I talked to him last night, he thought he might have gotten a drink with Jimmy after their meeting.

I pick up the phone to call Sarah. I have to talk to someone.

"Hello."

"Hey, Sarah," I say with a crack in my voice.

"Is everything ok? Are you crying?"

"Ian didn't come home last night."

"What do you mean? Is he okay?" She asks concerned.

"I don't know. No one has talked to him since about eight last night. I called the hospitals and now Jimmy is looking for him."

"Oh my goodness. Do you want me to come over and help you or wait with you?"

"No, I have to get to the studio soon. I have two classes today and I am working with a local dance group on some choreography. I can't cancel."

"I could wait at your apartment for him. Blake is out of town and I am working from home today."

"I don't want you to have to do that," I say and there is a long pause before I ask, "Do you think he met someone else?"

"Nia, Ian loves you. Maybe he went to the library to study and fell asleep. Don't start thinking the worst."

"He has been so distant and he won't talk to me about what is going on. I don't know what else to think."

"You need to get ready and go to the studio. When you get home, I am sure he will be there and you can talk to him about it. I'm sure there is an explanation."

"You're right. I know you're right," I say, but I don't know that at all.

"Call me when you hear from him."

"Okay, bye."

We hang up and I don't feel any better. I fight the urge to call and cancel my classes, but I know it is too late to notify everyone. I get ready and head to the studio. My mind is swimming with thoughts of Ian with another woman.

When I am finished working with the dance troupe there is a notification on my phone alerting me to a voicemail from Jimmy. He said Ian is fine and at home.

I drive to the apartment as fast as I can and rush inside. Ian is sitting on the couch with a law book in his lap. He looks up at me and smiles. I fight the desire to let last night go and jump into his arms.

"Where were you?" I ask without taking a step closer to him.

"I'm sorry. I was studying and lost track of time."

"You lost track of time? You didn't call or come home Ian. Do you have any idea how worried I have been? I called hospitals looking for you," I scream at him unable to keep my cool.

"Calm down. I'm sorry. I am under a lot of pressure right now. I didn't mean to worry you. Come sit down."

"I don't want to fucking sit down. Is there someone else? Just tell me and get it over with if there is," I say, the screaming giving way to tears now.

He puts the book on the table and comes to me.

"Of course not. How could you think that? I love you," he says with a look of alarm in his pale green eyes.

He reaches for me and I push his hands away. He tries again and I start slapping his chest.

"You can't do that to me. You can't stay out all night and not even call. You can't do that to me."

He gets ahold of my hands and pulls me into him. My anger waivers and I lay my head on his chest. He is holding me and rubbing my back when someone knocks at the door. I push away from him and look out the peep hole.

"It's Noie, Jett and the girls," I say quietly to Ian and wipe the tears from my face. "I forgot they were coming."

"Go to the bedroom and take a minute. I'll tell them you will be right out."

I hear Ian open the door and greet them. Noie's sing song voice asks, "Where is Auntie Nia? Her favorite girls are here for movie night."

I take a quick shower to wash the day off of me and get dressed. My face is still red from crying, but hopefully Noie will just think it is from the hot water of the shower.

"Look at Auntie Nia's two little princesses," I say when I walk into the living room. "They are wearing the jumpers I got them and they look so adorable. Now hand over the baby!"

Noie places Audra in my arms and I take in the powdery scent. I love these little girls.

"Auntie Nia," Audrie's tiny voice calls me as she pulls on my leg. "Hold me too."

I sit on the couch so she can slide up under my arm. With her little arms around me, I let go of the hurt and anger I was feeling earlier. That will have to wait for another time.

22 IAN THEN

Life has been getting more and more stressful. I need some kind of outlet. I can't figure out how to let go and let things be. I have spent the last three years in law school and they mean nothing if I do not pass this exam.

Nia has been going out of her way to take care of everything so all I have to do is focus on the Bar exam and work with Jett on plans for the practice.

Now she is pissed at me and I just want to fix it, but I can't talk to her about what is going on. I didn't mean to stay out all night. I was supposed to make it home before she woke up and then she would have never known I was gone.

I am glad we had plans with Jett and Noie tonight. Nia will be more relaxed after and hopefully she won't try to talk about it anymore. I will just be more careful from now on. I will have to make it home before she wakes up. I don't ever want to see her look as mad and hurt as she was earlier.

I love her and all I want is her happiness. I hope she

knows that. Keeping things from her that will just upset her, is my way of protecting her. I hope she can see that.

23 NIA DIARY

Dear Diary,

Ian has been so distant and after he stayed out the other night, I was sure he was cheating on me. Then I watched him play with Audrie and Audra and I don't see him being able to do something like that. He has too good of a heart. He kept looking at me and everything in me melted. I can feel his love when he looks at me like that. I am sure it is just the stress of the exam.

When the exam is over I think everything will be back to normal. What do you think?

Everyone goes through times when things don't really click. I just need to try harder to get the spark going. Maybe I should talk to Hadley about it. She would be able to give me advice without digging too deeply or getting very judgie about it like Sarah or Noie would.

Ian and I have never been in a long relationship before each other. We have to navigate all of the ups and downs of a relationship for the first time together. I just don't want to push him right now with everything he has on his plate. He takes the exam in two weeks. I will plan something amazing for the night after the exam.

I guess I just miss him. I miss us. I don't ever want to lose what we have.

24 NIA NOW

I can't sleep. I have been trying to fall asleep for hours now. I roll over and look at the clock which reads five o'clock. Frustrated, I roll out of bed and make my way to the bathroom to brush my teeth.

I go to the drawer I keep my dance clothes in. I pull out the first thing I see and get dressed. I need to clear my head and dancing was how I used to do it.

I make my way to the basement and turn on the lights. All the mirrors are clean and I don't see a sign of dust anywhere. Gertie must be keeping it clean down here. That makes sense, but I guess I just felt like this studio stopped existing when I stopped using it.

I walk over to the stereo equipment in the corner of the room and scroll through the IPod. I find the song for the first performance I choreographed myself during my freshman year of college. I hit play and put it on repeat.

I lift my leg onto the bar and begin stretching. Everything feels so tight. As I stretch, all my muscles feel foreign to me. Slowly, I start relaxing and my muscles begin to warm up. I close my eyes and breathe as I deepen into each stretch. I own my movements and let the music take over. Moving with the music, muscle memory takes over and every move becomes as natural as breathing.

I watch myself in the mirrors as I dance. I feel freer with each movement. I love the feeling of sweat seeping from my pores and flowing down my skin.

Out of the corner of my eye, I see something on the stairs and I freeze. Noie.

"Sorry. I didn't mean to interrupt. I just haven't seen you dance in so long and when I heard the music coming from down here…I just had to come see."

I walk over to the stereo and turn the music off. Grabbing a small towel from the shelf, I walk towards Noie. She stands and follows me as I go up the stairs.

I feel so winded. Chain smoking cigarettes is probably not the best thing for my stamina. I used to only be a social smoker, thanks to Jett. I always remind Noie her husband gave me my first cigarette when she says anything about my smoking becoming a full time occupation. Now, Noie brings me cigarettes and tries to mask her annoyance at it.

"I didn't know you were coming today," I say as I walk to my chair where my coffee is waiting for me.

"I wasn't planning on it, but then something came in the mail for you and I wanted to bring it over."

She reaches into her purse and pulls out a large manila envelope. I instantly recognize Sam's handwriting on the front. He sent the tickets. I hold the envelope in my lap without opening it.

"He called me the other day. He is really looking forward to you coming out there. I will miss you at

Christmas, but I think you will have a great time."

I close my eyes and take a few breaths to calm myself. The pressure is feeling too heavy at this moment. I love Sam, but I don't know if I am ready to spend three weeks away from home. What if he makes me do stuff every day and tries to make me talk more than I want to. I don't know if I can handle it. I don't know if I want to go. I open my eyes and reach for a cigarette.

"Have you fed Russell yet today?"

I shake my head no.

"Well good. I get to do it then. I would like to bring the girls over to meet him. Let me know when you are up for it. We could just come for a morning feeding on the weekend or something," she says as she walks towards the kitchen to get his food.

I open the envelope and pull out the tickets. December tenth until January fifth. That is almost a month. Noie walks back in and sees me staring at the tickets.

"He told me he has a lot of built up vacation time he never uses. He plans on being off the entire time you are there. He even told me about Maria. Sounds like she might last more than a few nights," she says with a small laugh.

Maria. That reminded me of Hadley's letter. She said they met at a support group. I hope nothing is wrong with Sam. He is the definition of a workaholic. Taking almost a month off work doesn't sound like him at all. The panic beings to rise. I can't handle anything being wrong with Sam. He is my rock. My breathing gets frantic and I knock the tickets onto the floor.

Noie jumps out of her chair and runs to the kitchen.

She comes back with a pill and a bottle of water.

"Take these before it gets too bad."

I knock her hand away from me and the pill flies across the room.

"Nia, calm down. Focus on your breathing."

I rock back and forth. Every possible ailment starts flashing through my mind. What if he has cancer? What if it is something else just as awful?

"No, no, no, no, no, no, no, no," I can't stop the word from coming out over and over again.

"Nia, focus please." She must have picked up the pill, because it is back in her outstretched hand. "Take this pill. You need to take it."

I calm myself enough to grab the pill and put it in my mouth. She hands me the water to wash it down with. I continue to rock and start fumbling for my phone. When I can't get the power on, Noie grabs it for me and turns it on. I grab it back and find Sam's number and hit send.

"Hey beautiful," his voice melts me and I begin crying. "What's going on?" he asks with worry. "Shh, honey. Try to take a breath. Are you alone?"

I shake my head, but I know he can't see me. I hand the phone to Noie.

"Hey Sam, its Noie." She pauses and I can't hear Sam's side of the conversation. "I just gave her a pill. I came over to bring the tickets you sent and she just started panicking," she pauses again and then says, "Okay," before handing the phone back to me.

"Nia, I didn't mean to upset you. You don't have to use the tickets if you don't want to, but I told you I was sending them. They shouldn't have been a surprise. Please just calm down and you can throw them in the trash."

I control the crying enough to say, "I'll be there." I hang up the phone before he can say anything else and power the phone off. I can feel the medicine kicking in. It makes me feel tired and heavy.

"Do you want to get in the tub and relax? I will stay with you to make sure you don't fall asleep."

I nod my head yes and stand. I pick up my cigarettes and ashtray before walking to the bedroom. Noie walks ahead of me into the bathroom and begins running water in the tub. She takes my cigarettes and ashtray to sit on the ledge above the tub. I strip out of my clothes and ease myself into the warm water. I sink down until my chin rests on the top of the water. Sam is okay. He has to be.

"Nia, I don't know what happened, but I am here if you want to talk about it."

She settles down on the floor and leans against the side of the tub. I don't want to talk to her about it. My suspicions will feel too real if I voice them. I just have to keep telling myself he is okay until I believe it. Maybe believing it will make it true.

25 NIA THEN

"Jett and I need your help this week. How does your schedule look today?" Ian asks me.

Ian and Jett opened their practice together about eight months ago. I help out as much as I can. I was pre-law in college, but I have signed up for a few paralegal courses at the local trade college to be able to help more.

"I have a class today and two private lessons this evening, but I will have a big gap in the middle of the day."

"Good. We have some things that need to be filed at the courthouse and I need you to set up a few meetings for us. I jotted down the people we need meetings with. Look at our calendars and fit them in where you can. I have to run," he says and kisses me before running out the door.

Two seconds later, the door flies back open and Ian drops his briefcase. He walks to me, wraps his arms around me and gives me a deep kiss.

"How did I get so lucky?" He asks and kisses me again.

I stare after him as he walks back out the door. I wish he didn't have to run off to work. That kiss makes me want to spend the day in bed with him.

Crap. I am supposed to meet with the realtor today. I forgot. I will have to reschedule with her later in the week. I want Ian to look at the houses with me, but with all the hours he is putting in building the practice, finding a house is left to me. It will be less stressful when we are out of this tiny apartment. We will have an office at the house that doesn't double as a dining room. Hopefully it will allow Ian to work from home some and we can see each other more.

My phone starts ringing and I run to the kitchen where I left it by the coffee pot.

"Hello."

"Hey girlie! What are you doing?" Hadley asks.

"Getting ready to head over to the studio. What's going on?"

"I'm coming for a visit next weekend and I even got Sam to agree to fly out. It has been a while since we have all been together and I miss everyone like crazy so clear your schedule."

"That's a tall order right now. Ian is busy and I have been helping out a lot, but I am sure I can break away for dinner or something. Where are you staying?"

"I'm staying at Sarah's and Sam is getting a hotel. He will only be in for one night. Saturday, I think. I will let you know and I will get us reservations somewhere."

"Sounds good. I have to run. My schedule is packed today. See you next week," I say and hang up the phone.

It will be a good escape to see them. We all talk on the phone as much as we can, but it has been almost a year since Hadley or Sam have made it to town. Sarah and I always talk about going to visit them, but we haven't found the time yet.

I make my cup of coffee and find the pack of cigarettes I have stashed away. I go outside to sit on the balcony and relax for a few minutes before starting my day. The neighbor's dog isn't allowing me any peace. They lock him on the balcony all day and he barks at every noise or movement. I guess I should be getting ready anyways.

I go to the dining room to grab the paper Ian left with the names of people he needed meetings set up with. I notice a scrap of paper falling out of his planner so I open it to tuck it back in securely and freeze when I see it.

Lunch with Becca – 1:30 p.m. Tuesday

Something about it bothers me. I know he has lunch with clients, but "Becca" feels informal. When he puts lunch meetings on his calendar, he will use first and last names. I search my memory for a client with the name Rebecca, but I don't remember anyone. I am being ridiculous. She is probably a new client and I haven't worked with every client file. It could be anything. I try to shake off the sinking feeling in my stomach and start getting ready for the day.

I arrive at the restaurant about fifteen minutes late. I was trying to wait for Ian to be free, but he and Jett are still stuck at the office. As I walk in, I look down at what I have on. A simple black dress and flats. I hope Sarah and Hadley don't give me too much grief.

The hostess shows me to the table and Sam slaps the open chair next to him as he says, "Do you sleep anymore?"

"Hello to you too. Next time you can just say I look like crap."

"Excuse me, but that is not what I meant. I never think you look like crap. I asked if you were sleeping out of concern because even in all your glory, it is obvious you are tired," Sam says backpedaling.

"Stop hogging her, Sam," Hadley says as she walks around the table to give me a hug. "You look wonderful. Boys are just mean and stupid."

"Now this is someone I am happy to see," I say smirking at Sam. "Sorry I am late. Have you been here long?"

"Not too long," Sarah says.

"Is this for me?" I ask pointing to the glass of wine in front of me.

"Yes," they all chime in.

"I tried to wait for Ian, but he couldn't leave the office."

"I don't know why you are house hunting. You should just set up a room at the office for you too," Blake says.

"I know but speaking of house hunting, do you want to look at some places with me this week? I need another opinion and Ian can't make it," I say to Sarah.

"If you let me know in advance, I will take off and just do some work from home before we go."

"You are the best. Enough of my stuff. What is

going on in the big cities with the two of you?" I ask Sam and Hadley.

"Me first," Hadley says. "I just got a promotion and it came with a raise big enough to move into the building I have been lusting after since moving to Chicago."

"Congratulations," we say and lift our glasses of wine to toast her.

"My news is not as good. I work all the time hoping to get noticed and that's it," Sam says.

"Boo hoo, I know you love your life out there in D.C. Don't act like you don't. Plus I am sure there is a steady stream of new women for you to chase," I say to Sam.

"Nia, my love, of course I love my life and I don't have to chase very hard," he says winking. "I do miss this. I miss getting to see all of you. I have friends in D.C., but they just don't compare. I think about moving back sometimes."

"Me too," Hadley says. "But now that I can get the apartment I want, I think you should all move to Chicago," she says laughing.

When dinner is over, Sam asks, "Nia, do you mind giving me a ride to the hotel so I don't have to be crammed into the backseat with this heathen again?"

Hadley playfully shoves him after his heathen comment.

"Sure."

We all say our goodbyes and Sam follows me to my car. It takes less than five minutes before we are pulling up in front of his hotel.

"Do you want to come in for a drink at the bar?" Sam asks.

"Let me call Ian. He might be out now and could

come meet us."

"Okay, give him a call. I'm going to talk to the valet so they park your car under my room and Ian's too. Let him know that if he is coming."

Two minutes later, I get out of the car and hand the keys to the valet.

"Is he coming?"

"Yes, I caught him right as he was finishing up. He should be here in fifteen minutes."

"Then let's get started," Sam says and holds out his elbow for me to hold as we walk in.

Ian joins us before we finish our drink and quickly orders one for himself after kissing me hello and doing that weird slap hug guys do with Sam.

"Sounds like you have been busy," Sam says to Ian.

"Man, I knew this would be a lot of work, but I had no idea it would be this rough. We are doing good and building a solid reputation for our practice. That's a good thing, I guess. Most days I am too tired to care."

"I hear that. I work all the time too and everyone says you reach a point where things are easier and you don't have to put in as many hours. That day cannot come soon enough," Sam says.

I sit back and sip my wine while they swap work war stories. Every once in a while, Ian will squeeze my knee and lean in for a kiss. As the night goes on, I can see the tension leaving Ian's shoulders. He looks happier and more relaxed than I have seen him in a while. I don't want to interrupt boy time, but I need some time with my husband while he is in this mood.

"Sorry to be a party pooper boys, but I need to get home and I need my husband with me," I say looking in

Ian's eyes. He sees the meaning and calls for the tab.

We leave my car at the hotel and barely make it through the door of our apartment, before we are ripping each other's clothes off.

"Nia, I hate to tell you this, but today is the last time I go looking at houses with you. We have been three times in the last two weeks and seen more houses than I could possibly remember. Almost all of them had everything on your list and you said no to them. After today, you are on your own or you can drag Hadley from Chicago to go with you," Sarah says with exasperation oozing from her voice.

"I have a good feeling about today. This is the house Ian and I will spend the rest of our lives in. We will raise our family in this house. It has to be perfect. I just need something about it to scream to me 'you are home.'"

"Blah, blah, blah. Choose one or you are on your own."

I laugh at the face she is making and walk out the door with her dragging her feet behind me.

Lucky for me and Sarah, I walk to the back window of the third house we go to and I see a beautiful willow tree in the middle of an expansive backyard. That is what I needed. That tree lets me know I am home.

I turn to Sarah and the realtor and say, "I want to make an offer. I'm home."

I wish I could have shared this moment with Ian. I hope he likes it as much as I do.

26 NIA DIARY

Dear Diary,

We moved into our house! This has been the most amazing month of our lives together. Ian and I broke in every room in the house. He took some time off work so we could shop for new furniture and decorations for the house. Everything feels rejuvenated.

Hadley called and she is coming next week to make sure I am not decorating the entire house in black. What she doesn't know is I have ten cans of paint in the garage with our names on it.

The contractors are starting on the studio today. It will be wonderful to not have to drive across town to the studio where I rent space. I wish we could put in a music area for Ian, but he said he didn't need one. I wish he would play the guitar more. Every once in a while, he will play and the look on his face can be described as nothing other than peace. It is such a pleasant change from the constant stress I see on his face when he is working on a case.

I feel like everything is falling in place for us. This next chapter of our lives is going to be even better than the last. The love I feel for him hasn't stop. I slept in the other morning after moving in.

When I woke up at eleven, I found Ian's signature sticky notes which led me to the backyard. He laid out my quilt and had a picnic set up under the willow tree. After we ate, we broke in the backyard too.

27 NIA NOW

"Nia, your bags are all ready to go," Gertie calls from my bedroom. "And the car should be here to take you to the airport in thirty minutes."

The day is finally here to go to Tennessee for Thanksgiving. I made arrangements to take a different flight and stay for less time than Noie, Jett, and the girls. They are spending the entire week, but I feel like I am keeping up my end of the arrangement as long as I am there for the actual holiday, so I agreed to stay for three days. This way Jett can still have his family get away from the crazy sister-in-law.

Russell has finished his morning food and I decide to go outside and play with him for a few more minutes. He is the first pet I have ever owned and I never expected to feel so attached to him. The thought of not seeing him for the next three days saddens me. I grab the stick with tassels hanging from one end out of the toy bin and go outside. As I swish it around in the air, he jumps and swats at it. This has proved to be his favorite toy and I can't help but smile at how excited he gets when I walk outside with it.

The temperatures are dropping lower and lower. I have tried to entice him to come in the house, but he hasn't taken the bait. Noie bought a cat house for him a few weeks ago so he would have somewhere to get out of the wind and escape the snow when it starts to fall. I am still hoping the warmth of the house will change his mind before that happens.

I stop swinging the toy and rub his head before going back inside. Gertie is waiting for me when I enter.

"Don't worry about him while you are gone. Odie is out of school for the holiday break and I told him he could come with me to look after Russell. He was really excited. I hope you don't mind."

I shake my head no. Odie is her eight year old son. He is a sweet kid with a quieter demeanor than most boys his age. There is some relief to know he will come and probably play with Russell until he falls asleep from exhaustion.

"I put your bags by the front door. Is there anything else you need?"

Shaking my head no, I grab my pack of cigarettes and head to the front hall when there is suddenly a knock at the door. It startles me and my heart begins to race when I realize it is most likely the driver.

Gertie runs up behind me and says, "I put your pills in the front pocket of your carry on. Noie wanted me to remind you to take one when you get to the airport. She thinks it will help you on the flight. She will be at the airport in Chattanooga to pick you up alone. She also wanted to make sure you turn your phone on when you land and send her a text message."

The knocking on the door starts again with a little more force and I reach for the knob. An older man with kind blue eyes greets me.

"Good morning ma'am. Do you have any luggage you would like me to grab?"

I reach for my carry on and point to the large suitcase next to it. Waving bye to Gertie, I walk out the door. As I open the door of the car, I notice Mrs. Oden checking her mailbox.

She sees me and says, "Hello Nia, Happy Thanksgiving."

I politely wave and smile before sitting in the car and closing the door. The driver left the car running with the heater on higher than necessary and I pull at my collar feeling a little suffocated. After my suitcase is safely in the trunk, he gets in the car and we are off to the airport.

I am lost in the scenery out the car window when we pull up to the drop off at the airport. I love the anonymity and energy of the airport. I take my suitcase from the driver and roll it through the doors to the counter and check it. I watch all of the families bustling around and struggling to keep their kids from running off to explore their new surroundings. Audrie and Audra come to mind. I haven't seen them in months and missed both of their birthdays. I hope they are not upset with me when I see them. Noie has reassured me over and over again about the resiliency of kids leading up to this trip.

I make my way through security and find a coffee shop. I still have twenty minutes before my flight boards, but I decide to pass up the shops and settle down into a seat at the gate. I decide to read until they begin boarding.

I am lost in the book when the announcement is made to board first class. I put the book back in my carryon bag and walk over to the door where a girl who appears to be in her early twenties scans my boarding pass.

I take my seat next to the window and pull out the bottle of water I bought when I got my coffee along with one of my pills. Placing it in my mouth, I take a large drink of the water to wash it down.

A man dressed in expensively ripped jeans and a concert tee takes the seat next to me. He appears to be close to my age, maybe a few years older, and is attractive with his dark brown hair falling just below his ears and his chocolate brown eyes. He smiles when he notices me looking at him. I smile back and look quickly back out the window. I hope he is not a talker. No such luck.

"Hi, my name is Tanner," he says and I detect a slight British accent. Possibly, he lived there when he was young, but he has been in the United States long enough where it is not overly pronounced.

"Nia," I say with a forced smile hoping he will understand I am not in the mood to talk.

"Well Nia, nice to meet you. What takes you to Chattanooga?"

"An airplane," I say sarcastically since he is not reading my body language which is screaming not to talk to me.

"I suppose that's true. I am flying out to spend the holiday with my old college roommate. I didn't have plans and he was nice enough to invite me. It's nice to have somewhere to go for the holidays."

I don't engage in the conversation. Instead I just nod in agreement and look back out the window.

"He is having a big family get together. I feel a little bit like an intruder, but he insisted it would be fine. The more the merrier or something like that."

At this point he is just talking to the back of my head. It is very uncomfortable when people do not get the point. Luckily the flight attendant comes by and interrupts.

"Miss, can I get you something to drink?"

"Coffee please, two sugars."

"And you sir?"

"Coffee, black."

She hands us our cups of coffee and I am thankful he has something to occupy his mouth for a minute.

"This is one of my favorite holidays. What is not to like about a day devoted to eating as much as you can?"

It looks like I am going to have to be a little more direct.

"Tanner, is it? Listen, I am sure you are a nice person who just wants to have a little friendly chit chat to pass the time, but I don't."

"I'm sorry. I just…" he trails off and finally understands. The rest of the flight goes by in silence except when the flight attendant comes by again to remove our empty cups and see if we need anything else.

The flight was smooth and I was happy to be back on solid ground. I pull out my phone and text Noie to let her know I have landed. My phone dings almost immediately.

Perfect. I am about twenty minutes away. That should give you time to get your bag.

As soon as they open the door, I step out behind Tanner and quickly grab my bag out of the overhead compartment. Walking as fast as I can manage without jogging, I make my way to the baggage claim just as the buzzer sounds alerting everyone the baggage is about to come out. My bag, with its red and black checkered strap is the fifth bag down the carousel. I pull it off the the rotating belt and make my way to the exit. Noie isn't out here yet, so I find a bench and dig around in my bag for a cigarette. I realize I didn't grab a lighter when I left the house and sigh in frustration.

"I don't want to disturb you but it looks like you need a light," Tanner says from beside me. Great, this guy again. I turn towards him and he has a lighter outstretched to me already lit. I place my cigarette in my mouth and light it.

"Thank you."

He doesn't move from beside me, but he lights a cigarette and stays quiet. Just then, Noie pulls up, jumps out, and comes towards me. She stops right before she takes the handle of my suitcase and looks towards Tanner.

"Tanner, is that you? Jake said you were coming, but he didn't mention I should pick you up."

You have got to be kidding me. This is Jake's friend. I never really liked Jett's older brother and I think the feeling is mutual. Now he is going to be really miffed when Tanner tells him what a bitch I was on the plane.

"Noie, it has been forever," he says giving her a hug. "I think Jake's wedding, right?"

"Yes, I think so. It looks like you met my sister," she says looking at me.

"We had the pleasure of sitting next to each other on the plane, but I didn't realize she was your sister."

"How are you getting to the house?"

"I was just going to grab a cab because I need to check in at the hotel before coming over. Jake told me there would be plenty of cars around so I could use his while I am here instead of getting a rental."

"Well let me drive you to the hotel then."

Tanner turns towards me and asks, "Do you mind?"

I shrug, grab the handle of my suitcase and walk towards Noie's rental car.

Noie and Tanner talk the entire ride to the hotel. I try my best to ignore the conversation. I'm regretting this trip but keep reminding myself it is only three days. I can get through three days. There is a slight panic building in my chest. I reach for my bag and take out another pill. I swallow it and notice Noie giving me a worried look out of the corner of my eye. I roll my eyes and look back out the window. I am just trying to get myself under control before I flip out in front of this stranger.

We pull up to the front of the hotel and Tanner jumps out thanking Noie for the ride. Then he says, "Nia. It was a pleasure." He closes the door and I watch as he disappears into the hotel.

"Tanner is such a nice guy," Noie says as she pulls out of the circular drive. "Did you talk much on the plane?"

I shake my head no and she purses her lips.

"Well I have seen him many times over the years. I don't think he has much family around because Jake invites him to almost everything. I'm surprised you haven't met him before. I guess you did only come to Jett's family's a few times. I guess it was the few times Tanner didn't come for some reason. Everyone is at the house already. A few of Jett's aunts and uncles are here with their children and grand-children. His sister, Jane, also came with her kids. Most people are staying at the same hotel as Tanner. The only people other than us staying at the house is Jake, Jane and their families. We have you set up in the pool house. I thought that would be nice for you to have a little privacy and quiet. There is a coffee pot out there with coffee and sugar. I also put a few cans of soup in case you didn't want to come in to the main house for every meal. We are not cooking tonight. Everyone wants to go to the Mexican restaurant that has a play area so we can have a nice dinner while the kids are entertained. It also gives Jett's mom a break from all the cooking since she will be up before dawn to cook Thanksgiving dinner tomorrow. I will let you take the keys to this car. We put your name on the rental agreement so you are free to use it for the next few days." She pauses, takes a breath after her nervous talking and places her hand over mine to give it a little squeeze before saying, "I'm really glad you came."

At this moment, I don't share that feeling, but I look at her and smile anyway. Its early afternoon and the two pills I have taken today are making it hard to keep my eyes open.

Noie pulls around to the back of the house so I can go straight into the pool house and nap before I have to face the hoard of people inside.

Closing the door, I walk straight to the bedroom. I pull back the covers and crawl into the soft bed.

"Auntie Nia." Audra's sweet voice wakes me. She is gently nudging my shoulder. I roll over and look at the clock. I have been sleeping for over three hours. I bet everyone is already getting ready for dinner.

Audra is looking at me with sad eyes and my heart breaks. I pull up the covers for her to get in next to me. I wrap my arms around her little frame. I missed this little girl so much. I hate how I may be the reason for the sad look in her eyes and I just want to make it go away.

"Don't tell mommy I came in here. She said we have to leave you alone because you still don't feel good, but I really missed you and just wanted to see if you were okay."

"Don't worry baby. You won't be in trouble. Auntie Nia is happy you wanted to check on me. I will tell your mommy that."

I hear a soft knock on the door before it opens. Noie is standing there and when her eyes fall on Audra's face she instantly looks upset.

"Audra what did I tell you about leaving Auntie Nia alone?" she says in 'a stern mommy voice. I know it well from my childhood. It is a voice she started perfecting at the age of eight.

"Sorry mommy. I was just worried about her and she said she was happy I checked on her."

Noie's face softens at the sound of her delicate voice laced with a whimper.

"Okay, sweetie, but you are still supposed to listen when I tell you something. Now run inside and get dressed for dinner. I laid out something for you and Audrie. Daddy will help you get ready and I will be in to brush your hair. I just need to talk to Auntie Nia for a minute."

I give her a soft kiss on her head and she slides out of the bed before heading to the main house.

"I'm sorry about Audra. I will make sure she doesn't come out here again without permission."

"It's okay."

"We are going to leave for dinner in about thirty minutes. Do you want to come with us?" she asks hopefully.

I rub the sleep out of my eyes and nod my head yes. I have to get this over with. If I go tonight then maybe I won't feel so guilty tomorrow if I stay away from everyone until it is time to eat.

A smile brightens her face and she claps her hands together. "Come inside as soon as you are ready and we can go," she says before heading out the door.

I pull myself out of bed and get my toothbrush out of my bag. Looking in the mirror, while brushing my teeth, I decide I am fine to wear the jeans and black sweater I already have on.

I timidly walk into the back door of the main house and the loud conversations I could hear from outside come to an abrupt halt. The first person I make eye contact with is Jett. I walk over to him and he wraps his arms around me. I can't hold back the emotion and tears start running down my face. This amazing man has been like a brother to me from the moment him and Noie began dating in college. I have completely shut him out and basically stolen his wife, but here he is holding me and trying to comfort me.

"Hey, Nia. It's okay. It's okay," he says in a faint whisper while rubbing my back. The quiet of the room which is full of no less than thirty people begins to dawn on me.

Audrie's voice breaks the silence, "Daddy is Auntie Nia still not feeling well?"

"No baby, but she will. She just needs time." He

pulls back from me and wipes the tears from under my eyes and says, "We are all really happy you are here. Now how about we go stuff ourselves with some Mexican food?"

I smile through the tears and nod my head. Just then I catch sight of Tanner with a look of concern on his face.

"Out front in five minutes everyone," Jett says to the room of staring onlookers.

I reach for a cigarette out of my purse and walk towards the front door and realize I am being followed by Tanner.

Feeling embarrassed, I look up at him with a meek smile.

"I just thought you might need a light," he says as he flicks the lighter to life.

"Thanks."

After a couple of drags, the door opens and everyone starts piling out.

"Nia, do you have the keys? Me, you, Jett and the girls will ride in the rental," Noie says.

I hand her the keys and look for a place to put my cigarette out.

"You can ride with me and finish that if you want," Tanner says.

Although I don't really want to be stuck in the car with him again, it seems like a better option than bunched in the back seat of the rental with the girls.

I shrug.

"Noie, Nia is going to ride with me," he says and holds up his cigarette as an explanation.

"Okay," Noie says and looks at me confused.

I just shrug and follow Tanner to Jake's car he is

borrowing.

"Jake is riding with us too. His wife and the baby are going with Jane and her kids."

Perfect. Car ride with Tanner and Jake. I should have just crammed myself into Noie's car.

I open the door to the backseat as Tanner and Jake jump in the front. Jake doesn't even acknowledge me. I say a silent thank you for that.

"So bro, how is everything in Louisville?" Jake asks Tanner.

"Good. Work has been busy which is always good."

"How are the women? We need to get you to join the married life. Then you might slow down enough to make it up to Cincinnati more and then Megan will have someone to occupy her while we hang out," Jake says with a laugh.

I roll my eyes. Megan is a sweet girl. Much too sweet for someone like Jake. I don't know how he lucked out. He is good looking, but how can you look past the machismo personality?

"That is not even on my radar Jake. My life is much too busy trying to build my business to have time for a wife or family right now. You can bring it up again when I turn forty."

"I hope you are still getting a nice piece of ass to keep you company."

Is he serious? Who talks like that? Jake, I guess. It shouldn't surprise me. I feel a twinge of sadness for his wife. I can't imagine how she is treated with his apparent lack of respect for women. I can tell Tanner looks uncomfortable with the conversation. Probably just because I am in the car. If he is friends with this asshole, he is probably just like him.

"Naw man. I just have Missy to keep me company," Tanner replies. He looks in the rearview mirror at me and says, "Missy is my dog."

I look back at him with a look that says, "Did I ask?"

"Do you mind stopping at a gas station on our way so I can get a lighter?" I ask. I do need a lighter, but I really just need a minute out of this car with Jake to calm myself. I wish they could just leave me at the gas station and let me call a cab.

"No, I got it," Tanner says as he hands me his lighter.

I take it and light another cigarette. I feel like a prisoner. I don't think I can do this. Why did I agree to come here? I just want to be in my house with my stuff. I don't want to be at the mercy of all these people for three days. I'm really trying. Would Noie realize I really tried if I left early? Would she feel like I was breaking my promise to her? I take another pill out of my purse and dry swallow it. I begin to rock and try to calm myself.

"Hey Nia, are you okay? Should I pull over?" Tanner asks.

"Bro don't worry about her she is just crazy," Jake says in annoyance.

I feel the screams begging to escape my throat and I rock faster.

"I'm pulling over. Jake call Noie and ask them to pull into the parking lot up ahead."

With the effort I exert to try to smother the screams, I begin to cry. Jake yanks his phone from his pocket.

"Jett can you pull over at the Speedway up ahead. Your freak of a sister-in-law is losing her shit," he says before hanging up.

"Not cool Jake," Tanner says in an angry voice.

"Whatever."

We pull over and seconds later Noie is jumping from her car before Jett has a chance to fully stop and comes running towards me. Tanner and Jake are already out of the car.

"Nia, have you taken a pill?" Noie asks.

I nod my head yes as best I can while continuing to rock.

"Tanner, I am going to have Jett and the kids ride with you so I can take her back."

"No, no, no," I scream and shake my head. I don't want to ruin their night. "Cab," I yell out.

"I am not letting you get in a cab like this," she says.

"Noie, come here for a minute," Jett says.

They walk a few feet away, but I can still hear them.

"You are not going back to the house. You promised me you would be present in our lives this week. I know she is your sister and she is going through a lot, but we need you. For this marriage to function, I need you. We have talked about this," Jett says in a fiery tone I never hear him take with her.

"Hey Noie, how about you let Jake ride in your car and I will take her back. I will sit with her while you have dinner and wait until you get back to leave."

"No, you can't do that. She needs me."

Jett walks up and Tanner asks if he can talk to him for a minute. They walk away where I cannot hear the conversation. Get ahold of yourself and just calm down. I keep repeating this to myself over and over again.

"Noie," Jett says softly. "Let me talk to Nia." Noie steps to the side and Jett squats down to my level. "Do you want to go back to the house?"

I nod my head yes again and more tears fall.

"Do you need Noie to take you?" he asks.

I shake my head no.

"Well we are not going to let you go back in a cab like this with a complete stranger and be alone at the house, but Tanner has offered to take you. He is a good friend of our family. He will make sure you are ok. Can you handle that?"

I reluctantly nod my head yes. I just want to be alone, but more than that, I don't want to ruin their dinner.

"Then it is settled. Thank you Tanner. You have our cell numbers. Please call if you need us and we will be right there. Come on Jake, you are with us," Jett calls out in his brother's direction. I hear Jake mumble something, but all I could make out was "bitch" and I am sure it was directed at me.

Noie lingers by the car door and rubs my back. Jett comes up behind her and encouragingly says, "Come on honey, let's go."

She backs away as if stuck in quick sand and goes back to her car. Tanner kneels down beside me. I have managed to stop the tears, but I am unable to control the rocking.

"Nia, try to stop rocking and take this." Tanner is holding a lit cigarette out to me. His voice has taken on a soothing tone.

It takes me another minute, but finally I slow the rocking enough to take the cigarette. He sits down on the ground leaning against the open car door with his back to me. Why is he doing this? I have treated him with nothing but contempt since I met him. I finish the cigarette and tap him on the shoulder. He turns around and I hold out the burning butt to him. He takes it and flicks it out onto the street.

"Are you ready to go?" he asks.

I just nod my head yes and lay down across the backseat.

When we arrive at the house he drives around back and gets out to help me inside. I lean against him under the weight of the medicine.

Once inside he starts to guide me to the bedroom and I point to the couch. He helps me sit and finds a throw blanket to put over me. The material is itchy unlike my throw at home, but the warmth it provides is nice.

He locates the remote for the gas fire place and clicks it on before settling in a chair next to me.

I struggle but then find the words, "Thank you. I'm sorry you are missing dinner. Jake will never forgive me for this." The words come out shaky.

"Don't worry about Jake. He is not always like that. I was actually kind of shocked. Plus, I don't like Mexican food very much. I am much more of a pizza guy."

The word pizza sent my stomach into a frenzy and I realize I haven't eaten anything today.

He hears the grumbling coming from my stomach and smiles, "Sounds like you are hungry. I could order a pizza. Sound good?"

"Yes," I reply. "Cheese."

"Cheese pizza is my favorite."

He grabs his phone and locates the number to a local pizza delivery place. After he hangs up the phone he walks to the kitchenette and comes back with a glass of ice water for me. I smile and take the glass. The liquid feels good running down my throat which is dry from a mixture of crying and the medicine.

I stare into the flames of the gas fire place and zone out thinking about Russell and wondering if he is cold right now.

There is a knock at the door and I can smell the pizza as soon as Tanner opens the door. He quickly pays him and carries the pizza to the coffee table before grabbing some napkins. I sit up as he opens the box and hands me a piece. The hot cheese warms my mouth and I close my eyes as I chew. I finish the first piece in record time and reach for another. When done, I wipe my mouth and hands then pull a cigarette out of the pack. There is an ashtray on the table. I am sure Noie put it in here, so I guess that means they don't care if I smoke inside. Still without a lighter, Tanner reaches over and lights it for me.

By the time I am done smoking, sleep is beginning to take over. I stretch out on the couch and quickly fall asleep.

I wake when the light starts coming through the windows. I sit up, my heart beating fast, and look around forgetting where I am for a minute. Then I remember falling asleep on the sofa after eating pizza with Tanner. I am alone in the room, the pizza has been put away and the table cleaned.

As I sit up, the door opens and Noie walks in.

"Hey, I just wanted to check on you and put on a cup of coffee."

She walks to the kitchenette and I go to the bathroom to freshen up. When I come back there are two cups of coffee on the table. Sitting on the sofa, I shiver in the cool morning air and reach for my cup.

"How are you doing? Do you want to talk about what caused you to get upset last night?" She asks

"No," I reply. It's a pointless conversation to have. It was probably just a combination of everything about this trip, but Jake sent me over the edge. I can't tell her that because it would just cause problems. I don't want to make things even worse.

"We are going to make hand turkeys with all of the kids. You can come over and make one of your own if you want," she says in a sing-song voice. "If not, just come over whenever. Jett's mom is already up and cooking. She says we will be sitting down to eat at three."

We sit quietly for a few minutes before she continues, "I'm sorry for leaving you with Tanner last night. Was it okay? Did you get anything to eat?"

I nod.

"Okay, I am going to go in and help with the cooking a little bit before the girls get up."

She stands and walks to the door.

"Russell?" I say questioningly.

She turns with a huge smile spread across her face and says, "I called Gertie last night. She and Odie are taking good care of him. Gertie says she is going to have to get Odie a cat now. He is in love. Don't worry. See you later." She blows me a kiss and walks out the door.

I refill my coffee and take a seat at a chair near the window. The trees beyond the pool have shed almost all of their leaves. I long to be at my house where I can watch Russell scamper around the yard. The last few weeks, I have been sitting outside using the fire pit in the evenings. Russell has been very curious about the flames.

He crouches on the chair and watches it like prey.

Lost in my thoughts, I didn't see who walked up and was now knocking on the door. I get up to answer, a little upset I was pulled from my thoughts of Russell.

I open the door and Tanner is standing there holding a CD case.

When I don't move aside or say anything he asks, "Can I come in?"

I move to the side and sweep my hand towards the living room in a welcoming gesture. He walks in and turns towards me as I close the door.

"How are you feeling this morning?"

"Fine." I answer shortly.

"I don't want to take up too much of your time, but I wanted to bring you this." He reaches out and hands me the CD.

"Maybe you already have this or maybe you hate this music, but it is a CD I listen to when I need to calm my nerves. I just wanted to pass it on and who knows, maybe it will help."

I flip the CD over and over in my hands before saying, "Thank you."

We stand there awkwardly for a while and then he makes a move towards the door. "Do you want a cup of coffee?" I ask.

"How about we go for a cup of coffee? There is a Starbucks near the hotel I am staying at. I saw it was open when I passed by on my way here. What do you say?"

I look down at the black workout pants I have on with a large sweatshirt.

"You look fine. It's just a cup of coffee. No one cares what you are wearing. It's better to be comfortable."

"Sure, I guess."

"Don't get too excited."

I smile and grab my purse. He opens the door and I walk out towards the car. When we reach the car, he comes to my side first and opens the door for me to get in.

"I can't do this." I say and run back towards the pool house. Opening the car door for me feels too intimate. It made me think of *him*. I'm not ready to have other men do things *he* did for me.

I am back at the airport to head home. I'm relieved the rest of the time here went well. Audrie and Audra came to the pool house after Thanksgiving dinner and we watched a movie together. Sitting there with both of them snuggled up against me, I felt very thankful.

Tanner didn't come to the pool house again, but he was pleasant when I saw him at the main house. Well as pleasant as you can be from across the room. He made sure to keep his distance from me. Luckily he is on a flight that leaves tomorrow morning so I don't have to worry about him showing up in the seat next to me on the flight again.

When I walk into my house, I take a deep breath. The soft scent of lilacs in the air welcomes me home. I drop my bag and run to the bedroom. I yank open the drawer of the dresser holding *his* sweatshirt. I put it to my face and instantly feel more peace than I have felt in days.

28 NIA THEN

I open my eyes to find Ian watching me sleep. He smiles and kisses my forehead.

"Why are you watching me sleep?"

"Because you are beautiful."

I pull the sheet up over my head and then peek out shyly.

"Let's have a baby."

"What?" I ask and sit up.

"We have all this room in this house and I think it's time we start filling it up. Jett and I have more help at the office now which means I can be home more. I want you to have my baby."

I knew we would have kids one day, but with how busy our lives have been, I haven't even considered the possibility in a while.

"So, my beautiful Snow White, are you going to give me some little dwarfs?"

"Yes, seven of them to be exact."

"Seven? Then we better get started," he says and

pulls me into him.

As the time comes for my period I am getting more and more anxious. Noie tells me to let nature take its course and not worry so much because people usually have to try for a while before getting pregnant. Since we decided to take this next step, I want it to happen now.

I wake up on the day my period should be starting and keep saying, "Don't come, don't come" to my uterus all day.

Ian comes in the door and to the kitchen where I am cooking dinner. He puts his hands around my waist and rubs my belly.

"Are we still in the running for a baby this month?" He asks.

"So far, so good. No period yet," I say with a smile and turn my head to give him a kiss.

We sit down for dinner and I can't contain my excitement. I want to start planning everything now.

"So are you hoping for a little Ian?" I ask.

"Boy or girl doesn't matter to me but if it is a boy, we are not naming him Ian."

"Then what are you thinking?"

"It depends. Is there a family tradition we need to stick to? Like Nia-Noie and Audrie-Audra, or was that just coincidence?"

"No, family tradition," I say with a laugh. "I think Noie just got sentimental when she had two girls the same distance apart as me and her and decided to do that."

"Good, then I like Lucas for a boy. We could call

him Luke, if we wanted. Jacob is a good name too."

"I like Lucas but I have to veto Jacob."

"Why? It's a good name."

"Jake, Jett's brother, is actually Jacob. It's a no go."

"I see your point and I will have to agree. Vetoed."

After dinner, we clean up and head to the bedroom to relax before bed. I jump in the shower while Ian reads over some work papers. I get undressed and stand in front of the mirror pushing my stomach out trying to see what I might look like in a few months.

I turn the water on and let the heat encase my body. I look down and tears instantly spring to my eyes. Blood is running down my leg. My period. I start sobbing and Ian runs into the bathroom.

"What's wrong?" he asks and then sees it. His eyes soften and he looks at me through the glass shower door. "Nia. I'm sorry baby. Come on and get out."

I clean myself up and get out of the shower. I get dressed and Ian leads me to the bed. We lay down and he holds me as I cry. I knew it was a long shot getting pregnant the first month we try but it didn't stop me from wanting it so badly.

"We will keep trying and trying. This isn't our only chance," Ian says trying to sooth me.

I cry until I fall asleep in Ian's arms.

29 NIA NOW

Russell has finally ventured into the house at night. He keeps his distance once he is inside, but when I wake up in the mornings, he is lying in bed next to me. I like to lay there for a few minutes to feel him purr against my chest. Then when I reach out to pet him, he stretches his legs out before getting up and running for the backdoor. It has become our routine. I take him outside in the morning to eat and he is always eager.

This morning is no different. I get his food and get ready while he eats. I have to get out of my pajamas because I made plans with Noie today. I finally decided it was time to get some jeans that fit me. I have been trying to eat more, but I haven't been very successful. I usually have to get dinner for myself and by the time for dinner, I just don't have the energy to deal with it.

I'm still brushing my hair when Noie gets here. She makes her way into the bathroom looking more chipper than normal.

"I'm am so excited! We haven't been shopping

together in a long time. We can go to the mall and then out near the river for lunch or we can go to Skyline like we would do in college. Girls day," she sings.

"I just need jeans that fit."

"I know you think you just need jeans, but you leave for D.C. in two days. Don't you want to get a couple of new outfits to take with you? You will be gone for almost a month."

Don't remind me is all I can think. I do want to see Sam and find out if something is wrong with him but a month? I don't know how I can do that.

"Tanner called," Noie says cautiously.

I turn to her, feeling confused.

"He just wanted to see how you were doing."

"I don't really want strangers checking in on my life." Who does he think he is?

"I thought it was nice and he is not a stranger. I have known him for over a decade. He seemed concerned about you and it wasn't in some strange stalker way. I think he is just a nice guy and you are semi related to one of his oldest friends. Don't get upset over this. Just because someone wants to check up on you doesn't mean they are judging you or just taking pity on you. It was really nothing. Just forget about it and let's go shopping."

I take a deep breath and check my panic.

"Let's go."

"Wait a second. While we are on the subject of Tanner, I want to say something. I am sorry for not taking you back to the house that night, but I had to go with Jett and the girls. Plus we have known Tanner long enough to know he would make sure you were ok. Do you forgive me?"

"I wasn't mad about that. I overheard Jett talking to you. Is everything okay?"

"You don't need to worry about us. We are fine," she says dismissively.

"I do worry about you. You can talk to me. You don't have to treat me like I will break if you don't have a smile on your face every moment of the day."

"Things have been hard for us. He is working more and I have spent so much time away from home, but we are working on it. We will get through this and please don't think it's your fault. It's not. Can we talk about something else?"

"I do have a question about Tanner," I say.

"Okay, go ahead and ask."

"If he lives here, why have I never met him? Do you see him often?"

"Jett sees him for dinner every so often. Not very much. They are both so busy. We mainly only see him at family functions. Jake keeps trying to set him up with one of their cousins but he never seems interested."

"He probably doesn't want to share a family with Jake, no offense," I say and instantly feel bad about it.

30 NIA THEN

When Ian wasn't in bed and the house was silent, I felt a rush of sadness. Sunday mornings were usually the one time a week I could count on getting Ian all to myself.

I get up and head to the kitchen to put on a cup of coffee before I give him a call to see where he is this early. As I walk past the back window, I notice Ian sitting under the willow tree in our back yard with his guitar. The sight of him brightens my mood. I haven't seen him pick up his guitar in years.

I continue to the kitchen and see he has already made coffee. I grab two mugs from the cabinet and fill them before joining him outside.

The soft melodic sound of his guitar fills my ears when I step outside. I sit next to him and set the cups down. He strums a few more cords and then lays the guitar down next to him.

"You don't have to stop. I miss hearing you play."

Ian just stares ahead but doesn't reach back for his guitar.

After a few minutes he says, "I am taking a long weekend this week starting Thursday. I have already cleared my schedule."

Excitement fills my mind as I instantly start planning a weekend trip away or something special for us to do together.

"I will be leaving Wednesday night," he continues.

"Where are we going?" I ask confused by him saying "I" and think he must have meant "we."

"Just me. Well me and Jimmy. We are going out of town," he says in a flat tone.

"Why haven't you said anything before now?"

"I just decided last minute. It's not a big deal. I should be back by Sunday night."

Feeling hurt, I say, "It is a big deal. We get very little time together as it is and now you are going out of town with Jimmy. Why can't we go somewhere if you are taking vacation?"

"I can't do this right now, Nia. I don't want to fight. Jimmy and Laura are stopping by later for some drinks. I hope you don't mind," he says before standing and walking back into the house.

I get the sudden urge for a cigarette. I haven't had one in almost a year. Ever since we made the decision to start trying for a baby.

I can't wrap my mind around this trip. Why can't it be a couple's trip? Laura and I could both go. Maybe I will bring that up when they get here.

Laura and Jimmy get to our house at six. I ordered a

few Chinese takeout dishes in case anyone got hungry. After we have a few drinks, I get up the nerve to ask about a couple's weekend.

"So Laura, what are you doing this weekend while the boys are away?"

"Oh, um," Laura stumbles and darts glances at Jimmy and Ian. "I, um, don't know yet."

"Where is it you two are going?" I ask Jimmy and Ian.

Jimmy says, "My dad's fishing cabin. Just a few days in the woods."

I see Ian nodding his head in agreement.

"Since Laura doesn't have plans, and, neither do I, how about we turn it into a couple's weekend? Laura and I could even go antiquing in town to give you some boy time."

"I don't think that's a good idea. Laura doesn't have set plans, but she has stuff she needs to take care of, right?" He says and looks at Laura for confirmation.

"Yes. I do have some stuff I need to get done."

Why isn't Ian chiming in on this? He is just sitting there with his drink in his hand and staring off like he isn't paying attention to the conversation anymore.

Finally he speaks and says, "I need a cigarette. I'm going to go out back."

Jimmy follows behind him and Laura starts talking about wall colors she is thinking about for their house. I don't like the vibe of this whole situation.

31 NIA DIARY

Dear Diary,

I keep feeling more and more like Ian might be cheating. Seeing that word as I write it, it feels like it's a word that exists in someone else's life, not mine.

I want to talk to someone about it, but I know they would just dismiss it like Sarah did when I said something to her. Everyone believes Ian loves me too much to ever hurt me like that or chance losing me, but they are not around him every day. They don't see how distant he is at times.

Sometimes I think I might be going crazy. We have been trying so hard to have a baby. Would he want to do that if there was someone else? The darker part of me thinks he wants the baby so I won't leave if I found out he was cheating.

I know he is stressed at work. I hope that's all this is. He is probably going away with Jimmy because he needs a boy's weekend to blow off steam.

Sarah and I finally made it to Chicago to spend a weekend with Hadley a few months ago. We felt like we needed a weekend away – just girls. How can I fault him for needing the same thing?

Maybe I should plan a trip to see Hadley while he is gone so I don't sit around and make up stuff in my head that isn't really going on.

32 NIA NOW

This flight was much better than the one over Thanksgiving. I didn't have anyone sitting next to me so I was able to enjoy my flight in peace. It was made all the better by being an early morning flight. I got to watch the sun rise over the clouds. It is one of the most beautiful sights in the world.

A yawn escapes my mouth as I walk up to the baggage carousel.

"There she is!" I hear Sam yell as he picks me up and swings me around. I grip tightly around his neck and don't let go even when he stops swinging me. He puts his mouth close to my ear and says, "I've missed you love."

He places my feet back on the ground and I let go. The smile on my face feels almost foreign. I look him over, looking for any sign he is ill, but he looks amazing. His blue eyes are glowing and his sandy blonde hair is a perfect mess. The type you expect to see on a model. I had forgotten how tall he is, my neck is starting to hurt looking straight up at him, so I take a step back.

We walk over to the carousel and wait for my bags. I wrap my arm through his and lean on him. All the anxiety about coming is gone for the moment as I stand here with him. Since that first day of freshman year, he has been my best friend and I know he will be for the rest of my life.

"Let me guess, yours are the bags with the red and black checkered straps? Are these the same ones you have had since college?"

"Yes, I like them." I say and nudge him playfully.

"Me too." He says and grabs them for me. "Let's get a cab and get back to my place. I have six bottles of wine with our names on them."

I grab one of the bags and roll it behind me as I follow him to the cab stand. The smile still hasn't faded from my face.

"Here we are. Home sweet home for the next month."

His apartment is amazing. I haven't been to visit since he moved into his new place. The wood floors are a dark bamboo which is complemented by the gray furniture with muted red accents.

"I love it."

"Follow me and I will show you to your room," he says and heads down the hallway.

He opens the door to a room with a queen bed full of pillows. I wonder if he got extra for me. Then my eyes fall on the two chairs in front of the window with a small round table between them. The chairs are covered in the same orange fabric as the ones in my house. Over the back of one of the chairs is a soft brown throw blanket. Tears fill my eyes and Sam comes up behind me, wraps his arms around me and sets his chin on my shoulder.

"How did you…"

"Noie helped. We couldn't find the same chairs you have, but since you had yours recovered, she knew where to get the fabric. I ordered it and got these recovered. I knew it would be hard for you to stay here for a month so I wanted to do something to make you feel like you are at home."

My eyes fall on the framed picture next to the bed and I smile. "Russell."

"And that is not the best part."

He walks to the chair and reaches over the back. He turns around and he is holding a stuffed orange cat.

"I know it is not the same as having Russell here, but this will have to do. I hope you like it."

"It's perfect."

"Okay, you get settled in. I am going to get the fire started and open a bottle of wine. Come join me when you are ready."

I slip off my shoes and crawl into the bed. Laying in the pillows, I let the tears come. This isn't the panic crying, but a cry of release. I lose track of time as tears soak the pillow. When all of the tears are drained, I wipe my face and make my way into the living room.

Sam is sitting on the sofa reading a book. The fireplace is casting dancing shadows over the dimly lit room. The wine bottle sitting on the coffee table is half empty and I wonder how long I have been crying. Sam looks up at me and smiles, then reaches for the wine to pour me a glass. I walk over and sit next to him. He pulls me back into his arms and hands me the wine glass.

Sitting here with him, I feel the best I have felt in longer than I can remember. I try to fend off the thought something is wrong with him, but instead I start trying to find a way to bring it up.

"So when are you going to tell me about Maria? How did you meet her?"

"Maria is great. We have a good time together. I was going to invite her over for dinner one night so you can grill her. Can't say much or if it is serious until I get your stamp of approval," he says and winks at me.

"You can at least tell me how you met her."

He doesn't answer right away and I finish off my glass of wine in an attempt to fend off the panic.

Finally he sighs and says, "I met her at this group I've been going to."

"What kind of group?" I ask and then hold my breath.

He reaches for the wine bottle and empties it into our glasses before taking it to the kitchen and opening another one. He comes back and tops off our glasses then settles back down and pulls me into him.

"I started going to this support group for friends and families of people dealing with depression."

I try to sit up and pull away from him, but he wraps his arms tighter around me.

"Just listen. After everything that happened and you just disappeared inside yourself, I didn't know what to do. You wouldn't talk to me or to anyone. I would come visit you and you would just stare out the window. I would sit there for hours and you wouldn't even look at me. I felt so helpless. Then Sarah lost it on you and I realized I needed help. I needed emotional support for how I was feeling watching you fall apart, but I also needed to learn how to help you. Maria had been in the group for a year before I started going. We ended up becoming friends and then one thing led to another until we were dating. That is how I met her."

I try to process everything he just said. First, relief rushes over me at the realization Sam is not sick. But the awareness that I am causing him enough torment for him to seek out the help of a support group saddens me and makes me feel overwhelmed with gut wrenching guilt.

What am I supposed to do? It is not like I woke up one day and said maybe I will lose all sense of myself and my life to the point I cannot even function. It isn't fair I am hurting those around me just because I am hurt, but at the same time, I can't just shut off this lost feeling of emptiness.

I understand more why I shut everyone out. Seeing them hurt is hard. It is easier not to see what they are going through. I have been so mad at Sarah for the things she said to me, but maybe she was right to stand up to me and step away. Maybe it was hurting her too much to see me in so much pain.

I look up at Sam and say, "I'm so sorry."

"No Nia. You don't need to apologize. I didn't tell you all of that to make you feel bad. I just didn't want to lie to you about it. Also, I wanted to talk to you about it because maybe going to a support group would help you as well. Knowing there are other people out there who feel like you do or have felt the way you do in the past can be a lot of help."

Anger begins to rage in me and I try to push it down. I don't want to lose my control. I know Sam is just trying to help me, but I have to put an end to this right now. There is no way I can stay here for the next month with him pressuring me to go to some support group. Now I wonder if dinner with Maria is just a chance for them to gang up on me and push their own agenda. He has to know he is pushing a line.

I take a controlled breath and say, "Sam, I understand you just want to help me, but I don't want to hear this right now. I don't want to hear how there are groups of people out there who understand my pain. They don't understand shit. Most days I don't understand it. Please don't push this."

"Hey, hold on a second. I know what you are thinking and that is not what this trip is about. I wanted to spend time with you, the end. But as your friend, I need to be able to tell you what is going on in my life and give you suggestions about support out there you might not have thought about." He lets out a breath and turns my face to stare into his eyes and they look as if they are pleading with me when he says, "Don't shut down on me. You haven't said more than three words to me in over eight months before today. I miss you."

Seeing the love and pain in his eyes is more than my anger can withstand. It melts me and I smile, "Okay."

Waking up, I don't hear any noise in the apartment. The sun is not peeking through the curtains yet, so I look around the room for a clock. Nothing. I am in the middle of the guest room bed with pillows flanking my sides like people do when they lay babies on a bed. Sam must have brought me in here because I remember drifting off on the couch with him while watching a movie.

I climb over the pillow mountain and tip toe down the hall to the kitchen. The clock on the microwave says it is six in the morning. Not wanting to wake Sam, I locate my cell phone and turn it on to search for a nearby coffee shop. I see there is one just a few blocks over in Dupont Circle. Perfect. I pull a long sleeve shirt on over my tank top and then cover it with a sweatshirt before slipping into my tennis shoes.

As I open the door I realize I don't have a way to lock it. I decide it should be fine since I will be gone for twenty minutes tops.

The morning air is brisk and I shiver as I leave the building. The streets are already packed with cars and the sidewalks are bustling with people. This is nice. At this moment I am surrounded by people, but I feel completely invisible. No one knows who I am or how my life fell apart. No one is throwing me looks of sorrow or asking me questions I don't want to answer. I am anonymous.

The three blocks go by quickly and when I see the coffee shop, I pick up my speed to get into the warmth. The smell of coffee is inviting as I walk in the door. A bubbly young blonde greets me and I quickly order a coffee for myself and a vanilla latte for Sam. After I add two sugars to my coffee, I head back to the apartment.

When I am about a block away from Sam's building I hear my name being screamed.

"Nia, Nia, Nia!" Sam's voice sounds mad. I quicken my pace and I see him. He is barefoot in pajama pants with a robe hanging open. When his eyes meet mine, he quiets until I am a few feet away. "Nia you scared me half to death. Where did you go?"

"I feel like the two coffee cups would be a dead

giveaway," I say a little annoyed. This seemed like an overreaction. I have been gone less than twenty minutes.

"Yes, sorry. I just woke up and you were gone. I got worried." He sighs and smiles. "Are one of those for me?" I hand him the latte and then follow him back into the building.

In the apartment, I walk past him to the bedroom and sit down in the chair by the window. My cigarettes are sitting on the small table next to an ashtray. Sam must have done that. I look out the window at the smoky blue sky while lighting a cigarette. I can feel Sam staring at me from the door.

"Are you just going to stand there?" I ask not masking my annoyance.

He slowly walks my way and sits down. "Are you ever going to quit smoking?" He asks with annoyance that matches mine.

I take a long drag and then exhale into his face.

"Real nice, but seriously I always thought it was weird when you would have the occasional cigarette in college. You are a dancer."

"I don't smoke when I'm dancing."

"I get it. I'll let it go."

We sit in silence while we drink the rest of our coffee. The sun is fully out now. Its brightness is deceptive because the heat of it is barely discernable outside. Although this city is beautiful, I miss my willow tree. Even now when all of the leaves have fallen, I will watch the bare limbs swaying and get lost in their movement. The thought calms me and I feel my annoyance with Sam waning.

He looks at me with his lip jutting out. "Are we

fighting?" He asks in a baby voice.

Rolling my eyes, I shake my head no.

"Good! Then it is time for you to get in the shower. I'm making breakfast."

With that he walks out of the room. I reluctantly dig through my bags for something to wear and my toiletries before making my way to the guest shower. Fifteen minutes later, I emerge from the steam filled bathroom with a towel wrapped around my wet hair.

I follow the smell of grilled potatoes and eggs to the kitchen where Sam is plating our breakfast, looking like a domesticated Adonis although I know he is anything but domesticated. I hope this Maria woman is up for the task because she has a handful with this one.

"Poached eggs, grilled potatoes and salsa is served," he says sitting the plate in front of me.

"What do you have planned today?" I ask with a little fear. It was nice being lost in the people on the street this morning, but I am not fully embracing the day right now.

"Nothing much. We can do whatever you want. This evening I have somewhere to go for a little bit and I told Noie that was a good time to have Dr. Gillis call you." I look up at him sharply and he continues, "Dr. Gillis still wants to check in with you while you are here so Noie scheduled phone times with him."

This was news to me and not good news. I like Dr. Gillis, but I feel like I have been really trying. I have been talking and doing more which I thought would mean a temporary pardon from these appointments.

"But after that, you can meet Maria if you are up to it. She can come by here. Nothing formal," he says and then looks at me as if waiting for an answer.

"I guess I will meet her sooner or later so why not get it over with," I feel guilty the moment it comes out of my mouth. I didn't mean it to sound so rude.

"That lacked the excitement I was hoping for, but I will take it. If you feel uncomfortable at all then just excuse yourself and go to the room. And try to be nice, not everyone appreciates your sass like I do," he says and tosses a potato at me.

I throw the potato back at him and we both jump up. He comes at me and a shriek escapes my mouth and I start laughing. Not a polite smile or a little giggle, but a full on belly laugh. I cannot remember the last time I have laughed like this. He reaches me and yanks me up before tossing me down on the couch and tickling me. I continue laughing and beg him to stop.

At the same moment we both become aware of our bodies. Sam has me pinned to the couch and he is laying over me. Our faces are only inches apart. He is staring into my eyes and I see the sparkle of laughter leave them as it is replaced by desire.

Panic rises in my chest and I turn my head. Sam quickly gets up and backs away. He runs his hands over his hair like he does when trying to dispel frustration.

"I need to get ready. I have that stuff, um, to do. Yeah. Um, there is a key in the drawer by the stove in case you go anywhere. Keep your phone on please." He turns to go to his room and then whips back around and reminds me, "Don't forget the doc is calling later." Then he is gone and I hear the door to his room slam behind him.

What just happened? I thought he wasn't leaving until later. Why did he look at me like that? I jump up and run to the room and close the door behind me. I don't want to see him before he leaves.

Sitting down at the window, I light a cigarette. I don't want to take a pill. Dr. Gillis doesn't like how I try to decide when I need the medicine instead of when my body tells me I need it, but I have been able to function a lot better. I want to be able to calm and control my emotions myself. For now, I just want to forget that happened. Sam and I have never had even a moment before today like that. Moments like that destroy friendships. I don't want to have to worry about any of that stuff right now. It is more than I can handle.

Sometimes I feel so alone and just want to be held so I know someone else is there, but that is it. That is where I draw the line. My heart is so irrevocably broken and most days the only thing I am sure of is I will never have to use it again.

Tanner is suddenly on my mind. Why was he checking up on me? I have known Sam forever so I know why he is so nice and caring with me, but Tanner is a stranger. A stranger who I treated like he had the plague after opening a car door for me.

Maybe I just misread the situation with Tanner and what happened earlier with Sam. Maybe it is just all in my crazy, fucked up head.

Unable to stop my thoughts, I give in to the need for medicine. I hear the door close as Sam leaves so I go to the kitchen for a drink of water. I find a cold bottle of water in the refrigerator and take a gulp to wash the pill down.

I look around at the dishes left from breakfast. Sam must be upset too because he is not the type to leave a mess. I decide to clean up and then put on a pot of coffee. When it's finished brewing, I make a cup and head back to the room. Suddenly I feel tired. The medicine is kicking in. I abandon my fresh coffee on the table and crawl into the bed for a nap.

The phone ringing jars me from sleep. I jump out of bed to find the phone.

"Hello," I answer groggily.

"Nia, its Dr. Gillis. How are you?"

"Sleepy," I say curtly.

"Well then, I will not keep you long. I just want to make sure we stay in touch while you are away. How has the trip been so far?"

"Fine."

"Can you explain what you mean by fine? We are at a bit of a disadvantage not doing this in person. There are no visual clues as to how you are feeling."

I guess the sooner I give him something the faster I can get off this call and go back to sleep. "Seeing Sam has been really nice. He went out of his way to make sure I am comfortable here. I had some anxiety today and I wanted to control it on my own, but I decided to listen to your advice and I took one of my pills. That is why I am sleepy."

"Very good to hear. That is progress. Do you want to discuss what brought on the anxiety?"

"No." I say. The last thing I want to do is take my mind back there. I just want to forget this morning ever happened.

"I see. Maybe you think on it and we can talk about it next time. Did you bring all of your medicine in case you have an episode that calls for something stronger or should I have a prescription called in for you?"

"Noie made sure I brought everything."

"Good. Have you been talking to Sam or keeping to yourself since you have been there?" He asks cautiously. Dr. Gillis knows I get agitated when asked about how much I talk. What kind of question is that? Talking all the time is not a requirement of anyone and I didn't see why I had to.

"I have been talking, but Sam doesn't have a problem if I choose to be quiet. He never has," I say a little brasher than necessary.

"Have you ever asked him how he feels when you don't talk to him?" He waits for me to answer. After a minute goes by and I say nothing, he says, "I will take your silence as your desire to change the subject. That's fine, but it is something for you to think about. Is there anything else you would like to discuss?"

"No."

"Then let's end this session and we can plan another short call for Thursday. Does the same time work for you?"

"Yes." I say relieved this is almost over.

"Then I will talk to you Thursday, but if anything comes up between now and then, just call the office and let them know you need me to phone you. Goodbye, Nia."

"Goodbye."

I hang up the phone and lay back on the bed. I hope he realizes the phone calls are not helpful and tells me I can just call when I need him the next time we talk.

I am feeling homesick. I miss Russell. I turn over to look at the picture of him on the nightstand. I hope he is staying inside. I know Gertie and Noie are taking good care of him, but I wish I would have brought him with me. I don't think Sam would have minded.

I lose track of time staring at the picture of Russell. The urge to have a cigarette and coffee pulls me from bed. The room is getting dark. There is barely any light coming through the window. I take the cold cup of coffee I left on the table before I fell asleep and make my way to the kitchen to put on a fresh pot.

Back in my room, I sit by the window and light a cigarette then pick up the steaming cup of coffee to wrap my hands around for the warmth. I will have to ask Sam how to work the fancy temperature control panel I saw in the hallway.

I hear the lock on the front door click open and then Sam's voice followed by a woman's voice I have never heard before. Maria. I forgot she was coming over tonight.

"Nia," Sam calls as he walks into the room. "Hey, Maria is here. Do you want to come visit in the living room? We were thinking about ordering some food from the deli down the street. Are you hungry?" He whispers from right behind me.

I turn my head up towards him and nod towards my coffee. "Let me finish my cup and I will be out. The pot is fresh if you two want any."

He squeezes my shoulder and walks out of the room. I don't really feel up to meeting Maria, but Sam is my best friend and I don't want to upset him. I take my final sip of coffee and think to myself, "Here goes nothing."

I timidly walk into the living room and see Sam standing at the kitchen island with a beautiful brunette. They are talking quietly with cups of coffee in their hands. Sam finally looks up at me and Maria turns to look at me with a warm smile on her face. She has straight hair hanging halfway down her back. It looks straight out of a Pantene commercial. I nervously push my hair behind my ears feeling a little self-conscience. I didn't even brush my hair after I got out of the shower this morning.

"Maria, this is my best friend in all of the world, Nia."

I haven't gotten close enough to make a hand shake possible so she just smiles bigger, which makes her chestnut colored eyes shimmer and says, "It's nice to finally meet you. Sam talks about you all the time. I almost feel like I know you."

But you don't. I think to myself and say, "Likewise." That wasn't entirely true, but he did tell me a little bit about her last night.

Sam reaches out his hand and asks, "Would you like me to refill your cup?"

I nod and hand it to him. There is an awkward silence as he pours the cup, adds two sugars and stirs it before handing me the cup back.

"Let's sit in the living room where it is a little more comfortable," Sam says and moves towards the couch where he sits and Maria sits next to him. I take the chair and pull my feet up underneath me. "Maria and I know what we want from the deli. They have a hot roast beef sandwich. Would you like that?" He asks me.

I just nod my head yes and take a sip of my coffee. Sam stands and grabs his phone to order the food.

"So I hear you are a dancer. What is that like? I wanted to grow up and be a dancer when I was a little girl."

"I am more of a teacher than a dancer at this point. Or maybe I'm neither anymore," I say. I should tell her I am now a professional cigarette smoker and coffee drinker, but Sam would think I was being snarky.

Another awkward silence so I decide to ask her something. If I can get her talking, then I won't be forced to.

"What do you do for work?" I ask.

"I own a small bakery. I am known for the miniature cakes I make. They are about the size of a cupcake but not shaped like one. I make a lot of wedding cakes too and then I send the bride and groom home with a miniature version of their cake to have on their first anniversary. I would love to make a cake for you. Just tell me what flavor you like and find a picture of any cake on the internet and I will make you a mini version of it. I even made a mini version of Elvis and Pricilla's wedding cake one time for this couple who were having an Elvis inspired anniversary party. That was a lot of fun." Maria says with untamed enthusiasm.

She continues talking about cakes and other desserts she makes while Sam is placing the order. She really does seem sweet, but I start to drown out what she is saying and hope she doesn't ask me a question. Finally Sam joins us again and picks up on the cake conversation. He says something about a mini turkey cake she made for Thanksgiving, but I'm having a hard time concentrating on what he is saying.

At some point this leads to a conversation about a

friend from their support group who is having a baby and she is making a cake for the shower. I am thankful when there is a knock at the door from the food delivery guy.

We continue on with small talk while we eat. Maria tries to get me more engaged in the conversation by asking me questions. I give short, but polite answers, and then turn the question on her. She is a bit of a talker so I get off the hook for a while. After we eat, Maria says she needs to get home.

"Do you want me to walk you to the Metro?" Sam asks as he helps her with her jacket.

She says, "Nope, but I will text you when I get home." Then she raises up on her toes to give him a small kiss before turning to me. "I am so happy I got to meet you. Please make him bring you by the shop this week."

"I will," I reply and give her a small wave goodbye.

Sam shuts the door and then goes back to the kitchen to grab a bottle of wine and two glasses.

"So what is the verdict?" Sam asks as he pours the wine.

"She seems amazing and very beautiful," I respond truthfully. Under normal circumstances, I probably would have stayed up all night talking to her. She has a bubbly personality which reminds me a little bit of Hadley.

"She is both those things. I know she talked quite a bit tonight, but it was just because she was nervous about meeting you. She is a really good listener and has been there for me a lot lately." He says with a fondness unlike the way he usually discusses the women he dates.

"I'm glad you found her then. I approve. When is the wedding?" I ask with a grin.

"There is the feisty girl I love so much, but just

because we made it past the fifth date doesn't mean I am ring shopping."

"And there is the commitment phob I love so much."

"I'm not a commitment phob. I just want to save that kind of commitment for the right person," he says and then pats the spot next to him on the couch for me to come sit.

With all the weirdness of the first morning gone, we spend the rest of the week holed up in the apartment catching up and watching movies. Maria stopped by one day to bring us some cakes and I was in awe. The cakes were the cutest things I had ever seen and the taste was off the charts delicious. Hadley was able to make it into town for one night and we all hung out at the apartment. That was a great night. Hadley is just one of those people who lift you up when you are around them. It almost felt like we were back in our first semester at college. We just needed Sarah and Blake here with us. I hated saying goodbye to her the next morning, but she promised she would come spend a few days with me if I was up for company when I got back to Louisville.

Finally, during my second week, Sam jumps in my bed to wake me up and says, "Let's go out for coffee this morning. We can grab a bagel and then take a walk around town and get some fresh air."

I pull the sheet over my mouth before answering so I don't assault him with my morning breath. "Sounds good, but I need a few minutes to get ready."

"Hurry up," he sings as he walks out of the room.

When I am ready, we leave the apartment and head to the bagel shop arm-in-arm. After eating, we stroll around town on a "Sam's Favorite Buildings" tour since I have already seen most of the main tourist attractions before. Sam is an architect and it is entertaining to listen to him talk about the buildings and their history with such fervor.

Sam is in the middle of telling me about a church we are passing when I look across the street and I see *him* walking. I gasp and begin to shake.

Sam stops his story and frantically asks, with a deep look of concern in his eyes, "What's wrong?"

"It's *him*," I say pointing.

"It's who?" He asks confused.

"*Him*. It's *him*!" I yell and take off running. Horns begin blaring as I jet across the street.

"Nia stop!" Sam yells from behind me, but I can't. I have to reach *him*.

All of a sudden, Sam catches up to me and wraps his arms around me to make me stop.

"Let me go. Let me go." I scream over and over again as I try to escape Sam's grip.

"Nia, calm down. Please calm down."

"No! It's *him*. Let me go."

"Nia, it's not *him*. Please just calm down."

I continue to scream and try to kick myself free of him. People are stopping to stare at us, but I don't care. He has to let me go.

Finally Sam gets me into his arms and starts walking

back towards his apartment, refusing to put me down no matter how much I scream or hit him. I am still screaming at him when we reach his apartment. Why won't he let me go? He takes me to the bedroom and lays me on the bed. The tears start streaming down my face with the choking screams.

"Nia you have to stop screaming and breath. What can I do? Please Nia, please stop."

The screams keep ripping from my chest. The aching pain has reached every cell in my body. I begin rocking and pulling at my hair. Then I hear Noie's voice coming out of Sam's speaker phone.

"Shhh, Nia. Calm down baby," Noie says.

"Noie, what do I do? She is pulling out her hair and she has been screaming like this for about fifteen minutes."

"There is a small black bag she brought in one of her suitcases. Find it and get out one of the syringes. They are in a plastic case, pre-filled with her meds."

"Okay, I found it."

"Am I still on speaker?"

"Yes."

"Nia, listen to me. You need to calm down. Sam is going to give you a shot. Don't fight him. Sam you will need to hold her arm as still as you can and pinch some skin together near the top. Then give her the injection. Hold her still so she doesn't break the needle."

Sam's hands try to steady my arm, but I can't stop rocking and he can't get a good grip. I am still screaming and trying to get him off of me. He gets up on the bed, lays me down and then pins my arms under his knees before he is able to get the shot into my arm.

"Noie, I got it but as you can hear, she is still screaming," Sam says exhausted.

"Just hold her and help her calm down. When she stops, light her a cigarette and give it to her. I'm going to hang up. Call me in a little bit and let me know how she is doing."

"Thanks, bye."

Sam lays me on my side and wraps his arms around me. I can feel the heaviness come and screams subside into weeping. I gasp a few times trying to get more air in. After a few minutes I am lying still with only a trickle of tears left streaming down my face. Sam slowly pulls away from me and lights a cigarette. I take it from him and focus on my breaths.

I don't know when I fell asleep, but I wake and Sam is asleep next to me. I can feel the rise and fall of his chest against my back. It is soothing. I roll over to face him curling up in the fetal position against his chest. He stirs with my movement and then wraps his arms around me. I start to silently cry again until I fall back asleep.

The light streaming in the window wakes me. I open my eyes and find Sam awake, but still holding me. I look up into his blue eyes. He just stares at me and then begins to gently brush the hair back from my face.

"Good morning," he mouths to me.

I just nod.

"Are you okay?"

Again I nod.

Neither one of us make a move to get up yet. My whole body is aching. I start stretching out my legs and Sam let's his arms fall away from me.

"Coffee?" He asks.

I nod and he sits up on the side of the bed. He runs his hands through his hair and yawns before standing up. After he is out of the room I get up and head for the bathroom. I grab the door frame to steady myself. Once I have my balance back, I brush my teeth. The reflection in the mirror is a mess. My hair is sticking up everywhere and my fingers tug at knots when I try to smooth it down. My cheeks and eyes are still red and puffy from the crying.

When I get back to the room there is a glass of water next to a pill. Noie probably told him to make me take one. I hear the phone ring and Sam quickly answers. His voice carries easily through the quiet apartment even with his attempt at whispering.

"Noie, I don't know. Everything was fine. We were walking around town and then she thought she saw *him*. Everything just spiraled out of control from there." I hear Sam say before pausing for Noie to respond.

"No, I'm not putting her on a plane. Especially after that just happened yesterday. I know you are worried, but I can handle it."

Another pause and then his voice has an edge to it when he says, "I said I can handle it. If I can't I will let you know. Don't fly out here. She will be fine. I'll call you later."

I hate hearing people talk about me like I am some child who cannot take care of herself, although, I guess that might be a fair assessment after what happened yesterday. I just really thought it was *him* strolling down the streets of D.C. which is almost comical now that my head is clear, if it wasn't laced with so much pain.

That episode ensured it would be days before he would try to take me out again and it turned him into a mother hen. He just hovers over me all day and he has been sleeping in my my bed every night. He will talk to me while I go to sleep without getting any response from me. It felt like the phone calls we have had over the past eight months. I think he even spends most nights lying awake because many times I have woken up for a minute and he wouldn't be sleeping. The fact I've been stuck in my head trying to figure out what happened hasn't helped to ease Sam's behavior. Why was I so sure it was *him*?

By day five of lock down, I am feeling suffocated. Sam is even waiting outside the restroom anytime I go in there. It was starting to feel like the hospital Noie sent me to when I first went quiet. I feel ready to talk and I hope it will help Sam to back off a little.

I'm sitting in the chair by the window having a cigarette when he comes into the room with two cups of coffee. I take my cup and set it down while staring at the light snow falling outside the window.

"Sam?"

His head snaps in my direction at the sound of his name, but he doesn't say anything as if his talking will stop mine.

"I'm okay Sam. You don't have to stay locked up in this apartment with me, follow me around or sleep in the bed with me where you don't even get to relax. You are wasting so much of your vacation time dealing with my shit. I know the last five days haven't looked good, but I really am getting better. Every day another broken piece of who I am seems to fall back into place. I don't want to disappoint anyone because I have a little set back," I say then grab his hand and squeeze it as I look him dead in the eyes. "I'm finding my way back. I promise."

As I say those words, I really believe them for the first time. I know my heart will take much longer to patch up, but I am no longer alternating between numbness and pain. More and more each day I feel a larger variety of emotions and can see further and further past the next cigarette.

Sam threads his fingers through mine and says, "Okay."

When I wake up on Christmas morning, Sam is already out of the bed. He has eased up on me, but he still sleeps in the spare room with me in case I need anything at night. He is afraid he will not hear me from his room.

I see a red sweat suit laid out at the foot of the bed with candy cane socks. I guess this is what he expects me to wear today. Smiling and rolling my eyes, I get changed and slide my feet as I make my way into the kitchen.

There are Christmas songs playing softly on the stereo and Sam is standing at the stove cooking breakfast.

At the sight of him, I start laughing. He is decked out in the same red sweat suit I have on right down to the candy cane socks.

He turns around and says, "Merry Christmas. What's so funny?"

I point to him and then me before doing a spin.

"I figured if we were just going to sit inside wearing sweats, we should at least be festive."

"I love them!" I say with another giggle.

"I hope you are hungry," he says as he pours me a cup of coffee. "I made waffles, pancakes and French toast to get us started. Then we will move on to the mushroom, potato, onion and cheese omelets I am still working on."

"Who all is coming today to eat this food? Please tell me at least Maria is going to help us," I say as I jump up on a stool and reach for a pancake.

"Nope, just us."

"Where is Maria going to be today?"

"She invited both of us to go to her family's house for dinner, but I didn't think you would want to go and I don't know if me and her are holiday serious," he says dismissively.

"Hmm. Not holiday serious. Didn't you spend Thanksgiving with her?" I ask in a teasing voice.

"Thanksgiving is just one step up from having lunch with someone if you really think about it."

"I don't agree but obviously something is up you do not want to talk about or you are just protecting me from the wild that lives beyond your apartment door. Whichever it is, I will leave it alone in honor of the holiday spirit."

"Well thank you for being so amendable this morning. Are you sure you were not abducted by aliens last night and lobotomized?"

"Stop it and serve me my omelet."

He finishes up the omelets while humming along and dancing to *Santa Baby* which is quite the sight to see.

The food is amazing. I have forgotten just how good of a cook he is. I should make him feel guilty for feeding me so much take out the last two weeks when he could have been cooking for me.

When we are finished eating, we put on a few more layers of clothes and take hot cocoa outside on the patio with us so we can holiday people watch.

I see Sam pull something out of his pocket before saying my name. "Nia, I got you a present," he says as he hands me the little box.

"I thought the jammies were my present. This isn't fair. I didn't get you anything."

"It was just going to be the jammies, but then I saw this and couldn't resist. We will call it a healing present more than a Christmas present."

I remove the red and gold wrapping paper and open the box. Inside there is a beautiful black chain necklace with a small black heart pendant. The heart is made of what looks like crushed up black stone.

"It's beautiful," I say as I admire it. "Thank you."

"The heart is made of all of those broken pieces but it is still a heart. That's why I thought of you and wanted you to have it. All of the brokenness you feel has made your heart different, but it doesn't change what it is. I just want you to have a reminder of that," he says and then looks away.

"Thank you," I say again.

"You know what, I am freezing! Let's head inside and find a Christmas movie to watch," he says through chattering teeth.

We settle down on the couch under a plush blanket before he drops the bomb on me.

"We have to go shopping this week."

"Why?" I ask coyly.

"Because I have rummaged through your suitcases and it seems you only brought sweats, sweats and sweats."

"That is not true. I know there are some jeans and sweaters in there because Noie made me buy them for the trip."

"Hadley is flying in for New Year's Eve and we are taking you out. She insisted I make you buy something nice. She said something about you not changing since college and since her and Sarah won't be here to dress you up the job has been passed on to me," He says laughing. "They were very strict orders and I have to follow them or else."

Taking one last look in the mirror before Hadley's cab pulls up and we have to go, I get a little nervous and decide to take half a pill and put another pill in my clutch just in case. The black and gold sequin dress is much too short for this weather, so I paired it with black tights and black ankle boots with heels. I hope we don't spend too much time outside after I check my coat at the hotel because there is a keyhole cut out in the back of this dress that exposes the majority of my back.

I hear the knock at the door and take a final cleansing breath.

"Nia, get your sexy butt out here," Hadley calls from the living room, sounding like she probably started drinking on the plane.

I walk out and roll my eyes at her. She runs over to

me and gives me a big hug.

"I am so happy I was able to make it here tonight and even happier we are going to a party. I know you have been locked up in this apartment since you got here," she says and looks at Sam with a glare. "It seems I have to fly here to take you out because Sam isn't being a very good host." After she has given him her best angry look, she reaches up and kisses him on the cheek. "Are you ready to take us out? You are going to be the envy of every man at the party showing up with us."

Hadley has never been modest, but she is so nice that her self-love never comes out catty.

"You are absolutely right, my girls look hot," Sam says before helping us with our coats and opening the door.

"Is Maria meeting us there?" Hadley asks as we walk to hail a cab.

"No, she had a girl's getaway planned for months. She will be gone for a week," Sam replies.

"That's too bad. I like her. I was hoping to get to see her again."

Sam says, "Maybe next time" as he opens the cab door.

I smoked two cigarettes before I was ready to go in. Sam waited outside with me while Hadley went in. She knows a few other people who are going to be here and wants to get in and say hi.

"Do you know a lot of people here?" I ask Sam.

"Yes, there will be some of my colleagues here and other people who run in my social circle."

I stub out my cigarette and say, "Let's go."

Sam opens the door for me and we walk to the coat

check. I tuck my coat slip in my clutch as Sam places his hand on the small of my back to guide me towards the elevator.

The party is being held in the penthouse suite of some swanky hotel. The suite was almost as big as my house and a lot nicer. From the balcony you can see the Capital building and Washington Monument. It is breathtaking.

Sam introduces me to his friends and co-workers. I am able to participate in the appropriate amount of small talk and once I have a few drinks, it got easier.

Hadley keeps trying to pull me onto the dance floor, but I am not ready to draw that kind of attention to myself. So, I just spend most of the night by Sam's side. Early in the night, Hadley was complaining about not having anyone to kiss at midnight, but she made fast friends with a friend of Sam's. I don't think it is a problem anymore. I, on the other hand, am only looking forward to midnight because it means the party will be over soon and I can get out of these heels.

A little before midnight people start gathering on the balcony to watch the fireworks and countdown to the New Year.

Sam and I can't find Hadley in the crowd so he grabs us two glasses of champagne and we head outside. The excitement in the crowd is reaching a boiling point as the countdown begins.

"Ten, nine, eight, seven, six, five..." The crowd chants. Until finally a loud "Happy New Year" rings out and the fireworks go into overdrive.

I look up at Sam with a huge smile on my face and he is already looking down at me. With the hand that has been firmly attached to my back all night, he pulls me into him. I look into his eyes just before they close. They are filled with the same desire I saw in them the first morning I was in town. I stand in disbelief as his mouth moves towards mine. I can feel the heat of his breath right before our lips touch. He is soft at first as his tongue coaxes my mouth for entrance. His kiss deepens as I begin to respond. I feel his hands move up until he is holding my face in an effort to make the kiss last long after the other party goers have finished their kisses. Our kiss finally breaks but before letting go of my face, he pulls me back in and places a gentle peck on my lips. His thumb rubs across my cheek and then he lets his hands fall back to his side. At that moment, my eyes fall on the shocked face of Hadley who quickly tries to divert her eyes.

My fingers cover my mouth as the tingling left by his lips fade. My mind is a whirlwind of confusion after that. Relief rushes over me when Hadley makes her way over to us and asks if we are ready to leave. She has an early flight and wants to grab a few hours of sleep. This means Hadley will share my bed so I can skip any possible conversation the kiss might bring up between me and Sam. He is my friend and I just want to keep it that way and forget the flurry of beating his kiss is causing in my heart.

Sam seems to be on the same page as me because he doesn't bring up the kiss during our last few days together and he stops sleeping in the room with me. Things are back to normal.

It's the last night I am here, we are staying in and Sam

is cooking chicken parmigiana for me. One of my favorites. We end up uncorking a few bottles of wine before I have to get into bed if I want any chance of sleeping before my flight.

We say goodnight and I get into bed. I toss and turn for a few minutes. Unable to sleep with the pending flight looming in my near future. I decide to see if I could sleep in his room. I am going to miss him so much and feel so thankful for this much needed get-a-way. I don't want to spend my last few hours here away from him. I tip toe down the hall. His door is cracked and I see his lamp is still on so I lightly knock on the door.

"Nia?" He says with a question in his voice.

I push the door open and look at him with a pout on my face.

He waves me in and says, "Come here. Do you want to sleep in here for your last night?"

I nod with the pout still firmly on my face.

"Then what are you waiting for? Jump in," he says and pats the bed.

He closes his book and places it on the nightstand as I crawl under the covers. He pulls me over to him so I can lay my head on his shoulder. I notice he doesn't have a shirt on and a spark I haven't felt in a long time ignites inside me. I rub my hand across the muscles of his chest and down his stomach. He is very still under my touch. I place a soft kiss on his chest and that is all the invitation he needs. He pulls me on top of him and begins kissing me. I lightly pull on his bottom lip with my teeth and he groans. His hands move up my hips and grab the bottom of my shirt before lifting it over my head. He crushes me against his chest and the feeling of skin on skin fully awakens my desire.

He sits up and wraps my legs around his back and stands. Turning to face the bed, he lays me on my back. His eyes stare at my body in the faint lamp light. Taking in every curve as he reaches for the waist of my pants and slowly removes them. He spreads my legs ready to explore every inch of my body.

33 NIA THEN

How am I going to get everything done today? We are having a Valentine's Day recital at the local community center and Ian made me promise I would be home by six. Looks like I am going to have to call in Mrs. Organization. I pick up the phone and dial Noie's number.

"Good morning, little sis," Jett says when he answers the phone.

"Good morning. Why are you not at work yet? Are you becoming a slacker in your old age?" I tease.

"I have a late meeting with some clients and I don't know how long it will take so I am going in late. I wanted to make your sister breakfast in bed so I wouldn't seem like a lousy husband on Valentine's Day."

"You better watch calling yourself lousy where Noie can hear. She doesn't like people talking about her husband that way."

"I know, to hear her tell it I am a flawless Prince Charming. Her delusions are why I love her so much."

"Who are you telling I am delusional?" I hear Noie

yell at him.

"It's my little sis," he replies and hands her the phone. I love how he never calls me his sister-in-law, always little sis.

"Don't listen to him Nia. You know I am the most grounded one out of all of us."

"I know and that is exactly why I am calling. I need some grounding today and your exceptional organization skills."

"Flattery? I like it. What can I help with?"

"I have the recital today and a million other things to take care of before six. I promised Ian I would be home for dinner," I groan into the phone. Why did I agree to a recital on Valentine's Day? Because the girls I teach begged to be a part of it with the local dance school and I can't say no to their cute little faces. Since I started teaching classes out of our house, I have to team up with other studios for recitals. I need to grow a backbone.

"Do you know what Ian has planned? Jett told me he is taking off early today and has been all hush hush about it."

"I have no idea other than I have to be home by six."

"I guess I will have to wait until tomorrow to hear about it. Jett is leaving in thirty minutes. I will be over after that."

"You are a life saver! Love you, bye," I say and hang up.

Relief washes over me. Noie is the best at this. I will probably even have an hour to spare for lunch with her help.

The recital went flawless and I had everything done in time to get coffee with Noie before it started. I could have passed on the coffee talk. She lectured me the entire time about switching to decaf while we are trying to get pregnant. I know she is right but functioning without caffeine seems impossible.

I make it to the front door at three minutes to six and can't wait to get inside to my man. There is a sticky note on the door.

Happy Valentine's Day.

I open the door and see the next note on the coat rack.

Take off your coat. Tonight is clothing optional.

I hang my coat up and scan the room for the next note. I see it on the coffee table next to a box that has been wrapped in a gold and red paper so pretty I almost don't want to rip it.

If you are opting for clothes, put this on.

I open the box to find a bathing suit with a matching sarong. This hunt better not lead outside. February in Kentucky is not bathing suit weather.

I take the box to the bedroom and slip out of my clothes before putting on the bathing suit. It is a black and red, retro style suit and I love it.

The next note is on the mirror.

I can already see you in it and I'm speechless. If you are feeling a little cold, you might find warmth in the kitchen.

I go to the kitchen and find a glass of wine next to a note.

Drink this to warm up your insides and find me in the place you feel most free.

I take my glass and head down to my dance studio in the basement. Ian is sitting in the middle of the floor surrounded by rose petals and candles. One of our favorite love songs is playing on the stereo. In front of him is a New York style cheese pizza, my favorite guilty pleasure.

"Will you be my Valentine?" He asks.

"I guess," I flirt then walk over to him.

He pulls me down into his lap and begins kissing me in a way that makes me wish I had opted to go without clothes. Before it goes too far, he pulls away.

"Let's eat and you open your present first."

"First tell me why I have a bathing suit on."

"Nope. You will figure it out," he says and hands me an envelope.

I sit back and open it slowly. Inside are two plane tickets to Hawaii.

"Ian, really? We are going?" I say a little too loudly for the romantic setting, but my excitement is boiling over.

"Yes. We didn't get to take a honeymoon and you always talk about wanting to go there and I thought it was about time I took you."

"You can get out of work this long?"

"Yes, Jett knows all about it and he is going to cover anything I can't reschedule."

In six weeks I will have this man all to myself in paradise. I can't wait.

He looks deep in my eyes and says, "The food can wait," as he begins to untie the top of my bathing suit.

34 IAN THEN

I can finally see the light at the end of the tunnel. Everything is going to be better. Nia is as happy as I have ever seen her. I have made sure of that. Everything is in place and ready.

35 NIA NOW

"Good morning, Noie," I say as she walks through my front door.

"Good morning. I picked you up a coffee. I hope that is ok. I know you have been going out for your morning coffee since you got back from visiting Sam. Gertie has been keeping me up to date since you still don't seem to know how that cell phone of yours works."

"Well, unlike Gertie, I didn't want to bother you while you were on vacation. Did you all have a good time?"

Noie shoos Russell out of the chair next to me and sits down. He jumps on the window sill and settles down to watch out the window.

"Look at you. That trip must have been good for you. Not only are you engaging in conversation, but you started it."

"Don't do that, Noie," I say aggravated. "I'm taking it day by day and I am finding my way. Just take it as it is and don't make a big deal out of it."

"Okay, deal. Our vacation did us a lot of good too. The girls were actually hoping to come by to meet Russell, see their Auntie Nia and tell you all about the vacation. Do you think you are up for that?" She asks hopefully.

"I think that would be good. I miss them."

"Then we will set it up sometime next week. They missed a lot of school to take the trip and are working overtime to get caught up. What are you doing today?"

"I am still going out for coffee. I made a promise to myself I would get out of the house every day. It makes it easier if I don't get out of the habit."

"Have you talked to Sam since you have been back?"

I don't like her tone. It sounds like she is fishing. Why is she concerned about whether or not I have talked to Sam?

"Um, I don't think so. He took so much time off work I figured he needed time to catch up." I say nonchalantly.

"Nia, I don't think he is too busy to talk to one of his oldest friend. He worries about you."

"Is there something you are not telling me?"

"He called a few times to check on you. He said you haven't called or answered your house phone since you left. Of course your cell phone always goes straight to voicemail."

"What did you tell him?"

"I told him you were doing well, as far as Gertie told me, and I would call him after I saw you, but I bet he would rather hear from you."

"One day at a time," I say to end the conversation.

"Okay, I am going to head over to the school. Call me if you need anything. Bye."

I know I should call Sam, but after what happened, I just don't know what to do or say. What happened should have never happened and after what he said, I just can't talk to him yet. I have to get it all worked out in my head first. What happened was just a mistake. We were drinking and things got out of hand. I don't know what he wants from me. I don't have anything to give him right now. There are just so many emotions running around in my head. I don't think he even knows what he wants. I think he just wants to save an old friend, but it's not his job to save me from myself. I have to save me. I'm the only one that can. That much I know for sure.

I need to get to the coffee shop. All of these thoughts are going to end up keeping me home. I get up and crouch down at the window sill to rub behind Russell's ears. He is the only man I need in my life right now.

I walk into the coffee shop and buy a cup. My normal table by the window is occupied so I find one in the back. I picked up a newspaper on my way in. I have been so closed off from what is going on the in world for the last nine months. I figure it is time to catch up a little although the stories aren't really the best thing for my emotional wellbeing.

Someone taps me on the shoulder and I look up into the smiling face of Tanner. I just give him a tight smile and look back down at the paper.

"Do you mind if I sit?" He asks, still persistent as ever.

"If you aren't leaving, you might as well."

"I sense a bit of hostility, but there are no other available tables so I guess I will have to deal with it."

Feeling a little bad about my tone, I say, "I don't mean to be hostile. I just have a routine and I am surprised to see you here."

"At least you haven't jumped up and run out of here. It looks like we are making progress. Do you want to talk about what happened in Chattanooga?" The faint accent in his voice seems exotic in a place like Louisville.

"Look you seem like a nice guy. You were really good to me at Thanksgiving when you didn't have to be. I am sure Jake gave you an earful about how crazy I am and I guess there is some truth to that, but right now I am trying to put myself back together and I'm not really open to new people."

"Jake says a lot and I listen to less than half of it. He is an old friend and he does have redeeming qualities even though he doesn't seem to want to show any of them to you. Aside from that, I am just curious why you ran away from me when we were in Chattanooga. If you don't want to tell me, fine. I am going to sit here and enjoy my coffee. I'll be on my way when I am done."

His chocolate eyes sparkle a little with his grin and then he pulls a small note pad out of his jacket pocket and begins writing. The way he just made my time and space his own makes my heart hitch a little. It takes me back to when I met...*him*.

I can't concentrate on the paper anymore. This day is not going the way I wanted it to. I need a cigarette.

"You can have the table to yourself for a few minutes. I'm going to step out for a smoke."

"No, I'm about done. I think I'll join you."

"Suit yourself."

I walk towards the door with Tanner close behind me. We find a bench and sit down. As soon as I pull out my cigarette, Tanner has his lighter out and ready for me.

"Thanks. I won't have to worry about carrying a lighter if you keep following me around."

"See I can be good for something."

I take a deep breath and decide he deserves a little bit of an explanation for the way I acted.

"I just got freaked out and that's why I ran off. When you opened the door for me it felt like a date. I know it sounds stupid, but it is what went through my head. I got scared and ran. I'm sorry about that and how I acted the entire time I was there. You just happened to meet me at a low point." An awkward laugh escapes my mouth and I say, "I used to be a pretty normal person."

"What does normal mean anyways?" He asks and flicks his cigarette. "Do you want to get out of here? There is this chain sandwich shop not far from here and it has a band play during lunch. It seems so out of place in there. Mostly business people go there for a quick lunch and then, in the corner, there is a band. I like to go watch them sometimes. The singer has a nice voice and they deserve someone to go there to actually hear them play."

"A daytime band in a sandwich shop?" I say questioningly and then think over the absurdity of it. "I'm in."

"I want to be clear about one thing before we go. This is not a date. If I hold a door open for you it is only because my mom raised me right. So no funny business."

We walk the few blocks to the deli and dip inside. It's

just as he said. Men in business suits are having lunch as if a band is not blaring right next to them. No one is even looking in their direction. We order at the counter and then take the open table right in front of the band as they finish a song.

Tanner begins whistling and clapping. I join in and we get a few stares. The singer bends down to say hi to Tanner.

"Are they friends of yours?"

"No, I just know them from here. I told you I come to watch them and I have talked to them a few times after their set."

Our number is called and Tanner jumps up to grab our food. It's kind of nice being with him. He may know some of my past from Jake, but he doesn't act like it. He doesn't have a frame of reference to compare my behavior to. There is no longing for the "old Nia." It helps me relax a little when I realize that.

I am lost in my thoughts when I hear Jett's voice, "Hey Nia, Tanner. What are you two doing here?" There is a layer of intrigue in his voice.

Shit. I can probably expect another prying conversation with Noie after this.

"I ran into Nia at the coffee shop and I asked her to come watch the band play with me," Tanner answers giving me another minute to curse how small the world is.

"Really? Well that's great," he says looking at me with a raise of his eyebrows.

I give him my best "not you too" look and then smile.

"I had to get out of the office for a minute so I just stopped in to grab a sandwich to go. Nia, you are looking good today. Noie told me you seem really well when she stopped by this morning."

Jett draws out each word as he talks, taking every opportunity he gets to raise his eyebrows and cock his eyes in Tanner's direction.

"Shouldn't you be getting back to the office?" I ask in a curt tone.

"Yes, I should little sis. We should talk soon. Maybe I will stop by one morning with Noie," he says with a wink and I get the urge to sock him in his winking eye.

Jett and Noie can be like two old ladies with their gossip. I can't even imagine how inflated this story will be when he calls Noie the second he steps out the door.

Jett says his goodbyes and leaves. I notice a little extra pep in his walk than normal. I am sure Noie told him Tanner has called and checked on me since Thanksgiving. They are surely going to make more of this than what it is.

"So about this routine of yours," Tanner says after Jett walks out, "is it just coffee or do you have other plans."

"Most days it is just coffee, but I want to add going over to the used bookstore once a week. They have a few stacks of used vinyl in the back. I used to make a habit of checking it out for anything new someone has traded in."

"That sounds fun. Do you mind some company?"

"Don't you have a job or something you should be getting to?"

"You say that with a little more judgement than someone who is also not at work should be using."

He does have a point there so I just roll my eyes and wait for him to answer my question.

"I work in the music industry doing a little bit of everything: back-up vocals, producing, mixing, and I travel with bands who need a guitar or bass player when they go on tour. Nothing too glamourous. It does take me to L.A. a lot and I have gotten the opportunity to work with some amazing people. I have sold a few songs, but probably nothing you would know."

"So kind of the music business jack of all trades?"

"Hey, I like that. I might need to put that on my cards."

"So are you happy doing what you do?"

"I am for now, but I have been working on my own album off and on for about a decade. I'd like to finish it one day," he says with a far off look in his eyes.

My thoughts take me back to college. *He* always wanted to be a musician, but the guitar became more of a hobby after graduation than anything else, letting me focus on dance while *he* took the stability track.

"Nia, are you still here with me?" Tanner asks.

"What?"

"I don't know where your head was. You checked out of the conversation for a minute."

"Oh, sorry. Old memories," I give as an explanation.

"You ready to head over to the book store?"

"Sure."

Gertie's car is in the driveway when I pull up to the house. Tanner and I ended up staying at the bookstore longer than planned. It was a lot of fun going through all of the vinyl with him. He knows a lot of music I have

191

never heard of before. He even talked me into buying a few albums because "the records deserved to have new ears experience them for the first time again." He made it sound like I was giving new life to the music. His excitement was refreshing.

Before he left, he agreed to scale back any stalking he had planned, but said, I have not seen the last of him.

"Gertie, I'm back," I call out when I enter the house.

"I'm in the kitchen."

I walk into the kitchen to see what she is cooking. The smell of garlic and other spices are hanging in the air.

"It smells good. What are you cooking?"

"Fettuccini Alfredo with grilled vegetables."

"Does Noie have anything to do with all of the pasta you have been making lately?"

"She just worries. She wants you to gain a little weight back."

"Well this looks delicious and I'm going to happily eat it, but let me worry about my weight. All this is going to do is pack on the fat," I say patting my stomach.

"You have a letter from Hadley on the table. Go take care of whatever you need to do. I will put on a fresh pot of coffee. When the food is ready, I will make you a plate and put the rest away. Then I'm going to head out."

"Sounds good. I'll see you tomorrow."

Gertie is amazing, but I need to stop depending on her so much. Noie also needs to stop using her for intel on me. I think part of taking a step back and focusing on her family should include her not badgering people for information, although I am sure Gertie doesn't mind telling her how I am doing.

I take Hadley's letter to my chair to read it. Russell is

outside playing with a ball on the patio. I got him some new toys last week he really seems to like, but I'm thinking about getting him a friend.

Lighting a cigarette, I open the letter from Hadley.

Hey Nia!

I guess this is the only way to talk to you since you still aren't using the phone. We need to talk girlie. I am coming to Louisville soon. Don't move the hide-a-key so I can get in if you are not there. Noie said you have been getting out more. I hope you don't get upset about me coming, but I have to come.

I have something else for you to think about before I get there. I am going to see Sarah and Blake when I come. You could come with me if you want. I think it would be good for you and Sarah to talk things out. I know she said things to you that were really hard to hear when you were already going through so much, but you have to understand it was hard for her to say too. She loves you and all she wanted was for you to let her in. She was hurting too when she said those things.

I'll see you soon.

XOXO,
Hadley

I wonder why Hadley couldn't just tell Noie she was coming to town. It also would have been nice if she would have given a date when she was going to be here.

The situation with Sarah is something I know I have to deal with at some point, I just don't know if I am ready to yet. I stopped blaming her a long time ago for what she said and started blaming myself. I hated her when she called me a selfish bitch who wasn't thinking about anyone except myself. After everything that happened, all I could see was how it affected my life. Now I know every one of our friends and family were affected. I fell apart so completely they couldn't even assess their own damage.

I wish I could have been different, but there is no way to prepare for what happened. There is no way to have a reserve of strength large enough for me to have been any other way. I just have to believe Sarah realizes that now too.

"How have you been feeling?" Dr. Gillis asks.

I sit in my normal chair with Russell perched in my lap. He purrs quietly as I pet him. I don't want to talk to Dr. Gillis today. My mind is stuck on going to the shelter to find a friend for Russell. Dr. Gillis says now is when the real therapy begins because I am in a better place to face what happened and start dealing with the emotions connected to it. I am just afraid looking too deeply into those emotions will just send me back to where I was before. What if I can't pull out of it this time?

"Nia, are you listening to me?"

"Sorry. I have been better. I am sticking to my new routine. I leave the house every day. I haven't needed to take any of the emergency medicine in over a week. I only took it then because I was starting to feel the panic coming on and I was going to stay home. I didn't want to do that." I spill out the words like a robot. I hope I hit every point he wanted me to so we can wrap this up.

"Do you know what caused the anxiety last week?"

"Yes."

"Can we discuss it?" He asks.

I could sense a little impatience in his voice. That's odd. He is usually devoid of emotion. Something I guess you have to learn how to do in his line of work.

"I ran into someone I met over Thanksgiving at Jett's family's house when I was at the coffee shop. The next day I got nervous about possibly running into him again."

"Did something bad happen? Does he scare you? What about this person causes you to panic? I want you to dig deep and explore the root of the problem so we can work out the real problem. If this person is a bad person who means you harm then the solution is to stay away, except, I think, it has nothing to do with him. I think it is something in you. These are the questions we need to start asking to really work on the root issues."

I know what the issue is, but it is not something I want to talk about or even think about. I enjoyed the time I spent with Tanner and it reminded me of *him*. I'm not there yet. I'm not ready for that conversation.

"I will think about what you asked," I say dismissively.

"That's all I ask, for now, but as you get stronger we will need to push more. You don't want to patch everything. You need to work through it."

"I understand."

"It appears we are done here today. Same time next week?"

"Yes."

"Now that you are getting out more we can start having these sessions in my office. Let me know if you want to start doing that."

195

"I'll let you know."

He stands and makes his way to the door as we say our goodbyes. I close the door behind him and sigh in relief the session is over. At least we are down to once a week now.

Russell saunters over to me and rubs against my leg. I wish he could come with me to pick out his new friend. The shelter said there is a return period in case it doesn't work out between the cats, but I can't imagine taking an animal back there.

"You are getting a kitten friend today Russell," I say to him in a baby voice.

I'm full of excitement as I pull up at the shelter. I park and jump out ready to pick out my new kitten when I am stopped dead in my tracks. Tanner is leaning against the building smoking a cigarette. His eyes are on me when I walk up to him.

"I let the coffee shop slide because that is an easy coincidence, but this feels like stalking," I say and it brings a grin to his face.

"The coffee shop was a coincidence, I swear," he says holding up his hands. "This is not, but the term stalking is a little harsh. Noie told me you were coming here today."

"What do you have on Noie to make her willing to give you my schedule?"

"Noie thinks it is good for you to have friends around."

"Noie means well, although she may have crossed a line this time," I say without covering how pissed I am.

"Take it easy on her. She is just trying to help you and me. Did you ever stop to think maybe I need friends too?"

I'm just making it worse arguing with him so I say, "I'm going inside. You can come if you want."

We walk inside and ask the lady at the front desk where the cats are. She points us towards a side hallway where they have play rooms and kennels. As we turn the corner I am a little overwhelmed by how many cats are there. Sadness washes over me because there will be so many left behind when we leave today.

"Are you looking for a certain type or color of cat," Tanner asks.

"Not really. I do think a young female would be the best fit for Russell."

We start looking in each of the kennels and reading the tags on the front to see their age and sex.

"Do you have any pets?"

"I do. I have a Weimaraner named Missy."

"That's right. I remember you saying something about her at Thanksgiving."

"I've had her for about three years. My ex and I adopted her from a rescue. When we broke up she took everything from our apartment except the dog. I was angry at her about taking everything, but, soon realized, she left the most important thing. Missy has become my best friend."

I know how that feels. I think Russell is the closest thing I have to a best friend right now. I feel like I should say something sympathetic about what he shared about his ex, but I don't want to open up a personal conversation.

I see a little gray cat rubbing up against the door of a

kennel. I open it and pull her out. She starts licking my fingers with her rough tongue.

"Do you want to take her into the playroom," Tanner asks.

I smile and nod my head yes. We take her into a room full of toys and towers for the cats to climb. There are about ten cats already in the room. They must let some of them hang out in here instead of being locked up in the kennels all day. I set the small kitten on the floor to see how she plays with the other cats.

I take a seat on the floor and Tanner sits down next to me. We sit in a comfortable silence interrupted by fits of laughter when the cats pounce on something or jump in fear when nothing is near them. I can't wait to get one home for Russell.

"She seems to be playing well with the other cats. That's a good sign, right?" Tanner asks.

"I think so."

"Do you want to grab any more cats to come in here?"

"No, I think she is perfect," I say as I watch her hopping around a larger cat. She is a little feistier than Russell, but I think her personality will be good for him.

"Then you need to name her," he says as he reaches over and pets the black and white cat who has taken up residence in my lap.

I stiffen a little at the closeness of his hand to my thigh and become aware of how close he is sitting to me. He is looking into my eyes with an intensity this situation doesn't require. It makes me nervous. I shift slightly and the cat jumps out of my lap.

Clearing my throat I stand up and go to where the

gray kitten is playing. Tanner walks up behind me and places his hand on my shoulder.

"Is everything okay? Did I do something wrong?"

"No I just need to get her home and I am sure there is a lot of paperwork."

"Nia, I don't know what I am doing wrong here. I just want to get to know you."

I turn to face him and say, "Why, Tanner? Do you see some broken girl you want to fix? Or do you see someone vulnerable and think you can get something out of that? I don't know you and the last thing I need is some amateur stalker trying to pry his way into my life. I have enough of my own shit right now."

"Wow," he says and backs a few feet away from me. "I know we don't know each other very well, but I haven't done anything to give you that impression of me. I'm not trying to fix you or take advantage of you. I just wanted to get to know you. Yes, I think you are beautiful and I would be lying if I said I wasn't interested in maybe taking you on a date one day, but I'm not going to pry my way into your life. Obviously this was a mistake. I hope you have a good life, Nia and I hope one day you try to open up to someone. Not everyone is out to hurt you."

He turns and walks out without saying goodbye. I stare after him for a few minutes absorbing what he just said to me. I know my words were a little cruel, but it's for the best. He doesn't understand what he is trying to get into with me. If he did, he would end up walking out just like he just did.

I turn back to the kitten and pick her up. I nuzzle her into my neck and allow the tears to fall.

"They are too cute together. Russell has much more energy than I ever realized," Noie says as we watch the girls play with the cats.

"Hey girls, have you picked out a name for her yet?" I ask.

"Yes, yes, yes!" they shout in unison.

"Okay, let's hear it."

They look at each other and giggle with excitement, then Audrie says, "Chloe."

"I love it. Chloe. I'm glad I let you girls choose her name."

They smile up at me and then go back to playing with Russell and Chloe. I needed this. It is hard to let any sadness take over when you are around children. My house hasn't been this full of life in a long time. I didn't realize how much I missed it.

"Noie, I have a favor to ask," I say nervously.

"Okay," she draws out in reaction to my tone.

I just need to say it and get it over with. "I need to find out where Tanner lives."

She relaxes and asks, "Why do you need to know where he lives?"

"Don't make this something it is not. I saw him at the shelter the other day, thanks to you, and I said some really ugly things to him. I just want to apologize in person," I say and grit my teeth. I hope she just helps me and doesn't dig.

"Nia, he is such a nice man. Why would you be unkind to him?"

"Can you help me or not?" I ask rolling my eyes.

"Yes. Let me give Jett a call. I think he picked Jake up from Tanner's apartment one time."

A few minutes later, she hangs up the phone and hands me a scrap of paper with his address on it.

I find Tanner's apartment building and walk around trying to locate his number. The place is located in a trendy area of town. It looks a little too modern for Louisville. When I get to his door I have to take a minute to get my nerve up to knock. I knock and wait impatiently. I want to get this over with before I lose my nerve.

A minute later he still hasn't answered the door. What am I doing here? I should have just asked for his number. I could have called and avoided the nerves wrecking my stomach.

"Not sure you can call me the stalker anymore after showing up at my place when I am sure I never told you where I live," Tanner says from behind me. I turn around and my eyes land on a beautiful gray dog.

"This must be Missy."

She starts wagging her tail at the sound of her name. I reach down and pat her on her head. Tanner walks around me and opens his door. He leaves it open after him and Missy go inside. I follow and close the door. Tanner removes Missy's leash and she comes over to me and begins sniffing up and down my legs.

"Hi, Missy. Do you smell my kitties?" I ask and pet her again.

Tanner walks to his kitchen and pulls a beer out of

the refrigerator.

"Do you want one?" he asks and takes a swig.

I shake my head no and begin to fidget with some papers on his bar. Tanner is just watching me. When I make eye contact with him, he looks away and moves into the living room to take a seat on the couch. His apartment is eclectic mix of furniture with multiple guitars hanging on the walls and others on stands next to the window.

He is not making this easy on me. I walk into the living room and sit down next to him. I don't know how to start.

"Do you want to tell me what I owe this pleasure to?"

He has an ashtray on his table so I pull out a cigarette and light it to give me another minute to gather my thoughts.

"I felt bad about the things I said to you the other day and wanted to come apologize and maybe explain myself a little bit."

"I'm listening."

"I shouldn't have said those things and I don't think those things about you. You are actually pretty great and that scares me. It scared me to have so much fun with you the day we went to the sandwich shop. My life is complicated and I have done things recently to make it worse. I'm trying to prevent anything that might upset the shaky ground I am standing on." I don't know if I am making any sense.

Tanner reaches for my hand and doesn't let me pull away. "Come somewhere with me. Don't over think everything. Just let it go and come somewhere with me."

"Okay."

He gets a thick blanket from his bedroom and grabs a

guitar off the wall before dragging me out of the apartment. I feel a sense of déjà vu remembering the first time I went to watch the planes at the airport.

He pulls up to a park and we get out of the car. I don't see anyone else out. The weather is still too cold to enjoy the day outside. That explains why he brought the thick blanket. I follow him to a group of trees where he lays the blanket out.

"Sit down and wrap the blanket around you. I don't want you freezing."

I comply and then ask, "Why did you bring me to the park?"

"I love it here. I come out here a lot to play my guitar. It relaxes me and helps me find my center. I want to play one of my songs for you."

He begins to play and it's beautiful. His voice has a raspy soulful sound to it. The song is about lost love. He connects so fully with the lyrics as he sings, the pain is relived on his face. The sound of the guitar is haunting and I get lost in it. I'm taken aback by how talented and passionate he is.

When the song is over, I don't know what to say so I listen to the faint sound of cars passing in the distance. I can see why he likes it here so much. I relax and the tension I was feeling earlier melts away. If I close my eyes, it would almost feel like I was here with *him* and this was our tree.

He lays his guitar down and sits in front of me on the blanket pulling the other side around his shoulders.

"What did you think?" He asks.

I look into his smoky eyes and say, "It was amazing. I think you should get around to finishing your album."

He smiles and leans in towards me. I back away and stand up.

"Hey, I'm sorry. I get it. Just forget I did that. It was stupid. You keep telling me to back off and then I just misread the moment."

"Just friends," I say flatly.

"Just friends."

I walk into my house and am instantly greeted with Russell and Chloe's meows. Russell puts his chin in the air welcoming me to scratch his neck. I reach down and love on him a little before picking Chloe up to kiss her tiny face.

My stomach starts to growl. I forgot to eat anything today. Hopefully there are still some leftovers because I don't want to cook. I feel emotionally exhausted and I feel the urge to get in bed. I settle for sitting in my chair and watching out the window as the sun finishes setting.

A knock at the door yanks me from my thoughts. I'm not expecting anyone. I hope it isn't Tanner. Although it would be fair game for Noie to give him my address, I don't think she would send someone over here without me knowing. I figure it is a sales person until I hear the key turning the lock.

"Nia!" I hear Hadley's voice yell.

I let out the breath I was holding and feel slightly annoyed my peaceful evening has been invaded on.

"In here," I call back to her. She comes in and drops a few bags on the floor. How long is she staying?

"There you are," she says as she bends down and

gives me a hug. "Are you surprised to see me?"

"I got your letter, but I didn't know you would be here today."

"The way you have been dodging everyone, I was afraid you would leave if you knew when I was coming," she says as a reprimand.

"I'm not dodging you. I've been busy. Not your type of busy, but much busier than I am used to anymore."

"What about Sam? Are you dodging him?" She gets right to the point.

"Is that what this visit is all about?"

"Hold that thought. Let me open a bottle of wine and I will be right back."

She comes back with two large glasses of wine and hands one to me. I take a sip then sit is on the table and light a cigarette.

"My plan was to loosen you up with some wine before we jumped into the heavy stuff, but I can't wait. Spill about Sam," she says leaving no room for negotiation.

"Why don't you tell me what you know?"

"Do you really want to know what I know?"

"Yes, I asked, didn't I?"

"What I know is Sam has been in love with you since freshman year of college. He held it in all of these years out of respect for your friendship. Then you sleep with him and he finally opens up to you and tells you he loves you. After that, you said maybe three words to him before leaving town and you haven't spoken to him since. That's what I know."

I stand up and look at her with anger radiating through my entire body. "Did you really come all the way here to throw this on me? Look at my life Hadley. I feel like it is a win if I leave the house or if I can even carry on a conversation with someone. My life is gone. I know what I did with Sam was wrong, but all this love talk is bullshit and I don't want to hear it."

"Bullshit? Are you really that blind Nia?" She asks in disbelief.

"It was a mistake Hadley. He was caught up in the moment with a friend. He has Maria. She is who he loves or is falling in love with. I am just a friend who is going through some shit and took my need to feel something other than pain too far."

"He broke things off with Maria the second you left. He wasn't in love with her. They just bonded over some shared trauma. I hoped things would work out with them because I know you are not ready for a relationship right now and it has been heart breaking watching him pine over you for all these years. When I saw the two of you kiss on New Year's, I was pissed because I know your heart is broken, but, I knew, in that moment his heart was about to be broken too. Now you are telling me you slept with him because you just needed to get laid or something. I am not diminishing anything you have gone through, but you do not make yourself feel better at someone else's expense. Especially not a friend's."

"That's not what I said."

"Yeah, well you don't say much," she says and walks into the kitchen. Two seconds later she stomps back out and continues, "You know what? I am not done. You might want to tell Noie to keep this whole Tanner thing under wraps when she talks to Sam. No need to twist the knife."

"What Tanner thing?"

"Noie is so excited about how well you are doing so she just goes on and on. When I called her to let her know I would be in town today, she informed me you might be out with Tanner when I got here. I don't know who he is, but I don't want her bragging about your new friend to Sam right now," she says disgusted before walking back to the kitchen.

It's all too much and I can't hold back the tears. They start flowing down my face as I sob. Hadley hears me and comes running back in the room and falls on her knees in front of me.

"Nia, calm down," she says in a soft tone. "I didn't mean to yell at you like that. I know you don't need that right now. It has just been building up. Sam called me right after you left and he calls or texts me every day to see if I have heard from you. Since I never do, it has just built up and I exploded."

She is rubbing her hands on my knees trying to calm me. I whimper out an, "I'm sorry." I have never seen Hadley yell at someone in all the years I have known her. She is always the one you can depend on to be happy and upbeat. I hate being the one to finally push her over the edge.

"No, Nia. I am sorry. I let all of that out without even checking on how the situation affected you. I am your friend too, not just Sam's. I shouldn't have attacked you and put you on the defensive because I know it's the only reason you said what you did. No one sleeps with someone they have been best friends with for over a decade to just blow off steam or have a little fun. At least I know you don't do that kind of thing."

She wipes the tears off my cheeks and smiles up at

me just as my stomach lets out a loud growl. We both start laughing.

"Have you eaten anything today?" she asks disapprovingly.

"No, the day just got away from me."

"How does pizza sound?"

"Perfect."

She orders the pizza and we sit quietly sipping our wine while Russell and Chloe play near our feet. By the time the pizza arrives, we have finished off the first bottle of wine and opened the second.

"Can we start over?" She asks.

"I would like that," I say genuinely. I do love having Hadley around and I don't want to fight the entire time she is here.

"Then it is girl talk time. I want to know who Tanner is and I am not asking as Sam's defender. I am asking because I am curious," her manner is playful now and I am thankful for that. I could use a girl friend to talk to about him.

"He was roommates with Jett's brother in college. I met him over Thanksgiving. He got to witness me lose it a little bit and he took care of me. After that he started calling Noie to check up on me and then I ran into him at the coffee shop when I got back from D.C. We have hung out a few times, but I have made it clear we are just friends."

"Does he want to be more than friends?"

"We don't really know each other. He tried to kiss me today. So I guess the answer to your question is yes."

"How do you feel about him?"

"Afraid. I think about Ian a lot when I am with him."

That is the first time I have allowed myself to say his name. It almost feels like a relief. I have been trapping it away for so long. So scared of what the sound of his name would do to me, I have banished it from my every thought. As it came out of my mouth I realized trying so hard to never hear or think his name has caused more damage than saying it ever could.

"He plays the guitar. Today we went to a park and he played for me. It almost felt like I was with Ian. Or the version of him if he would have followed his dreams of playing music instead of opening the law practice with Jett. When I'm with Tanner, it's like I am with the person Ian was always meant to be." A tear runs down my cheek and I see Hadley's eyes are tearing up too.

"I keep trying to push him away from me, but he is determined to get to know me. There is this part of me that feels drawn to him, but I know it's unfair. I can't treat him like a do-over, but I don't know how I can treat him any other way. Does that make sense?"

"Yes."

"Then I also feel like if I am ever able to really consider letting someone into my life again, it needs to be someone like Tanner. Someone who doesn't know every moment of my past. Someone who doesn't long for the person I used to be but wants the person I am now. A fresh start."

I pause and look over at Hadley. She looks like she is trying to process everything I am saying. I figure she needs a minute to formulate what she wants to say to me. I pour a little more wine in my glass and light another cigarette. Russell jumps into my lap and lays down. He does this when he needs a break from Chloe's never ending energy. I rub my hand along his back and relax to the vibration of his purr.

Hadley finally asks, "Are you ready to talk about what happened with Ian?"

My eyes refill with tears and I nod my head yes.

36 NIA THEN

I think this is the happiest I have ever been in my life. The last week in Hawaii with Ian has been just the rejuvenation we needed. Ian works so much and is always so stressed so having him to myself for an entire week felt like Christmas. Even with me feeling a little sick, it was perfect because I expect the sickness has been for an amazing reason. I can't wait for us to get home and for Ian to go to bed. I want to take the pregnancy test I picked up without him knowing so I can surprise him with it. I would tell him, but there is no reason for both of us to be disappointed if it is negative.

He reaches over for my hand and laces our fingers together before pulling my hand to his mouth. He kisses my hand and says, "I love you, my beautiful Snow White. No matter what, always know how much I love you."

"I love you too."

My heart is overflowing with joy. I look over at him, at his gorgeous face and imagine what our child will look like. I hope he or she has his green eyes.

"Home sweet home," Ian says as he pulls into our driveway.

He kisses my hand again and then releases me so we can get out of the car. We both grab a couple of bags out of the trunk and head inside. We make a bee line to the bedroom and sink into the bed.

He leans over me and starts kissing my neck. My body instantly reacts to his touch. I stand up next to the bed and slowly start to remove my clothes while he watches me. I can feel his eyes as they take in each piece of skin as it is exposed.

I start to climb back into the bed and he stops me. "Let me look at you."

He sits up on the side of the bed and runs his hands up and down my body as if trying to see me through touch. I reach down and pull his shirt over his head then he pulls me into him to run his mouth over my stomach.

He stands to remove the rests of his clothes and then guides me down to the bed. Taking his time, he makes love to me savoring every moment of pleasure.

I sneak out of bed once I know he is asleep and pull the pregnancy test from my purse. The next five minutes may change our lives forever.

I go into the bathroom and read the instructions to make sure I do everything right. Once I am done I pee on the stick as instructed and place it on the counter to begin the waiting game.

I scroll through pictures of our vacation on my phone to pass the time. When the five minutes is up, I take a deep breath and pick up the test. Two lines. Pregnant. I fight the urge to jump up and down screaming. I debate waking him up right then, but decide to stick to my original plan and tell him over breakfast. Tomorrow is his birthday and I can't think of a better present to give him.

I hide the test under the sink and then go to bed dreaming of our green eyed baby.

The sun is shining in the window when I open my eyes and feel my hand across the bed for Ian. I wanted to tell him happy birthday right away, but he is already up.

My hand stops when I feel a little sheet of paper. I grab it and open my eyes to read the sticky note he left for me.

Good morning beautiful.

I sit up and stretch my arms looking around for the next note. He shouldn't have done this today. It is his birthday. I should have made a note trail for him.

The next note is on my nightstand.

You are the most wonderful thing that has ever come into my life.

On the chair I spot another note.

My love for you transcends the physical world and nothing can ever change that.

The mirror over the dresser holds another note.

Look up. You are looking at the only woman I have ever loved.

The bathroom door has the next note.

Seeing you dance around the bathroom in the morning when you get ready is the best part of my day.

I open the door and step in to find another note on the shower stall.

Some of the most passionate memories we have made together happened in here.

I smile as I think about some of those moments and I can't wait to make some more. The next note is on the closet door.

Call Jimmy, he should be on his way over. Wait for him before you go any further. I love you.

I should have figured Jimmy would be coming over today. I just wished we could have our time together before all of the birthday festivities started.

I go back to the nightstand and grab my phone to call Jimmy. He answers on the first ring.

"Good morning, Nia. How is our birthday boy?" He asks.

"I haven't seen him yet. He set up one of his note trails and said I have to wait for you before I go any further so you need to hurry," I say to him with excitement.

"You won't have to hold your horses too long little lady. I am pulling onto your street."

"Okay, I'll meet you at the door."

I pull my robe off the hook on the wall and tie it around me before going to the door. Jimmy's hand is raised to knock as I open it.

"What does that boy have planned for us now?" He asks.

"You never know with him. I was just a little surprised he wanted you in on his little love note trail. I thought that was our special thing," I say with a mock pout on my face.

He laughs and says, "Believe me, the love notes are only for you. He saves the noogies and things like that for me."

"Follow me. The last note I read was on the closet door so I am guessing he has outfits in there for us to wear to whatever he has planned."

Jimmy follows as I skip back to our bathroom and stand outside of the closet.

"Okay, are you ready?" I ask Jimmy before throwing open the door.

All the air rushes from my body and I collapse. Jimmy's arms are around me before I hit the floor. Screams begin erupting from my mouth. Jimmy tightens his hold on me as I begin to swing my arms at him. I can barely hear Jimmy's sobs with my screams echoing through the room. My hands find my hair and I start ripping at it and shaking. Jimmy tries to hold down my hands, but he is too weak from his own shock to stop me.

Jimmy pulls his phone from his pocket and tries to quiet me while he calls for an ambulance. I am no longer in control of my body and I cannot force the screams down.

He is still holding me and trying to calm me down when the paramedics arrive. They follow my screams to the bathroom and find us staring at Ian's body hanging lifeless in the closet wearing his favorite college sweatshirt, a self-made noose around his neck.

They lower him to the floor and try to revive him, but I know it's hopeless. His wide open green eyes had no sign of life when we opened the closet door.

One of the paramedics try to help Jimmy to calm me down and and get my screaming to stop, but they can't. I just rock back and forth, holding chunks of my hair in fists as I bash them into my face.

Suddenly I feel a needle in my arm and my hands become too heavy to lift to my face. They help me to the bed where all I can do is let the tears fall like a flood onto my pillow.

I fall in and out of sleep as strangers fill my room. I think I hear Jimmy's voice telling someone what happened, but I drift away before he is finished.

I wake to Noie sitting next to me crying and stroking my hair. My stomach is cramping and I try to tell her, but I can't get the words out of my mouth. I need the pain to stop, but it just keeps getting worse.

Noie finally notices me clutching my stomach and asks if I am okay. All I can manage is to shake my head no.

She moves my arms to look me over and then yells for the paramedics.

"She is covered in blood between her legs."
I finally manage to speak, "I'm pregnant."

37 IAN THEN

I hope I made her happy. Nia has always wanted to go to Hawaii and I was determined to take her on that trip before I left. Watching her lie in the sun was one of the most beautiful sights anyone will ever see, next to her smile.

I think I have everything in place to make sure she is okay. I have stashed money away for years. That combined with her family inheritance should keep her secure without my income. Jett will also have to buy out my portion of the practice which will help.

The smile on her face last night before I fell asleep gives me peace. All I ever wanted to do was make her smile.

I know she may have a hard time understanding what I have to do, but, in time, I hope she will forgive my weakness.

I texted Jimmy to make sure he comes over first thing. He will know what to do and be able to help her through this.

I need to read through the letters one last time to make sure I said everything I need to.

Dear Nia,

I remember the first time I spoke to you like it was yesterday. I knew from that moment I was hooked. This was the woman I was going to spend the rest of my life with. I had hoped our life together would be longer, but the inner demons I have carried with me for so long would never let me rest.

Please know you have done nothing except make my life better and my decision has nothing to do with you. I don't want you to hold on to the thought you could have done something to stop this inevitable end.

I will take this next step with memories of you to comfort me. When I am gone, I want you to remember me with love and I hope one day you will give your heart to someone who cherishes it like I do, but who is strong enough to face this life at your side. You will forever be my Snow White.

Ian

I take a breath and pull out the note for Jimmy. He is the strongest person I have ever known. I have always wished I could be a little more like him. He has always been able to take on any of life's trials with poise and determination. Nia will need that.

Jimmy,

You have been the best friend anyone could ask for and I hate I had to ask you to bear this burden. I just couldn't let Nia find me alone.

Please look after her for me and help her to understand. Tell her everything one day.

Thank you for always having my back. I am sorry I can't be here to have yours, but you are the only person who saw how hard I have struggled to keep myself level which means you might understand why I had to do this.

Ian

38 NIA NOW

Hadley folds the letter back up and sets it on the table. Tears are streaking her face and she doesn't even attempt to wipe them away.

"I am left feeling like my life was a lie. I was planning our future while he was planning to end his. I keep replaying that night in my mind. Wondering if it would have been different if I had told him about our child." I have to stop and choke back the tears. I light a cigarette and take a few drags before continuing. "Every thought of him makes me feel absolute love and hate at the same time. He took my life with him that night and I can't help but blame him for taking the life of our child too. He is gone. His pain is over and I am left with a fucking letter. I ask myself if he would have known how completely he was going to destroy me, would he have still done it. The only answer I can come up with is yes because I don't know how he could have shared in the love we built together and think it was something I could just move past. I can't rectify the feeling of love and hate I have for him."

My tears are falling without abandon now. The next thing I want to say is one of the hardest parts of this new reality I have had to accept.

"He knew every facet of my love and he walked away from it. I don't know how to love a person who was worth so little to the person who knew her best. If I can't find a way to love me again, how did he ever think I would be able to love someone else?" I stop after that. I need a few minutes to pull myself back together before I fall apart again. The glue I have been trying to hold myself together with hasn't cured yet. Every moment I am waiting to fall completely apart again.

"I want to go to bed," I say to Hadley and she follows me into the room to sleep with me. Neither of us able to be alone right now.

I am sitting in my chair staring at the willow tree when Hadley comes out of the bedroom.

"Did you sleep," she asks with the roughness of sleep still in her voice.

"A little."

She sits in the chair next to me and Russell gets up from my lap to jump into hers.

"Good morning, Russell," she says as she scratches behind his ear. "We are not going to sit here all day. Let's get out of here now before we talk ourselves out of it. No big adventure. Let's just grab a coffee and maybe some breakfast on our way back."

"Gertie will be here soon. I want to wait for her so

she doesn't try to make me any food."

"Okay. I'll get ready while we wait," she says and disappears with her bags into the bedroom.

About fifteen minutes later I hear Gertie come in the door. She walks over to me to say hello but stops when she sees my bloodshot eyes and puffy face.

"Nia, are you okay? Should I call Noie?" She asks concerned.

"No, Hadley is here. She is getting ready. We are going to go out for breakfast."

"That's nice. I might not be here when you get back. I have to take Odie to the dentist in a little bit."

"Alright. Are you coming tomorrow?"

"Yes, in the morning."

"You can bring Odie with you if he wants to see the new kitten."

"He would love that."

"Then I will see you two tomorrow. I need to get dressed so we can leave. Bye, Gertie."

We walk arm-in-arm into the coffee shop with my head leaning on her shoulder. Taking my last few minutes of rest before Hadley makes me talk.

"Grab a table, I will order," she says.

"Do you mind if we sit outside? I want a cigarette and the weather seemed nice enough when we walked in."

"Okay, but you know I am a wimp when it comes to the cold. We will have to sit in the car with the heater running if I can't handle it."

"Yes, ma'am," I say and roll my eyes before walking

outside.

I find a table and sit to watch the people walking by. It seems like every other person is walking a dog. I wonder if Russell would let me walk him. It's a funny thought. He would probably try to scratch my eyes out.

I spot Tanner and Missy right as Hadley walks out with our coffees. Hadley sits down and hands me my coffee. She sees me looking behind her and turns around. Tanner waves.

Hadley waves back and then asks, "Do we know him?"

"That's Tanner."

"Good morning, Nia. This is two days in a row. I might have to file a restraining order," he says with his brown eyes piercing mine.

"I was thinking the same thing. Tanner, this is my friend Hadley. Hadley meet Tanner."

"Hi Hadley. I'm surprised to meet you. I wasn't sure if Nia could be nice long enough to actually have a friend," he says to her with a mischievous smile.

"It's not easy being her friend, but sometimes you get stuck with people," Hadley replies. "And who is this pretty girl?"

"This is Missy. Unlike Nia, she makes for a wonderful friend."

"Have you both gotten in enough jabs this morning or would you like to continue?"

"I'm good now," Tanner replies.

"Me too," Hadley says with a laugh.

"I'm actually very happy to see you here. Do you mind watching Missy while I grab a coffee? I hate leaving her out here alone."

"No problem."

He hands Missy's leash to me and goes inside.

"So, that is Tanner? He is cute and has an accent. Does he have any single friends?"

"I don't know and I don't want to encourage him to hang around."

"Fine. We are having a girl's day anyways."

Tanner comes back out and I hand Missy back off to him after petting her head one last time.

"Thank you for watching Missy and Hadley it was nice meeting you," he says and starts to walk away. A few feet away, he turns and says, "I'm going to hold off on the restraining order for now. I hope to see you again soon."

"Wow. There is no doubt he is interested in you. I'm still team Sam all the way, but team Tanner is kinda hot."

"Hadley, please stop it."

"Sorry, I'm just trying to lighten the mood. I want to finish our talk from last night and I thought we could relax a little before we got back into that."

We keep the conversation light over coffee and breakfast. I don't want to risk a public meltdown, so we are waiting to finish our talk when we get back to my house.

Gertie is already gone when we arrive, but I can hear a pot of coffee brewing in the kitchen. We must have just missed her.

"I'm going to grab a cup of coffee, do you want one," I ask.

"Yes, please."

When I walk out of the kitchen, Hadley is making goo-goo gaa-gaa noises at Chloe as she squirms in her hands. She sits her down when she sees me and takes her coffee.

"Nia, I don't know exactly how you feel, but I think the thoughts you are having are understandable, although misguided. You will never find a new way in this life if you carry all that guilt and anger with you. Ian made a choice *for himself* not because of you. Now you need to make choices *for* you and not *because* of him. You can't let him take your life with him and it is time to stop pushing everyone away. We love you and want to be here for you. You don't have to do this alone."

In my head, I know she is right, but the pain that comes with each beat of my heart holds me prisoner in this hell. Sometimes it feels like my heart is working triple time to beat for Ian and our baby ever since their hearts stopped.

"You are getting much better at the motions of life, but at some point you have to choose to start living life. I came here originally to talk to you about Sam, but not because I think you need to fall in love with him and start a new life like nothing happened. I don't even care if you do or don't open yourself up to someone like him or Tanner. I just don't want you slamming the door in the faces of people who care about you. From the things you said to me last night, you could use more people in your life who want you to know you are worth waking up for each day."

I start to block her out as she tries to reason with me. The pain is the only connection I have left to Ian and it is the only connection I have ever had with our baby. My instincts tell me to protect it at all costs.

I let pain take over and I begin to sob. Hadley is instantly at my side. I pull my legs up in the chair and wrap my arms around them. All of my favorite memories of Ian start flashing through my mind. I see us laying together in bed for hours looking into each other's eyes while discussing our dreams for the future. A future that only exists in the past now.

I am sitting on the back patio staring at the flames in the fire pit when Hadley gets back from Sarah's house. She tried to get me to go, but after all of the emotions that have drained out of me since Hadley has been here, I just didn't have anything left to give to Sarah.

Hadley walks outside and takes a seat in the chair next to me. Her face is flush and she looks like she has been crying.

"Are you okay? Is everything okay with Sarah?" I ask.

"I'm fine and so is Sarah. She misses you and we were talking about the things she said to you. It just got emotional. She is really sorry and wants the chance to fix it, but she doesn't know how to." She lets out a small laugh and continues, "Her belly is getting really big and the burning question was finally answered."

"What question is that?" I ask confused.

"She was in heels. Swollen feet and a belly big enough to tip her over and she still had heels on."

"That's Sarah for you. If she has a girl, it will be the first child in history to take her first steps in heels, I'm sure."

The only time in all the years I have known Sarah to not wear heels was when she went to the gym. Hadley jokes about it, but she is almost as bad. All three of us are close in height, but I always looked like the short friend when I was with them.

"Sarah wanted me to tell you if you ever want to meet for coffee or lunch, she would really like that. Also, she is having a baby shower next month and is going to send you an invitation. She would love to have you there."

"I'll think about lunch and I will send a gift for the shower."

"She doesn't care about the gift. She just wants the chance to see you."

"I know, but I will still send a gift anyways. I don't think I want to go to the shower."

"While we are on the topic of repairing relationships within our little group, can we talk about Sam?" Hadley ask apprehensively.

"What do you want to talk about?"

"What happened? I just want to know where your head was when you were there and where it is now."

"Sam was just being Sam. You know how he is always so touchy and cuddly. I have always been so comfortable around him and it was nice to be held and it just went too far. I don't know what else to say. I don't want to ruin my friendship with him. I couldn't live without it. So right now I am just hoping it can be fixed and we can go back to before that moment."

Hadley is quiet for a few moments, taking in what I said.

"Nia, I want to make a few things clear where Sam is

concerned so you have all the facts as you try to work out what happened in your head. First, he is not touchy and cuddly with everyone. That is not just Sam being Sam. That is how Sam has always been with you. Second, he was not just caught up in the moment when he told you he loves you. The only person who sees this as new information is you. He said it because he felt like it was finally safe to say to you."

I light a cigarette and think about what she said. I know she wants me to respond, but how do I respond to that? I have been with Ian for almost the entire time I have known Sam. I have never considered him as anything more than a friend. Of course I love him, but that is different from being in love with him.

"If that is truly how he feels then how do we go back?" I ask.

"You can't," She says truthfully. "But, it doesn't mean you can't still have a friendship with him."

"Would he be okay with being only friends now?"

"Yes. He has been torn up since you left. He is so upset with himself for letting that happen. Sam wants you in his life. If he has to put those feelings aside, he will. He has been doing it for eleven years already."

39 NIA NOW

I am waiting for Dr. Gillis to get here. I am looking forward to talking to him today because I have some answers he will like to hear. That is if he isn't too upset with me cancelling our appointments for the past two weeks.

I hear the knock at the door and jump up to answer it. Dr. Gillis greets me and walks in.

"Can I take your coat?" I ask.

"I can take care of it, but if you have a pot of coffee made, I would appreciate a cup."

"Absolutely," I say and make my way to the kitchen.

I walk back in and hand him a cup before taking a seat in my normal spot.

"You look well. Did you cancel our appointments because you have been feeling better?"

"Not exactly. Hadley came to visit and I spoke to her about Ian. I just needed some time to process before we met."

"Would you like to discuss it?"

I take a breath and say, "I finally put words to how angry I am with Ian. So angry it feels like hate, then, at the same time, I love and long for him. I am really confused about everything. He took me on an amazing vacation before he did it. Everything seemed perfect. He actually seemed more relaxed than he had in a long time. How could he be so happy and then do that?"

"What I am about to say may be hard for you to hear. It is not uncommon for someone who commits suicide to be relaxed or calm before they do it. Ian probably had a sense of peace because he had made up his mind to go through with it. He possibly saw the end to his pain in sight and it calmed him."

"Why would he ruin things the way he did? He left notes for me to find him. That was something he had done over the years for good things and he tainted all of those good memories by leaving those sticky notes."

"I can't speak for Ian. I don't know why he would have chosen to lead you to his body in that way. I know you are left with so many questions, but these questions can never be answered. You have to come to terms with the unknown."

"It's just really hard," I say.

"It is a hard situation with complex emotions. It is not going to be simple to face," he says and lets it sink in before continuing. "Have you allowed yourself to think about the baby?"

"Yes, but it almost feels like a dream. I knew I was pregnant for less than a day. I suspected for longer, but only confirmed it the night before. I think the memory of Ian is so real it overshadows the baby and almost makes me feel like I made it up in my head. Then other times the pain of what could have been is so intense and it is those times when I hate Ian the most. When my mind is blaming him for me losing our baby, I can almost block out any love I had for him. It's a strange feeling. The people around me feed into the baby feeling unreal as well. They didn't know I was pregnant before I lost the baby and with everything happening at the same time, no one even considers how hard losing the baby was on me."

"I have someone I would like you to talk to. She specializes in the loss of a child and I think she can help you work through those feelings. Would you be willing to meet with her?"

"Yes."

"Then I will set it up and let you know when the appointment is. Are there any times I should stay clear of? Are you working, yet?"

There it is. The question he always comes back to.

"I am not working yet. I have been contacted about a few girls who need private help. I am thinking about scheduling some time with them, but it will be in the evenings. I was going to start a class, but have decided to hold off for now and see how the private lessons go."

"What about helping Jett out? Are you planning on taking any legal work on?"

"That is one decision I have made for sure. I am going to let Jett buy out Ian's portion of the practice. I may go to work for another practice in the future, but I think I should cut those ties for now. I feel like it will bring up too many thoughts of Ian and affect the work I do."

"I like it. A firm decision. That is progress," he says with a proud smile.

"Don't slam the door in my face," Tanner says from my door step as I stare at him in shock. "I realize showing up at your house confirms stalker status, but please just hear me out."

"I'm listening," I say unamused.

"Your studio is listed in the directory. I haven't run into you in a while and I just wanted to say hi and," he pauses as he pulls up the bag he is holding, "I brought some toys for the cats. I wanted to see how they were getting along."

He waits with a look of anticipation on his face or it might be fear I am going to call the cops or hurt him. I think for a minute before stepping aside and letting him in.

"Me letting you in is not an open invitation to stop by here unannounced. I don't like that. You could have called Noie and at least given me a heads up."

"I promise it won't happen again," he says genuinely. "I just wanted to see you and it was time sensitive."

"Really? Why is that?"

"I have a gig in town and wanted you to come. It's tomorrow."

"Where at?"

"The sandwich shop."

I laugh and ask, "Are you being serious?"

"Yes, I am."

"Then absolutely. It's one of my favorite venues."

We both laugh and it relaxes me from the shock of him showing up on my door step.

"Are you playing alone?" I ask.

"No, I asked the band who usually plays there if I could play with them sometime. They said yes and we finally set it up for tomorrow. I have been practicing with them to learn their music and we are going to do a few cover songs."

"Sounds fun. Now do you want to see Russell and Chloe?"

"Please, lead the way."

I take him to the back window where Russell is perched on the ledge. Chloe is on the floor swatting at his tail as he flips it back and forth.

"Isn't that cute," Tanner says. "Let me see what I have here," he says as he digs through the bag.

He pulls out a mouse with tiny wheels on the bottom. He flips a switch on the bottom and then sits it on the floor. The mouse starts rolling across the floor and when it hits the wall, it turns in the other direction. Chloe is instantly fascinated and starts chasing it around. Russell hangs back watching it intently.

"Thank you. It's perfect for Chloe. She never runs out of energy."

"I have a few other motorized toys in here. Hopefully Russell will like some of them."

Suddenly there is a knock at the door.

"Who now?" I say frustrated. "Are you expecting someone? You show up on my door step so maybe you gave out my address to random people on your way."

"I did, but it was only to a few homeless people without transportation. I don't think they could have made it here this quick"

"Ha, ha," I say and roll my eyes as I head for the front door.

Opening the door, I am shocked again and heat moves up my face.

"Sam. Hi," I say and continue to stare at him.

"Hi, Nia," he says with a slight tinge of sadness in his voice.

"What are you doing here?"

"I came in for Sarah's baby shower. Well actually to hang out with Blake while the shower is going on and drop a present off for the baby," he says before adding, "and to see you. Can I come in?"

"Oh, yes. Sorry," I say and step aside. "A friend just stopped by. I'll introduce you."

My stomach is doing flips. It's as if the world sees I am doing better and figures I need a curve ball. I walk into the living room with Sam following behind me. Tanner is sitting on the floor trying to get Russell involved with the toys. I can see Sam's body tense out of the corner of my eye.

"Tanner," I say and he looks up. "This is Sam, one of my best friends since college. Sam, this is Tanner. He was Jett's brother's college roommate. We met at Thanksgiving."

Tanner stands and shakes Sam's hand. The tension in the air is stifling. We all stand and stare at each other for a minute.

I finally say, "Tanner came by to bring the cats some toys."

"And to invite you to my gig. You haven't forgotten already, have you?" He asks.

No I haven't and thank you for bringing it up again, I think to myself.

"Gig? What kind of gig?" Sam asks.

"I play guitar. There is a sandwich shop in town where a local band plays during lunch. I am just playing with them tomorrow for fun. You should come too, if you are in town," Tanner offers.

"Maybe I will," Sam says and looks at me.

"That would be great," I say. Or it could be as awkward as this moment is.

"I need to be going. I told Blake I would stop by as soon as I got into town. I was going to stay here. I can get a hotel if it is a problem."

"No problem. You know that," I say giving him a look that begs him not be weird about this.

"Okay, then. I will see you later. It was nice meeting you Tanner."

"You too."

"Let me walk you out," I offer and then follow him out the door.

When I close the door, Sam turns to me.

"Is there going to be an issue with Tanner if I stay here?" He asks coldly.

"No. Like I said, he is a friend. That's it. He just showed up here today with stuff for the cats. He doesn't stay here or hang out here. This is the first time he has ever been in my house," I say feeling I needed to explain.

"Just know, I am fighting for you this time," he says and walks to his rental car.

I am still trying to process what Sam said to me earlier when he gets back from visiting Blake. I want us to be able to have a nice weekend without any weirdness from what happened between us over the holidays.

"Hey, can I put my stuff up in the spare room?" Sam asks when he walks in holding two large bags.

"Yes. There are fresh sheets on the bed. Gertie changed them this afternoon when she found out you were going to stay here."

"Thanks."

Small talk. This is a good sign. He seems much more relaxed than he was earlier. I decide to go in the kitchen and open a bottle of wine. Hopefully that will keep things light. I pour two glasses and make my way to the spare room.

He is hanging up some clothes when I walk in and say, "I brought you a glass of wine."

"Can you set it down? I'll get it in a minute."

I place the glass on the bed side table and start to walk out.

"You can stay," he says. "I have something for you."

I sit on the edge of the bed and let him finish situating his clothes. When he is done, he grabs a bag out of the suitcase and hands it to me. Inside is a hoodie style sweatshirt that says "I love Washington D.C. Boys" on the front of it.

I start laughing and he smiles at me.

"Thank you."

"You are welcome. I saw it in the airport and couldn't help myself. I thought it might break the ice."

He picks up his glass of wine and says, "Let's go to the patio. You can use your new hoodie if it is too cold out there for you."

"Sounds like a good idea, but I also have a fire pit."

"Fancy. When did you get that?"

"Noie got it for me to encourage me to get out of the house a few months ago."

We go out back and Sam tells me to sit while he gets the fire going. Russell is standing at the back door looking out at us.

"Do you mind if I let him out?"

"That's fine. Just don't let Chloe out. She is still young and I don't want her running off."

Russell jets out the door when Sam opens it and hops right into the chair.

"Hey buddy, that's my seat," Sam says before picking him up so he can sit. He places Russell in his lap and begins stroking his back after he sits down.

"I finally get to meet Russell in the flesh. Does he know I named him?"

"It has come up during our long talks," I say jokingly.

We sit in silence for a while sipping our wine. There is no tension in the air, although I feel slightly uncomfortable. There is part of me that wants to curl up in his arms, then Hadley's voice is in my head telling me to be mindful of his feelings. We used to cuddle up together. Now it may be laced with a sexual undertone or the action could say something I'm not ready to say.

Sam breaks the silence and says, "You look good and I am not just talking about looks, your energy looks good."

"I have been a lot better. I realized I basically lost six months of my life and then was barely sleep walking through a few more. I decided to wake up every day and try to actually live. It is a process, but I am getting there."

"Hadley told me she came out for a few days."

"She did. She can claim a lot of credit for how I am feeling. We talked about a lot of things I needed a sounding board for and it helped."

"I hope she didn't give you too hard of a time about me. I shouldn't have, but I talked to her about us and she got a little hot headed."

"She gave me an earful when she got here," I say trying to sound playful.

"I'm just going to bring it up once. We don't have to talk about it. We can just move on, but, if you want to talk about what happened, how you feel about everything, we can," Sam says.

"Is that what you want?"

"What I want for me matters very little in comparison to what I want for you."

"And what is that?"

"I want you to heal and find your way again. I want you to experience true joy again. I would be lying if I didn't say I wanted to be a real part of that, but, if I am not, I just want your happiness."

"I need time right now to continue working on me. I'm not in a place to fully process what happened between us and I want to focus on our friendship for now," I say.

"I understand. I am a patient man, Nia. I consider it one of my super powers," Sam says with a wink.

The friend in me wants to ask about Maria and see if he is okay, but, I feel like after what happened, I lost the ability to ask those questions without them meaning more than me just being a concerned friend.

"I've had a long day. I think I will turn in to bed. Are you sure you don't want to go to the baby shower tomorrow?" He asks.

"I'm sure. Maybe we can all get coffee or something after. If Sarah is up to it."

"I think Sarah would be up for anything if it meant the two of you talking again. I'll let you know. Good night."

"Good night."

I watch as he goes back inside and decide I will wait until I am sure he is asleep before I go in.

I attempt to whistle, but I can't get any noise out so I settle for clapping my hands. It takes me back to my college days when I would watch Ian and Jimmy play. Ian would get the same intense look on his face. It is probably the way I look when I dance.

"Thank you everyone. We are going to take five," the singer says.

I laugh at how serious his thank you was when I was the only one clapping or even paying attention. I wonder why they continue to play here. They are good and this does not seem like a confidence booster.

"So what did you think?" Tanner asks.

"I thought it was great. I can tell you belong on a stage. You are very intense, but you also look at peace. It's nice watching you play."

"It's nice being up on stage again. I have been doing so much work with other bands and in the studio so I haven't played live in a long time. This is not exactly the same feeling when you only have one person in the place who is paying attention, but it is still nice. Why didn't your friend come?"

"He already had plans today. I am meeting up with him in some of our other friends later."

"Do you want me to tagalong?" Tanner asks. "I would like to meet your friends."

"This probably isn't the best time. There was a little bit of a falling out between me and Sarah and this will be our first time seeing each other or talking in a really long time. I think it would be best if there weren't any new people around, no offense."

"None taken, I get it."

The band starts piling back on stage and Tanner looks at me and says, "Well, duty calls." He brushes his hand over mine as he walks back on stage.

My nerves are starting to get the best of me as I wait for Sam to show up and let me know if we're meeting Sarah or not. I wish there was some way to just forget about what happened between us and move on. I know after what Ian did, nothing in my life is going to be exactly what it would've been, but, I realize now, different doesn't have to mean bad. Maybe I can find my way through this life without him and make something good of it. Maybe I go on living a happy life because he was never able to and honor his memory by just trying to be happy. That happiness has to start with repairing things with Sarah.

"You know, you really shouldn't leave your door unlocked," Sam says as he walks in the door.

"I basically live in Mayberry. Nothing bad ever happens here."

As soon as the words leave my mouth, I realize what a lie they are. The problem is a lock on the front door doesn't keep the bad things that happen here out. Sam must have had the same thought because he looks away and doesn't respond.

I clear those thoughts from my head and ask, "Are we meeting Sarah for coffee?"

"No, but they are coming by here. I hope that's okay. They should be here soon. They are stopping somewhere to pick up dinner for us and then coming here."

I look down at the sweatshirt and yoga pants I have on and think about changing, but I don't really want to.

"You look fine," Sam says. "It is just Sarah and Blake."

"Do you mind putting on a pot of coffee and then coming to get me when they get here? I'm going to go outback to smoke."

"No problem."

I go outside and light a cigarette trying to clear my mind. I take one drag before the back door opens and out walks a beautiful and very pregnant Sarah. I reach to put out my cigarette, but she stops me.

"No, don't. I will just stand over here. You can finish."

There is an awkward silence as I rack my brain for something to say. I just don't know how to start.

"I wanted to talk to you alone for a minute, if that's okay with you," she says.

I nod my head yes.

"I'm sorry for the things I said to you. It was mean. You were trying to deal with what had happened the best you could. I couldn't get past my own grief to understand how to be there for you. Since finding out I was pregnant, I understand even more what you lost. We were all sad about losing Ian and then basically losing you. I didn't consider how you were trying to cope with losing the baby as well."

My eyes begin to tear up. I don't want to break down right now. I muster up every bit of strength I have to keep the sobs at bay.

"I was selfish. I see that now. I should have tried to apologize earlier, but I was so ashamed of my behavior and didn't think you would want my apology."

We just stare at each other as I finish my cigarette. I know I am probably making it worse by not saying anything, but do I just say I accept? Or tell her how she made me feel? Since words are failing me, I stub out my cigarette and walk over to give her a hug. As our arms wrap around each other, she begins to cry and I start laughing.

"Why are you laughing?" Sarah asks through her tears.

"I can barely hug you over this belly!"

She starts laughing too and I pull away to touch her stomach.

"Do you know what you are having yet?"

"No, we want it to be a surprise."

"Boy or girl, it is going to be a big baby," I say with a smile.

"Is that your way of calling me fat?"

"Not at all. You look amazing. Do you want to go in and eat?"

"We can go in, but I don't know if the food is here yet. I was so excited to see you so I wouldn't wait on the pizza. We just ordered and told them to deliver it."

"Pizza, my favorite."

"I was craving pineapple and jalapenos. Don't'

worry, I got you a cheese."

We walk in to a heavy discussion between Sam and Blake.

"Nia, I need your help on this. I have been trying to reason with them about what they name this baby. I think Samuel for a boy and Samantha for a girl. They keep saying no. Obviously they are being unreasonable."

"You are alone on this one."

"You are all being unreasonable, I guess. I think those are great names," Sam says in defeat.

"Can we talk about something serious?" Sarah asks.

"Yes, please," Blake says.

"Sam, how is Maria?" Sarah asks in a mushy voice.

Sam looks at me and then back at Sarah before saying, "Fine, I guess. I haven't spoken to her in a while."

"Why not? I was excited you might have finally found a keeper."

"Anyone want coffee?" I ask as I walk into the kitchen. I don't want my face to give anything away. The last thing I want right now is anyone else knowing about me and Sam.

"I have found a keeper. It's just not Maria."

I can't breathe. He cannot be doing this right now.

"Forget Maria, then. Tell me about the new girl."

"She's amazing, but she is not looking to get into a relationship right now. I'm going to stick around and hope one day she is ready."

I have the sudden urge to run out there and punch him in the face. He is playing with fire here. Sarah is persistent. She is going to start questioning me and Hadley.

"That is crazy. You are a great guy and you don't

usually have trouble in the women department. If she doesn't want you then there are a million other fish in the sea." Sarah says.

"She's worth the wait. I'll just leave it at that. I'm going to go see what is taking Nia so long with the coffee."

I'm sitting in my chair sipping a glass of wine while Sam walks Sarah and Blake out. Chloe is perched at my feet waiting for Russell to jump down from my lap. I don't think she is going to get her way anytime soon. Russell is purring contently in my lap. I might end up the old cat woman. I got Chloe to give Russell someone to play with, but, with all of Chloe's energy, I am starting to think she needs another friend. That is not going to happen. I need to set up some of the other toys Tanner brought for them. Maybe one will keep her attention.

I hear Sam come back inside and the anger flares up in me again. He grabs his glass of wine and takes a seat in the chair next to me.

"I can tell you are mad at me. You have been giving me the cold shoulder all night," Sam says.

"Is this a joke to you? This thing that happened. Is it some kind of game?" I ask allowing the anger to fully penetrate my voice.

"No. I don't think this is a game at all. My friends asked me a question and I answered it. I understand you don't want our business out in the open and I am respectful of that. I can't tell them anymore than I did, but I think it should be okay for me to be as honest as I can with our friends. I know it is hard for you to see right now, but one day you will be ready to open your heart up to someone again and I told you, I plan on being there. Maybe I am not the one you will open it to, but I meant what I said to you that night and I'm not going to pretend like I didn't."

With that, he stood up and took his glass to the kitchen. When he passed back by me, he stopped.

"I leave early in the morning. If I don't see you before I go, I will see you when Sarah has the baby. I told them I would come as soon as I could get away after they called. Good night."

"Good night."

40 NIA NOW

"I heard you spoke to Sarah. How did that go?" Noie asks.

"It was good. She apologized and I tried to act like nothing happened."

"Why did you do that?"

"Because it doesn't matter. I want my friend back and I don't need any more awkward situations with friends. I have enough real things to deal with then to hold a grudge against Sarah."

"Good. You two have been such good friends for so long. You need that right now. I have hated how you were on the outs with each other."

"Can you tell me why we are here again?"

"You need a haircut. It will be good for you. Go crazy. Dye it a wild color or shave your head for all I care. I just want you to do something new. I am in store for a change as well."

"There is a change I have been thinking about and I don't need pink hair to do it."

"What's that?"

"I have been thinking about selling the house."

I said it out loud. Saying it makes it feel real and I begin to panic. I close my eyes and take a few deep breaths to calm myself. I haven't had to take a pill in over three weeks and I don't want to have to today.

"Are you sure about that? It's a big decision." Noie asks cautiously.

"I'm not sure. I have just been thinking about it. There is so much sadness there and I am afraid I will hold on to the sadness instead of the good memories if I stay there."

"Maybe we can start looking at places and see if there is anything you like. It might help you decide."

I think about that for a few minutes. Noie is right. That is probably the best way to get comfortable with the idea.

"Sounds good."

"What about your studio? Do you plan to quit teaching?"

"No, when we lived in the apartment, I rented out studio time. I can do that again. There is always the possibility I find something I can put a studio in."

"I will set up some appointments for us next week and see how you feel about it."

"Okay."

"Now, let's talk hair. What are you going to do? I am thinking about a brown color with a hint of eggplant in it. What do you think?"

"I like it for you, but I think I will stick with a trim."

I have a few private lessons set up for this week. Two are with girls I have never met, but one is with an old student. The old student gives me a little bit of anxiety. I don't want to answer any questions. Luckily she is very intense and dedicated to her dancing. She will probably be too focused to think about it.

I walk into the kitchen to make something for breakfast. I need to do something nice for Gertie. This week, I have realized how much she has been doing for me. She is only coming three days a week now and I hope to cut back to the regular two days a week soon. Noie tried to talk me out of it because she thinks I am taking on too much too soon.

I am startled by the sound of my cell phone ringing. I forgot to turn it off after I made the calls about the private lessons.

"Hello," I answer guardedly.

"Hey, it's Sam. I'm surprised the phone is on."

"Why did you call if you didn't think it was on?"

"I call every once and a while to check. I figured it would be on one day. What are you doing?"

"I am going over my schedule for the week. I set up a few private lessons." I say feeling a little strange being on the phone like this. It has been around ten months since I have carried on a normal phone conversation with a friend.

"That's awesome, Nia. I'm really happy to hear that. How are you feeling about it?"

"Are you my shrink now?"

"No, I know it is unfamiliar to you, but this is called friendship," he says sarcastically.

"I'm sorry. I go back and forth on how I feel, but I know it will be good for me and get easier as I do it. Noie wants me to start giving the girls private lessons. I think she is worried about me taking on too many clients and thinks bringing the girls for private lessons will help fill my schedule and be easy spots for me to cancel if I need to."

"Didn't the girls come to your classes in the past?"

"Yes, but never private lessons."

"You have to let Noie be Noie a little bit. She would probably go crazy if she felt like she wasn't doing anything to help you."

"Okay, okay. Since I am getting back into this friendship thing I should ask. How are you doing?"

"Well Nia, thank you for asking," he says with too much enthusiasm meant to be annoying. "I have been busy. We just got the contract for a new condominium building. I am the lead architect on the project. I am excited about it."

"Is this your first project as lead?"

"Yes, ma'am, it is. I have a good team working with me. It's not a skyscraper, but it will get me a lot of exposure and hopefully more opportunities," he says proudly.

"That's really cool. I am happy for you. I have some news you may like."

"What could be better than the news of private lessons?"

"I had coffee and went shopping with Sarah the other day. I also sent a letter to Hadley asking her to take some time off work and come stay with me around the time Sarah is due."

"That is good news. The three amigos back

together."

"I am still waiting for Hadley's letter to see if she can make it."

"You could give her a call. We are living in a century with phones and email. One of those options would get you a response a lot faster than snail mail."

"You are the first non-work person I have spoken to. Plus I like the letters I have received from Hadley over the last ten months. It feels like pen pals. Or one way pen pals until now."

"I guess it is good any way you do it. Where am I going to stay if Hadley is staying with you? I was going to come when the baby gets here too."

"My house is big enough for all three of us. You will stay here."

"Sounds good. I get to torment both of you at the same time. That's what I call a good time," he says jokingly.

"Great, I can't wait."

"I'm glad you answered the phone. I hope you keep it on. I have to get back to work. We'll talk again soon, right?"

"Right," I answer. "Goodbye."

"Bye."

After I hang up, I reflect on how normal talking to Sam on the phone felt. When I make my daily trips to the coffee shop, it is full of people staring at their phones. That is how I used to be as well. I kind of like my new phone free life, but it was nice to have a quick chat with Sam. Maybe I should start leaving it on.

I wanted to head out to the coffee shop, but I suddenly want to dance. No, need to dance. I need the freedom it brings me.

I head to the studio and turn the stereo on to one of my favorite songs to warm up to. Once I am done, I put the music on shuffle and let each song take me away.

I walk around the apartment with the leasing agent close behind me. The floors are hardwood. That will be good for Russell and Chloe. I hate the idea of them on carpet.

"Do you allow pets?"

"Cats and dogs under forty-five pounds."

I take a look out at the balcony. It is very small. I'm not even sure if my new chairs would fit out there, much less the fire pit. It has two bedrooms and a nice size kitchen. It just doesn't feel right.

"I'll take some information with me and let you know," I say.

"Not a problem. The first two bedroom we have available for move in is March. March will be here before you know it and these don't stay open very long. You will want to let me know soon if you are interested."

I get the information, thank her and leave. I don't think I could live there. It didn't feel like home. Although, looking for a place that is not my home to feel like home is probably a lot to ask.

The apartment is a short walk from the coffee shop and I decide to walk instead of getting in the car.

As I walk, I think about the next apartment to see on my list. It is the same complex Tanner lives in. I'm not sure if I even want to look at it. It just feels closer than I want to be to him. I like Tanner, but I don't know him very well. I feel drawn to him because of how much he makes me think of the happy times with Ian. It makes me like being around him at times and then other times, it feels wrong. It feels like I am reliving moments of my life that don't exist anymore.

I pull open the door to the coffee shop and my eyes fall on Tanner. He is sitting at a table in the back with his laptop out. I am starting to wonder if I summoned him with my thoughts. As if hearing me, he looks up and smiles when his eyes meet mine.

I give him a short wave and walk up to order my drink. I pay and grab my cup before walking over to Tanner's table.

"No autographs right now. I am trying to enjoy my coffee."

"One gig and you don't have time for the fans. Getting a little full of yourself Tanner."

"One gig, you say? I will have you know I booked a second gig."

"Ohh, when should the fan club be at the sandwich shop?"

"Actually, it is at a local bar. It will be with the band from the sandwich shop. I will be playing a few of my own songs as well," he says serious now.

"That's awesome."

"Yeah, it's pretty cool. They are going on tour and will be playing a few bars around town before they go. I asked if I could play with them to get some stage time. They are nice enough to let me. I also decided to put the finishing touches on my album and try to get it out there. I figured this was a good way to get a little local support."

"Looks like you will be living the dream soon."

"We'll see. I hope so," he says as he stares into my eyes. He holds me there for a few minutes before I break away.

"I should be going. I have some things planned today," I say.

"Would you like to celebrate with me when you are free?"

"Celebrate, how?"

"Dinner. My treat."

This feels like a really sneaky way to ask me on a date. I absolutely have to take his complex off my list.

"I am starting to work this week and I don't know what time I will have available."

"You have to eat. We can make it early or late."

"Okay, I'll let you know, but only if it is my treat."

Tanner reluctantly says, "Fine, but how will you let me know?"

"I discovered this device called a phone today. I might start using it a little."

He pulls out a pen and scrap of paper. After quickly jotting down his number, he hands it to me and says, "I'm looking forward to my free meal. Don't forget to call."

I take the number and quickly leave. Why do I feel so guilty about agreeing to dinner? Anytime I let Tanner in a little bit, I have guilt. I feel like I am betraying Sam, which is ridiculous because we are not together and I feel like I am betraying Ian and he isn't here to betray.

I shake the thoughts out of my head as I pull into my driveway. I notice the mailbox and realize I haven't been checking it on days Gertie doesn't come.

I check the box and pull out a few envelops and

notice the handwritten one in Jimmy's handwriting.   It's
been a while since he has written. I rush inside to open it.

Dear Nia,

    *You have been on my mind a lot lately.   Sorry I haven't
written. Laura said she saw you in town the other day with a man.
She had to do a double take because at first glance she thought you
were with Ian. She wanted to say hi, but didn't know if you would
be okay being disturbed. She was just happy to see you out and it
was good for me to hear.*
    *You have an open invitation to our house. Just because I can't
be in your house again doesn't mean we don't want to see you. I
would like to talk one day, when you are ready. Please let me know.*
    We miss you.

Jimmy

I close the letter and sit back in my chair. I miss
them too, but the thought of seeing Jimmy and Laura
stings. Ian and I always hung out with them together.
Laura and I became good friends, but we never did things
just the two of us. My friendship with them is so
connected to Ian and seeing them will make the space next
to me feel that much emptier. I know it is something I will
have to face one day.

From the letter, I know I will have to face questions
about Tanner as well. I can see he wanted me to know he
and Laura are okay with me seeing someone. I want to
correct that assumption, but it is nice he wanted me to
know they support me.

I need to write him back. He deserves it. More than

anyone, I feel bad I haven't been there for Jimmy at all. He and Ian were friends since childhood. I can imagine he has been made to feel worse by my silence. I hate the thought of that.

41 NIA NOW

"Girls, your mom is not going to be happy with me if I don't make you work hard in here. She is looking forward to the mini recital I promised her, so let's get serious for the rest of our time and then we will have ice cream before your mom comes to get you," I say to Audrie and Audra.

I shouldn't bribe them with ice cream, but I have missed so much time with them and I want to spoil them a little bit. I will hear it from Noie, for sure. I might need to find a few more girls to join them. They may focus better if there are other girls learning too. They never ran wild on me like this in the past when they were part of a large class.

"Alright, grand jete. Take turns across the floor."

I make them take turns until I am sure they are good and tired, then wrap up their lesson and head upstairs for ice cream.

I get the bowls made and two seconds later, Noie walks in the door.

"This looks like bribery. Am I correct?" She asks me sternly.

"It is as it seems," I say to her with a huge, don't hate me, smile.

She shakes her head at me and then looks at the girls and says, "Auntie Nia should not have bribed you. You get good things for choosing good behavior in the first place. I don't want to hear you are not listening or staying on task during your lessons."

"Yes, ma'am," sounds out in unison.

Looking back at me, Noie says, "Don't I get any ice cream?"

I laugh and make us both a bowl.

"So, when is Hadley getting in?"

"She flies in on Friday. I'm going to pick her up at the airport at three, I think."

"How long will she be here? Until the baby is born?"

"Yes and no. She is staying for nine days. We have to make sure the baby comes out in that time frame because she doesn't want to leave without seeing the baby and she can't stay any longer than that."

"I want to plan a night for me and Jett to come over. We need a night out of the house. I will see if Gertie is available to sit with the girls. And speaking of Jett, he has all of the papers drawn up for the practice. He wants to go over everything with you and talk about other options. He doesn't want you walking away. He was really hoping you would start doing some work for him one day."

"I can do work for him without owning a portion of the practice."

"Just hear him out."

"Okay."

I feel exhausted. It has been good to work again, although my body and mind have some catching up to do after laying dormant for so long. I can't wait until the weather warms up a little bit. I want to lay beneath the willow tree and stretch out with the cats. On cue with my thoughts, Russell jumps into my lap and presses his head to my neck and begins to purr.

I want to relax today away from everyone. Dr. Gillis is scheduled to come over. I don't feel up to having a session today. I pick up the phone and dial his office.

"Dr. Gillis' office, how can I help you?" A woman with a child-like voice answers.

"This is Nia Erickson, I have an appointment today with Dr. Gillis and I need to cancel."

"No problem, would you like to reschedule?"

"I will just wait until my appointment next week to see him."

"Okay, Ms. Erickson. Is there anything else?"

"No, thank you. Goodbye."

I hang up the phone and feel relief I have no plans today. Hadley will be here tomorrow and I need some alone time before she is dragging me around everywhere.

I reach down and pick up Chloe and head for my bed. Russell follows and curls up next to me while I lay on the bed petting Chloe.

After a while, I get up and go to the dresser drawer where I keep Ian's sweatshirt. I pull it out and walk back to the bed. I breathe in his scent and curl my body around the sweatshirt until I fall asleep.

Hadley is glued to her phone, which is odd for her. When she is with people, she is always one hundred percent in the moment. Something is up with her.

"I've never seen you on your phone this much and I don't think I have ever seen anyone smile at a phone as much. What's going on?"

"I didn't want to say anything because I am afraid I will jinx it, but," she pauses and takes a breath before saying, "I met someone. It's new and I actually like him. Not my normal – he's okay to pass the time with, but more of a – I can't wait to see and talk to him."

"That's huge. I didn't think a man existed who could hold your attention, much less make you gush like a love sick puppy," I tease.

"Hey, I am not love sick. I am like sick. That's different. Now can we move on to something else before we jinx it?" she pleads.

"I guess, but this is juicy. I kind of want to stay on topic."

"If you won't change the subject, then I will. How are we going to get this baby out of Sarah? I read online eating spicy food can help. I say we suggest Indian food for dinner tonight," she says raising her eyebrows.

"Stop it. I am not plotting to push her into labor with you," I say laughing.

"We might still need to eat Indian food because now that I said it, I am craving it."

"Sarah and Blake like the Little India Café on Richland Avenue. I think they would be happy to go there."

"I'll text Sarah and let her know to meet us there at six. You go get ready in something that doesn't double as pajamas," she says and points towards my bedroom.

"I am stuffed," Blake says. "This was a good call. We haven't eaten here in a while. I forgot how good it is."

"Sarah, are you okay?" I ask. "Did you eat too much?"

"The food isn't sitting very well on my stomach. I hope I didn't eat something bad. I am cramping a little bit," she says and starts fanning her face.

"I ate the Chicken Tikka Masala too and I feel fine," Hadley says.

"I think I need some air. Will one of you come outside with me?"

"You two go with her. I will take care of the check," I say.

Sarah rushes outside holding her stomach with Blake and Hadley on her heels. I call the waitress over so I can take care of the check.

As I am signing the credit card receipt, Hadley rushes in and yells, "It's time! Hurry!"

Everyone in the restaurant turns and stares as we run outside.

"Where are they at?" I ask looking at the empty sidewalk.

"Blake took her to the car. They are already on their way to the hospital."

We jog towards my car and I pull out my cell phone to dial Sam's number. He answers on the first ring.

"Hello."

"Sam, it's time. We are on our way to the hospital."

"I'll be on the next flight I can catch."

"See you soon."

"You don't think this is my fault, do you?" Hadley asks as we sit in the waiting room.

"No, I don't think your evil plan worked. I just think it was time."

"Are you sure about that? We have been in this hospital for almost eighteen hours and there is still no baby. I am feeling responsible."

"Calm down. The nurse said some babies take their time."

"I wish they would have found out what they were having. We could be in the gift shop buying everything pink or blue they sell to pass the time."

"Why don't you try to get some more sleep? I will wake you if anything happens."

With that, Hadley grabbed the blanket and pillow the nurses gave us and cuddles up in the chair. I wish I could sleep. My mind will not stop switching between anxiety, sadness and extreme happiness. I want the baby here and to know it's healthy and then I can relax. For now, I keep worrying and thinking about the baby I lost. He or she would be a couple of months old right now. Sarah and I would have been able to raise our babies together. Tears start to pool in my eyes again when someone comes crashing through the waiting room doors.

"Is the baby here yet?" Sam asks as he tries to catch his breath.

I start laughing and say, "Not yet. How did you get here so fast?"

"I said I would be on the next flight here. I stuffed a bag full of who knows what and went straight to the airport when you called. I lucked out and got a flight this morning. I could have checked before I left the apartment and slept at home, but I was too excited. Then I ran up the stairs when I got here because the elevator was taking forever."

"All you missed was almost eighteen hours of watching waiting room walls. Do you want me to see if she wants you to go back there? They will let you in. Hadley and I have been trying to give her space, but she would probably like to see you for a minute."

"No way. I will wait for the baby to be here before I go in. As a man, I am not sure I am prepared for anything going on in there."

"Such a man," Hadley grumbles as she opens her eyes. "Are you going to give me a hug or what?"

Sam walks over to her and wraps her up in his arms. Hadley giggles as she is pulled from the chair.

"Why do you look like you have been in a hospital waiting room all night too?" Hadley asks.

"Are you trying to say I don't look good, missy?"

Hadley winks and says, "Put me down."

Sam sets her down and ruffles her hair with his hand.

"Now be nice and go get us something to eat," Hadley says batting her eyelashes.

"Vending machine cuisine?"

"No, I want a shrimp caesar salad."

"Sorry, but that is not happening. I stayed the night in the airport so I could get here to see this baby. I got lucky enough to get here before it was born so I will not miss it for a salad when there is perfectly good chips and candy bars in the vending machine."

Hadley's face scrunches up at the thought of vending machine food. It's fun to watch them bicker with each other. They really do seem like they could be brother and sister. Even their blonde hair, blue eyes and stunning looks make them look like family. I hope we don't get kicked out of the hospital before the baby is born because now they are trying to put each other in a head lock.

I hear someone clearing their throat and turn to the door where Blake is looking at Hadley and Sam with the happiest confused look on his face.

I jump up from my chair and say, "Knock it off kids."

They stand up looking embarrassed when they see Blake.

"We have a baby boy! Are you all ready to meet him?"

My eyes tear up and I nod my head yes along with Sam and Hadley.

"No fighting in the room," Blake says eyeing Hadley and Sam seriously.

We follow Blake back to the room and lay our eyes on a glowing Sarah holding her snugly wrapped baby.

He is so beautiful. He has Blake's curly hair, but it is a few shades lighter than his brown. His skin is softly tanned. A perfect mix of Blake's dark skin and Sarah's olive complexion. I can't believe our group has a beautiful baby.

"What is this little guy's name?" Hadley asks.

Blake and Sarah look at me and say, "Lucas."

"I love it," I say with tears coming back to my eyes.

"Are you sure?" Sarah asks me.

"I think it's perfect."

Sam slides his fingers through mine and gives my hand a squeeze. When Ian and I started trying for a baby, we told all of them we would name the baby Lucas if we had a boy. I know this is Sarah and Blake's way of honoring us and the baby we lost who might have been a boy. If I ever found myself in the future with kids, I know I could never use that name because it was the name Ian and I picked together. I am so happy the name gets to go to this precious boy.

"Do you want to hold him?" Sarah asks me.

I nod my head yes and walk closer to her. She places Lucas in my arms and I am overcome with the love I feel for him.

"We have something to ask you and Sam," Blake says.

Sam and I look up at him.

"We want the two of you to be his God-parents. Would you do that for us?"

"Absolutely," Sam says.

"I would be honored."

This weekend has been amazing. After we held and loved on Lucas for a while, Sam, Hadley and I left to go shopping. We all went a little overboard. That little boy will not have to wear the same outfit twice for the first year of his life. We even went to Pottery Barn and ordered everything we could think of with Lucas' name embroidered on it. After stopping in at the Mommy and Me store and almost buying ten sets of matching pajamas for Lucas and Sarah we realized we needed to stop.

I am lying in bed, I should be falling asleep after not sleeping last night, but I can't. My thoughts are on the baby I lost. Tears fill my eyes and run down my face. I reach for my cigarettes and light one, trying to calm myself, but it doesn't work. The tears turn into sobs.

I hear a tap on my bedroom door and then it opens.

"Can I come in?" Sam asks.

I just nod my head yes because I can't get words out through the tears.

"I'm sorry to bother you, but I heard you crying from the living room and wanted to make sure you are okay."

He sits down on the edge of the bed and brushes my hair from my face.

"Can I get you anything?"

I just shake my head no and the sobs grow louder. He takes my cigarette and sets it in the ashtray and then scoots closer to me. He wraps me in a hug and I lean into his shoulder.

The exhaustion from the day is finally taking its toll on me. I lay back and Sam kisses me on the forehead before standing up to leave. I grab his hand and silently ask him to stay.

He pulls the cover back and slides in beside me. I turn my back to him and let him slide his arms around me. He cradles me in his arms until we fall asleep.

42 NIA NOW

My chain smoking is back in full force as I prepare for what I have to do today. Gertie is here this morning and keeps checking on me. I hope she hasn't called Noie. I know how it must look to her with me sitting in my favorite chair, chain smoking and not wanting to make conversation with her.

I keep picking up my phone and putting it back down. Finally I get myself to open up my contacts and scroll to Jimmy's number. All I can think about is how the last time I dialed his number, my life felt perfect.

After staring at his number for a few minutes, I hit send.

"Nia," Jimmy says sounding concerned, "Is everything ok?"

"Yes. How are you?" I ask trying to keep my voice steady.

"Hanging in there. I'm better now that you called," he says sincerely.

"Do you think we could meet?"

"Sure. Today?"

"If that works for you."

"No problem. Where do you want to meet?"

"Sunergos for coffee in an hour."

"I'll be there."

"Thank you. See you soon."

Jimmy is already at a table with two cups of coffee when I walk in. He lifts one cup towards me to let me know it is mine.

"I'm guessing you still take your coffee the same way."

"Yes, thank you."

"What do you want to talk about?" He asks tentatively.

"First, thank you for writing me over the past year. I'm sorry for being unresponsive until the last letter."

"Nia, don't apologize. I understand."

"You wrote and said you needed to talk to me about Ian and I am ready to listen. Tell me everything."

"There is nothing I am going to say that will make things better. Ian just wanted me to help you understand what he was going through and I wanted to honor that request. The worst part of what Ian did was trying to hide his issues from you. I have known since high school there was a possibility Ian would take his own life. I always hoped it would never happen, but I also prepared for the possibility. He didn't give you the chance to prepare. I am not saying that would have made any of this easier for you,

I just think you may have been better equipped to deal with the aftermath."

I think about what Jimmy is saying to me. For the first time I really consider what knowing would have been like. Would I have walked around every day feeling like I was holding a live grenade? Would our whole relationship have been different? Would we have had eleven amazing years together?

"Ian was always so intense. I used to think he felt pain deeper and love with a deeper passion than anyone else I knew. It was an attractive quality of his, but it caused him a lot of internal turmoil. Ian planned to kill himself after high school. I found a letter in his room for me. He was going to drive to the Golden Gate Bridge after graduation. I wouldn't let him go without me. I glued myself to him and eventually he stopped trying to get away from me."

Jimmy pauses and I can tell he is trying to hold back the emotions this is bringing up. I let the tears fall down my face as I listen to him and think about the time Ian and I were on the Golden Gate Bridge.

"Do you mind if we sit outside? I could use a cigarette," Jimmy asks.

"Let's go," I say getting up from the table and heading outside to find a table.

After we settle into the seats, we light a cigarette and take a few minutes to just watch the world around us. It gives Jimmy time to collect himself.

"Ian would never want you to think this had anything to do with you. You were the best thing that ever happened to him and boy did he love you. He felt so lucky to have found you, although, underserving. That's why he hid the side of him that was in so much pain. He was afraid to lose you and he didn't want you to deal with the worry he saw me deal with. He just wanted to be perfect for you. I told him time and again you loved him and that wouldn't change if he let you in on what was going on. It's sad he felt so determined to make you happy while he was alive, but couldn't comprehend the level of sadness it would cause you when he died. He didn't see himself as worthy. I think he felt like we would all be better without him. He had to convince himself of that to leave us."

Ian was so smart and talented. It is hard to think he saw himself as anything less.

"I apologize for the part I played in hiding things from you. I didn't want to, but he was my best friend. I know you suspected something at times because of your questions. The time you tried to go on the fishing trip to the cabin with us, Ian was actually going inpatient at the hospital his psychiatrist worked out of. She was changing up some of his meds and wanted to keep him under observation."

"I thought he was cheating on me, but couldn't bring myself to confront him about it," I say flatly.

"What?" Jimmy blurts out. "Ian would never have done that to you. Why would you think he would ever cheat on you?"

"Things like the fishing trip that seemed bogus. I found a note reminding him of lunch with someone named Becca. Then all the times he would disappear and not answer calls. I thought he might be with someone else."

"Nia, I am not saying this to preserve his memory. He never cheated on you. Not even almost. He loved you with everything he had in himself to give. Becca was a therapist he was seeing for a while. I think her last name was Montgomery. I can't remember for sure, but I could find out. When he would disappear, it was because he was cracking under the pressure he was putting on himself to seem perfect. He had to be alone and decompress."

I would have thought confirming Ian wasn't cheating would have been a relief, but instead, it makes me want to scream at him. I could have been a support for him. He didn't have to go through all of that without me.

"I think we need to stop for now. I am feeling a little angry," I say.

"I get that. I have had to work really hard to deal with the anger I have towards him. It's hard to love and hate someone at the same time," Jimmy says looking down as if ashamed of his feelings.

"Yeah, the anger is hard because it doesn't feel right to be angry with someone you love and will never see again. I don't know how to get out all of the mixed feelings I have. On one hand, I am so devastatingly heart broken and filled with an overwhelming love for him. Then, I also hate him for leaving me. I hate him for leaving me notes to find him. I know he felt like leaving me with a special thing he always did for me, but now I cannot look back on those other times without thinking about being led to his body. I also hate him sometimes for the baby. I blame him for losing the baby, but that always leads to me hating myself because what if I woke him up that night and told him. Maybe he wouldn't have done it.

I have to live with that choice now," I say as tears begin to choke my voice.

"I know you can't turn off those feelings with a switch, but you have to find a way to live in happiness. There is no happiness in those thoughts. The other option is to live in the pain like Ian did. It's not a place anyone can live in forever. All Ian ever wanted is for you to be happy. If you see a chance at happiness, take it. Don't let anything hold you back," Jimmy says as he stands and reaches his arms out to me for a hug.

I stand up and hug him. He is a wonderful person and was always such a good friend to Ian. I hope I don't lose touch with him.

"Remember, the invitation to stop by is always open. You can bring the friend Laura saw with you, if you want."

"Jimmy, he is a family friend of Jett's who I met at Thanksgiving. He is just a friend, but he reminds me a lot of Ian and that is nice to be around sometimes. He is still only a friend."

"No explanation needed. I just want you to know you don't have to hide away if you do find someone special. Laura and I hope you are able to open your heart to someone again."

"Thank you, Jimmy. Please tell Laura I said hello."

"Will do and if you want to come, we have something planned for Ian's birthday."

Saying Ian's birthday is so much easier to handle than anniversary of his death.

"We are going to his grave to say a few words about him and then releasing balloons. You are welcome to join us. We are planning to go at ten in the morning."

"That's nice. I'll see."

I have seen twenty apartments over the past two days. Noie did the planning or I would have never gone to that many. How can I not like any of them? I am starting to think I just don't want to move out of my house.

"I do have something else I can show you," the real-estate agent says. "It is not a rental apartment. It is in a building, but everyone owns their unit. It will need some work. Are you interested?"

"What do you mean by needs some work? Is there fire damage or has it not been updated?" Noie asks.

"It is a clean slate. It is an old industrial warehouse building and the owner decided to section it off and sell the units. Each unit has electrical and cable outlets ran. There is also one small bathroom. Everything else is open. It is about two thousand square feet. Very large space. There is also garage parking with storage on the first floor under each unit. It is a two story building he partitioned off into four units. Living space on the second floor and the storage area on the first floor could be converted into livable space. I have seen what the other people have done to their units and they are very nice. It is just a lot of work and I didn't know if you were looking for a project."

Clean slate. It sounds like the fresh start I am looking for.

"What about a kitchen?" Noie asks.

"No kitchen, although plumbing is roughed in where the owner thought a kitchen would work and there is roughed in plumbing for a second bathroom."

Noie is shaking her head no, but, I say, "I want to see it."

I know I am going to take it the moment I walk in the door. The floors are stained concrete and look perfect with the exposed brick on one of the walls. The windows are rows of small panes of glass that look restored. I walk over to one of the windows overlooking a green space next to the building. A beautiful old oak tree shades most of the area. It is not my willow tree, but I can still picture how it will look when the leaves change colors in the fall and know it will be breath taking.

The realtor comes to see what I am looking at and says, "The green space is for use by this building only. It is fenced for people who have dogs. They are able to take them off the leash down there."

"If this is privately owned units, who maintains the area?" Noie asks.

"The man who originally owned the building, lives in one of the units. He has a dog and chose to make the green space nice for other people with dogs or for any of the people who live here to have outdoor space for parties or kids. There is a maintenance fee that comes with living here to help with the cost of the upkeep."

"Nia, I will admit this place is nicer than I thought it would be, but this is too much work. Don't you want something move in ready?" Noie asks.

I hear what Noie says, but I can't stop my day dreaming long enough to respond. I am already moving in my mind. Plus, I could build a studio up here or in the storage space on the first floor, if it is big enough.

"Can I see the storage space?" I ask.

We follow the realtor through a door near where the kitchen would go and it leads us down a set of stairs to a garage.

"I didn't realize we would be able to access the garage from the second floor. That's nice," I say. "And this garage could fit three cars easily."

"The majority of the space under the unit would be yours. The only other thing down here is a maintenance room which takes a little space from each unit. Through this door is the storage space. Very large area."

I walk through the door and say, "I'll take it. I want to put an offer in now."

"Nia, we should talk about this. Don't be rash."

"There is nothing to talk about. This is perfect for me. I could even build out a studio down here eventually. I don't want to risk someone else putting in an offer."

"Okay, here is the information with the asking price and the cost of maintenance fees. Look at it as you go home and give me a call to go over the offer you want to put in. I am heading to my office to wait for your call."

I haven't been able to sleep all night and I can't help but dwell on the thought of how this day could be so different if I wouldn't have been able to sleep this time last year. Today is Ian's birthday and I have decided to meet Jimmy and Laura at the grave. I want to get there early to talk to Ian before they get there.

I finish my cup of coffee and stub out my cigarette before rushing out the door. I don't have to rush, but I feel like I need the extra momentum to push myself out the door today.

This is the first time I will see his headstone. I haven't been here since the funeral and I don't remember much of that. I will never forget the location he is buried because I choose a spot under the largest willow tree in the cemetery. It is towards the very back and I was surprised it was available. I left the monument up to Jimmy and Noie. I've never asked them about it. I hope it honors him the way I would have wanted.

I park my car in the closest paved area to Ian's grave. I can see from the car they chose shiny black granite for his stone. As I approach, I see the back of the stone first. "ERICKSON" is engraved across the back in large block letters. I walk to the front of the stone to see "Ian Patrick Erickson, Devoted Husband and Friend in Life, Eternal Peace in Death."

I kneel down next to the fresh flowers laying in front of the stone to look at the picture that is set into the granite. It is a picture of me, Ian and Jimmy from college. It was always one of my favorites of Ian. Noie must have chosen this picture for me.

I notice a card on the flowers and open it to see who they are from. The card reads, "She misses you, we all do. Happy birthday little brother. Love, Noie."

She must have dropped them off before work. I'm so lucky to be her sister.

"Happy birthday Ian. You have been gone for a year and I have missed you every moment of it. There are still days I wake up and forget you are gone. For a few seconds, I feel whole again. Then it all rushes back and my heart breaks. Most of the past year, I have spent my days trying to piece my heart back together. I couldn't understand why you would leave me. It was like everything we had built together meant nothing. Every moment of happiness was a lie because you were lying to me. You were struggling and didn't trust me enough to stand by you through it. I began to hate you. Do you know how it feels to hate the person you loved most in the world?"

I need to tell him what I came here to say, but this is not how it was supposed to be.

"I came today to tell you what I wanted to tell you a year ago."

I reach into my purse and pull out the pregnancy test I took last year and hold it out towards his headstone.

"I was pregnant. We were finally going to be parents. I wanted it to be a birthday surprise for you. I took this after you went to bed that night. I lost the baby soon after Jimmy and I found you. I hope you already knew this because I imagine you are with our baby and you two are happy and at peace."

The tears begin to fall thinking of them together. Part of me wants to join them. There were times over the past year I thought I would.

"As sick as it sounds, I spent a lot of my times wishing you would have taken me with you. I didn't want to live without you. But, finally, I noticed the world again. I saw all the people who love me joining together to get me through the wreck you left me in. I realized I can't let them feel the way I have felt. I had to start living for them and somewhere in that, I started living for me. Everyday something happens I want to share with you, but you took that from me. That was your choice. I thought it meant you didn't love me, but my heart knows that isn't true. The same way I thought moving on with my life would mean I didn't love you, but that isn't true either. Our love is forever frozen in the past and it will always live in my heart. I love you, Ian and I will live for you and our baby."

I lay down on the grass over his grave and close my eyes to pretend I am laying with him one last time.

"Nia. Nia, wake up," I hear Jimmy say.

I open my eyes, he and Laura are standing over me with three balloons. Jimmy reaches his hand down to help me up.

"How long have you been out here?" Laura asks as she pulls me in for a hug.

"Not long. I think I just fell asleep."

"Do you want to get started?" Jimmy asks.

"Yes, I'm ready."

We stand in a circle over Ian's grave. Jimmy hands me the extra balloon. We wait for a minute to think about Ian.

"I'll start," Laura says. "Ian you welcomed me in with open arms when I started dating Jimmy and I will be forever thankful for that. I will also always try to live by the advice you gave me at our wedding. I miss you."

"Happy birthday brother. Life isn't the same without you. Sometimes I drive to the parking lot we used to hang out at in high school. I feel closest to you there. You left a hole in my life I may never be able to fill, but, for nineteen years, I had the best friend anyone could ever ask for. I hope you found your peace."

"Ian, you had a beautiful heart and you spent every day showing that to me. That is the part of you I will carry with me. I love you."

We all look to the sky and let the balloons go. We watch until they disappear and I wish they would take all my pain with them and only leave the happy parts of the eleven years I spent with Ian.

"Hello," I say as I answer the phone.

"Hey, how are you doing today?" Sam asks.

"I'm okay."

"Are you just staying home today?"

"I met Jimmy and Laura at Ian's grave this morning. It was nice to see them. I don't feel like doing anything else. I just plan on hanging out with Russell and Chloe."

"Do you want me to let you go so you can relax?"

"Yes, I might take a nap if I can get Russell to lay down with me."

"Call me if you need anything and if you need someone with you, make sure you call Noie or Sarah."

"I will," I pause for a minute and then say, "I miss you."

"I miss you too, love."

We hang up and I coerce Russell into the bedroom with me. Chloe follows us and swats at Russell tail as he lays down next to me. After a few minutes of watching her pounce around the bed, I close my eyes, but I don't fall asleep. Instead I think about how far I have come over the last year. A year ago, I never thought I would get out of this bed again. Now I see possibilities of what the future can hold.

43 NIA NOW

I have completely over scheduled myself today and here I am drinking my coffee and playing with Russell and Chloe. This may be why I am always late.

I am meeting with the realtor Noie found for me. I have to start the process of selling the house because I am closing on the loft this week. Gertie came yesterday and cleaned the house in case the realtor needs to take pictures. Then I have two lessons scheduled back to back plus I promised Tanner I would come to his show tonight.

"Nia," Noie's voice rings out as she walks through the door. Perfect. Lecture time.

"I knew you would be sitting there when you have a thousand things to do," she says shaking her head at me. She grabs Russell off my lap and sets him on the floor. "You didn't even want me to come over. Did you sleep in those clothes? Please get dressed."

"I will not be in the pictures. Why do I need to get dressed? I have two lessons today. I will put dance clothes on after she leaves," I say a little whiny.

"No, you put clothes on when strangers are coming to your house. Up. Now," she says as she pulls me out of the chair. "And please make sure all of the ashtrays are put away. You might want to stop smoking in the house if you want to actually sell it."

I reluctantly walk to my room to get dressed. I pull open the dresser drawer to grab out a pair of jeans. In the drawer is the picture of me and Ian that usually sits on the dresser. I had to put all the personal pictures away for the realtor. I look at our smiling faces and think of the day we moved into this house. I thought I would live here for the rest of my life. I pictured our children and grandchildren playing under the willow tree in the backyard. It feels unreal to be selling this place.

I take a deep breath and close the drawer. I have to get ready for this day. No looking back today or I will never get through this.

Why did I agree to go tonight? It has been a long day and I am exhausted. I tried to pull Sarah away from Lucas for a few hours to come with me, but Blake has a work dinner.

I look in the mirror one last time and then head out.

I spot Tanner through the crowd as soon as I walk in, but it takes me almost five minutes to fight through the people to get to him.

"Hey, Nia," Tanner yells over the music. "I'm glad you made it."

He reaches toward me and kisses me on the cheek. I freeze and then try to act normal, but my insides are in knots. He has never done that before and I feel a rock of guilt in my stomach. I think of Ian and then Sam's face pops into my mind. I shake those thoughts away and try to pay attention to what Tanner is saying.

"Let me introduce you to the guys. This is Ray, Michael, Rand and Rion. We are about to go on. Michael and Rand's girlfriends are at the booth over there," he says pointing across the room. "Guys, I will be right back. Let me go introduce Nia to the girls."

Tanner grabs my hand and pulls me to a booth with two young women. I suddenly feel old. They look barely old enough to be in here. I pull my hand from Tanner's to wave a hello at them as he introduces us.

"Nia, this is Payton and Alex. Get ready to rock. I'll see you in a little bit," he says with a wink.

I take a seat and we nervously make small talk as we wait for them to take the stage. The girls are nice, but I feel uncomfortable sitting at the table of "band girlfriends."

The crowd begins to cheer as the music starts playing. It sounds like a song I have already heard them play at the sandwich shop, but there is a lot more energy this time. The band is feeding off the crowd and it is a much better vibe for them. After two more upbeat songs, Ray tells the, now adoring, fans they are taking five while Tanner does a solo song. I feel excited about hearing his music. The song he played for me before is a lot closer to the style of music I enjoy.

He begins strumming his guitar and the sound feels like silk. I close my eyes and until he starts singing, I almost feel like I am back in college listening to Ian.

I listen to the first few lines of lyrics and then open my eyes confused. After a few more lines I realize the song is about me. I feel the panic rising in my chest and it gets hard to breathe. I reach my hand in my purse to get a pill. I can't find them and remember I stopped carrying those weeks ago because it has been so long since I needed one. My legs feel like they won't hold me, but I force myself up and run for the door. When I feel the fresh air on my face it gets easier to breathe.

My phone starts ringing and I slide it out of my pocket figuring it is Tanner, but Sam's number is flashing on the screen. It calms me enough to pick up my pace towards my car and answer the phone.

"Hello," I say with my voice full of tears.

"Nia, are you okay? What's going on?" Sam asks sounding alarmed.

"Nothing. I'm just… I'm just. Everything is inside out."

"Okay. Are you home?" His voice has taken on a soothing tone.

"No."

"Are you somewhere safe?"

"I just got in my car. I need my pills, but I left them at home."

"Alright, just stay calm and talk to me while you drive."

"You talk. I just want to listen to you talk."

"I talked to Blake yesterday. Little Lucas is not giving them a moments rest. Sarah is supposed to go back to work in a month, but he thinks only someone who loves Lucas like a parent does can handle him right now. They are trying to see if they can afford for Sarah to take a few more months off."

It feels good listening to his voice. It makes me think of all the times I would call and he would just talk to me without trying to make me talk.

"I am thinking about flying in as many weekends as I can and give them a little help. Blake's mom has offered, but the last thing Sarah can handle right now is having his mom living with them. I figure I could stay nights over there so they can get some sleep and maybe you could keep me company. We could live up to our God-parent roles," he pauses and then says, "and we could see more of each other."

I like the idea of seeing him more. I wish he was here now. I wish he could hold me. The last time he was here, I felt so secure in his arms.

"I would like that," I say.

"How would you feel about me flying out this weekend? You sound like you could use a friend."

"I could."

"Then your wish is my command," he says in a princely voice. It makes me laugh and I realize the panic is subsiding.

"I am home now."

"Do you want to talk a little longer?"

"I think I need to get in the bath and relax."

"Then I will call you tomorrow with my flight details and I will let Blake and Sarah know we will be at their disposal one of the nights."

We get off the phone and I take my normal spot to smoke and relax before I get in the bath. I am about to head to the bathroom when there is a knock at the door. I take a deep breath before answering it.

"What happened?" Tanner asks.

"I had to get out of there."

"Can I come in?"

I step aside and let him in.

"I thought you were playing for an hour."

"I was supposed to, but you ran out. I had to make sure you were okay. Can you tell me what happened?"

I walk to the kitchen and put on a pot of coffee. I need a few minutes to figure out what to say to him. I peak around the corner and see he has taken a seat next to my chair.

"Do you want a cup?"

"No," he says flatly.

When the pot is finished brewing, I pour myself a cup and head back to my chair. Chloe has found her way into Tanner's lap. He is petting her tummy as she licks his fingers. I smile at the sight.

"Are you ready to tell me what is going on?"

"Tanner you have been nicer to me than I deserve since the moment we met. I am grateful for that, but I can't do this."

"Do what?"

"I like hanging out with you and listening to you play. You are really talented, but, when I am with you, I am always reminded of Ian. I picture you as what Ian would have been if he could have had the peace in his soul you have and followed his dreams instead of responsibility."

"What…" he begins to ask, but I cut him off with my hand.

"Let me finish. Was that song about me?"

Tanner nods his head yes.

"I can't be with you in the way you want and you don't want me to be because I will always be reminded of Ian when I am with you. I can't let you be the fill in for what I lost. So that is what I can't do."

He stands up and walks out the door without saying a word.

The sun is flooding through the curtains in my bedroom. I want to shut them, but I can't will myself out of bed. Too much has been happening lately and I think it is catching up to me. I am starting to feel sick. I hope Gertie is coming today, but I can't remember.

My head is pounding. I reach for the bottle of ibuprofen next to the bed. There are only two left. That is not enough to knock a headache this bad out.

Suddenly the phone rings and I silence it. I see Noie's number, but I can't talk right now. I roll over and cover my head with the sheet and fall back asleep.

"Nia! What is going on?" Noie is yelling from next to my bed.

"Shh, I have a headache," I say in frustration.

"Is that why you cancelled your appointment with Dr. Gillis again?" She asks in a softer tone now.

"I wasn't feeling well last night. I didn't know if I was getting sick so I left a message cancelling. Did they call you and tattle on me?" I ask annoyed. I hate when people act like she is my keeper. "Please tell me you brought coffee."

"I did," she says rolling her eyes. "I'll bring it in here. I was going to make you get out of bed to get it, but, since you are sick and not just hiding away, I will give you bedside service," she says and walks to the living room to get my coffee.

Maybe it's not so bad having her as a keeper.

I reach for my coffee and ask, "Can you close the curtains? And get me some ibuprofen from the kitchen?"

"You have a bottle right there," she says pointing to the night stand.

"It's empty."

My phone starts ringing and I think about chunking it at the window, but I see Sam's name and answer it.

"Hey," I say as pitiful as I can. I want the sympathy.

"Wow, you sound like crap. You okay?"

"No, I'm not feeling well and I have a huge headache."

"That's too bad."

"Now someone is knocking at the door. I was already woken up with Noie screaming in my ear. I don't need any more people coming in being loud."

"Are you going to answer the door?"

"Noie is still here. I just heard her open the door."

"Nia," Noie's voice sings out. "Look who just showed up on your door step."

Sam's smiling face is standing behind her with his phone still to his ear.

"Sam, I have to go. An intruder just showed up at my house," I say and hang the phone up. "What are you doing here? I thought you were coming tomorrow."

"Well good thing I got an earlier flight because you look like you need someone to take care of you."

"Noie is more than happy to do it. Right, Noie?"

"Nope. Sam can take over. You are a big baby when you are sick," she says and hands me the new bottle of ibuprofen. "I'm going to go. I needed to be at the school this morning. Sam, do not let her run you ragged. I don't think she is as sick as she is putting on."

Noie says goodbye and leaves. Sam sits on the bed next to me and brushes my bangs from my eyes.

"You need to get these cut," he says.

"I like them like this."

"So is this a movie and take out kind of day?"

"What if I am getting sick? You can't be around me if you are going to watch the baby Saturday night."

"I have two nights between now and then. If you are sick, I will have to tell Sarah and Blake they don't get sleep for a few more weeks and let them know they have you to thank for that."

"Thanks. Sarah might stop talking to me again."

"I just remembered something. Didn't you have a meeting with a contractor today?"

"I forgot. I cancelled my appointment with Dr. Gillis, but I can't cancel with the contractor. I have to get construction started on the loft. The realtor is listing my house in two weeks. If it sells right away, I might have to move within a month or two."

"Do you think he can come here?"

"No, it has to be at the loft."

"Consider me your personal chauffeur. Drink your coffee and let the medicine kick in. What time do you need to be there?"

I look over at the clock and am shocked it is almost noon already.

"I have to be there at two," I say with a whine.

"You have time. I have some work calls to make. Yell if you need anything and get ready as soon as you start feeling better. I want to get some food in you before we go. I'll make something."

Almost two hours later we are pulling up at the loft. I hit the garage door opener and Sam pulls in. Every time I come here, I am shocked by how perfect it was to find this place.

"This is an awesome building. I can't wait to see the inside."

"There isn't much to see yet. Hopefully that will change soon after today."

My head still has a dull throb and my body feels weak. I hope this doesn't take long.

We head up the stairs into the main space. I have been envisioning how it will look so much I feel like I can see how it will look already.

"Wow, you did say blank slate, but I wasn't expecting this."

I walk up to the window overlooking the tree and stare out. I feel Sam when he walks up behind me. I find myself leaning back on him for support. He wraps his arms around me to help keep me steady.

"I bet this tree was what sealed the deal."

I can feel his breath against my ear and my heart speeds up. There is a knock at the door and Sam releases me. I walk over to open it and feel the heat flushing my face.

"I can't believe it will only take four weeks to do all the work you want done there," Sam says.

We are sitting on the back patio letting Russell have some outside time. The weather is beautiful today. Luckily it hasn't gotten too hot yet this year.

"There is no demo. That takes a lot of time off."

"When are you going to turn the downstairs into a studio?"

"I want to see how having the studio space works upstairs first. Depending on if I hate it or not will determine when I do it."

"Do you want me to come back in town when you move to help?"

"You don't have to do that. Gertie and Noie will be around to help pack and I will have movers for the big stuff."

"Let me know if you change your mind. I would like to help," he says and flexes his bicep muscles.

"I bet you offered just so you could show off your muscles," I say laughing.

"I texted Blake earlier and they don't want either of us over there if there is even a slight chance you are sick. So it looks like you won't have to share me with Lucas this weekend after all," he says jokingly.

"I think I can handle that. Didn't you say something about a movie and take out?"

"Yes, I did. Maybe even some cuddling, if you are lucky."

I lock eyes with him and don't look away. His expression changes from playful to soft and all I can think about in this moment is how much I want his arms around me. I need the comfort they bring and I want to feel the spark inside of me they cause. A spark, I realize, I have become more welcoming of than afraid.

44 NIA NOW

I officially have four offers on the house and I have to accept one soon. I know I am moving and it will be good to have this new start. Realizing I will never walk into this house again after a couple of weeks, is hard to swallow.

The construction is a week from completion and the loft looks amazing. I plan on moving everything I can into the storage space as soon as possible to be ready for move in, but I just look around at everything to do and it makes me not want to do anything. Gertie has already packed the non-essentials from the kitchen, linen closets and even packed all décor items I am taking. It is looking a lot less like a home here.

"Nia," Gertie says walking up behind me. "I know it is overwhelming to move so I am sorry to be the messenger, but Noie wanted me to walk you through what you need to do."

"It's fine Gertie. I know how Noie is and actually some direction would be helpful right now. I don't know where to start."

"Okay, she wants you to go through your clothes and pack what you won't need and sort out what can be donated or trashed. Then she wants you to sort everything in the office. Anything that needs to go to Jett should be boxed and set aside. Jett will send someone to pick it up. She said everything else in there can be packed up because you won't need anything except your laptop from there until you move. She also wants you to pack up the studio, but I took care of that. The stereo is still out with some hand towels. I didn't think you needed anything else between now and then. Do you?"

"No, I have lessons over the next couple of weeks, but that is all I should need."

"The kitchen is packed except coffee, sugar, soup and a few dishes. It's all you really eat here, but, I can grab some other easy things from the store, if you want. Last thing Noie wants is all the packed boxes going to the loft to be placed in the garage and for you to put stickers on any furniture you want to donate instead of take with you. There are red dot stickers on the kitchen counter. I am leaving, do you want me to write any of her instructions down?"

"No, I can remember, but, I will warn you, I will not have all that done today. I still have two weeks until I have to move in and I will have access to the house for probably four more weeks."

"Actually three weeks. Noie has scheduled people to clean all of the grout and touch up paint three weeks from now," she says like she was afraid to tell me.

"I wish she would have ran that past me," I say with a shake of my head.

I hear Gertie leave and all I want to do is crawl back into bed. Sorting and packing is not a fun way to spend the day. I might as well have one more cup of coffee. I get up to head for the kitchen and start screaming quickly followed by cursing.

"Good thing I didn't bring Lucas. He doesn't need to know his Auntie Nia talks like a sailor," Sarah says.

I hold my chest trying to recover from the shock of Sarah, Blake, Hadley and Sam all standing in my living room.

"I hope everyone got a good laugh. I guess you had Gertie in on this surprise attack."

They are all smiling and saying yes.

"What are you all doing here?" I ask as I walk over to give each of them a hug. When I get to Sam, the hug lingers longer than it should.

"What do you think we are doing here, girlie?" Hadley asks. "We are helping you pack. Did you think we would leave you to do this alone?"

My eyes start to tear up and I say, "Thank you."

Sam walks to me and wipes away the tear beginning to fall and softly says, "No tears right now. Think good thoughts."

I take a deep breath and nod my head in agreement.

"It looks like we are supposed to start with clothes," Sarah says holding a piece of paper.

"Noie must have gotten to you."

"Of course she did."

"Boys, grab boxes, tape and markers out of the garage. Now we are off to throw all of your clothes away," Hadley says.

"No ganging up on me. I like my clothes."

We spent most of the day working on the house and manage to complete all of Noie's list. There was one thing missing from the list that needed to be done. I had to go through Ian's stuff and decide what to do with it. No one spoke of it, but we all avoided anything of his.

Hadley walks up as I am staring at one of his guitars.

"Not today. We will be back tomorrow," she says.

"What do you mean tomorrow? Aren't you staying here?"

She glances in Sam's direction and then back at me and says, "Nope, I want some time with the cutest boy in the world."

"Hadley, I don't know if I'm the cutest, but if you say so," Blake says in jest.

"You know I mean that baby of yours!" Hadley says and swats at him.

I feel a little sad. Hadley and Sam always stay with me. I want to ask Sam if he is going too, but not in front of everyone.

"We need to go. I told Noie we would pick Lucas up by five," Sarah says and gives me a hug. "See you in the morning."

We all start walking towards the door. Blake and Hadley hug me goodbye too, but Sam hangs back and says bye to them, as well.

"I guess I should have asked, but you are okay with me staying here, right?" Sam asks hesitantly.

"Yes," I say with a roll of my eyes.

He flops down on the sofa and motions for me to sit next to him. I sit down and he guides me to lean back on him with his arm around me.

"Long day. How are you feeling?" He asks.

"I'm okay. It helped with you all being here. I guess I needed the help after all."

He starts running his fingers up and down my arm and I feel heat from his touch.

"Are you hungry?" He asks.

I look up at him and say, "Yes."

I don't look away and I see the questions in his eyes so I nod my head slightly. He bends his head down and gently kisses my lips and then pulls back up. It felt so natural and part of me wanted it to last, but I'm afraid where it might go. I don't know if I am ready for what happened at his apartment to happen again.

"I'll cook," he says.

"All I have is soup."

"Hmm, soup. No. That doesn't work. We need more sustenance after all the work we did today. Do you want to go out or order in?"

"Can we order in? I have something I need to do and could really use your help."

"Absolutely. Do you mind ordering while I get cleaned up a little bit?"

"Not at all. Does Chinese sound good?"

"Yes. Give me fifteen minutes and I will be all yours."

I sit up so he can get off the sofa, but I grab his wrist before he walks away. He pulls me up to him and leans down for a kiss with much more passion behind it. I pull away when I feel the urge to lift his shirt to touch his skin.

He kisses me on the forehead and turns to go to the spare room to get ready.

I go to my chair and light a cigarette. What am I doing? The more I am around him, the more drawn to him I feel. Then there is this guilt that fights against the way I am feeling about him. The love I still feel for Ian makes me feel guilty, but also the possibility I will lose one of my best friends if things went badly between us rips at me.

I just have to figure out if what I am feeling towards him is enough to chance everything.

"Are you sure you want to do this tonight?" Sam asks.

"I need to."

Sam heads to the garage to get more boxes and I head to the bedroom. It is time for me to go through Ian's things. I don't want to do it with too many people around. Everyone will have an opinion about what I should or shouldn't keep. I need to make those decisions on my own. I wish Jimmy could help with this, but I understand that he can't come back to this house. I will pack up everything I decide not to keep and take the rest to him.

Noie talked to Ian's parents and asked them if they wanted any of his things. They have all of his childhood mementoes and everything else he left there when he moved for college. They don't want anything else.

I walk to the dresser and pull out his sweatshirt. I lift it to my nose and inhale his scent. I don't know if his scent is still there or if I am just imagining it.

Sam walks in the room with three boxes.

"You can sit those there," I say and point to the area next to the bed. "I want to go through his clothes first. Most of it will be donated, but I want Jimmy to have all of his concert tees. Do you mind pulling his clothes from the closet while I go through the dresser?"

"No problem," Sam says and walks to the closet.

I put Ian's sweatshirt back in the drawer and close it. I am not ready to pack it away yet. It's the only piece of his clothing I want to keep.

Sam quietly pulls Ian's clothes off the hangers and places them in the donation box. All of his concert tees are in the bottom dresser drawer. I pull them out and neatly pack them in the box marked for Jimmy. It takes us less than twenty minutes to pack away all of his clothing other than the suits. Sam thinks it is best to keep them on the hangers.

"What do you want to go through next?"

"I want to take his guitars and vinyl to Jimmy. I still need to sort through his nightstand and drawers in the bathroom. His watches are in there. Do you think Jimmy would want those or should I donate them?"

"Don't you want to keep anything?" Sam asks with a look of concern on his face.

"I am keeping his sweatshirt along with every moment I spent with him. His watch, guitar or anything else are just things. They aren't him. Ian is the first really cold morning in the fall. He would go outside in his boxers for about ten minutes. His toes would be freezing when he came back in and he would find me and stick them on me to warm up. Not one of his possessions will make me remember that. The same as nothing will erase the last memory I have of him in that closet."

My eyes fill with tears and I look down. Sam sits next to me on the floor and puts an arm around me. I lean into him and allow him to comfort me as I cry.

"My favorite memory of Ian is the night we all played charades about three years ago," Sam says and laughs. "He was trying to get Hadley, Jett and Laura to guess the movie, *Shawn of the Dead*, but none of them had seen it. They kept guessing names to those mummy movies. I swear I could see the steam coming out of his ears. He made us stop the game to watch that movie. He laughed so loud throughout the movie even though he had seen it probably twenty times. I miss his laugh. It was infectious."

A smile spreads across my face thinking about his laugh. I can almost hear it at the thought.

"He loved funny zombie movies. Have you seen *Life After Beth*?"

"No, what is that?"

"Another funny zombie movie he liked. We should watch it."

"He would want me to watch it right now. We can finish this tomorrow. Let's go put it on."

Sam stands and reaches for my hands to help me up. We go into the living room and put the movie on. I feel so much peace in this moment. I know Ian is smiling down at us right now.

301

I am sitting in my chair looking out at the swaying limbs of the willow tree. I will miss this when I move. Dr. Gillis agreed to come here for our appointment today. I only have a few more days here and even though it is feeling less like home with almost everything packed away, I still want to spend as much time here as I can before the move.

I hear the knock on the door and get up to answer it.

"Good morning, Dr. Gillis."

"Good morning, Nia. You look well today."

"I feel well. I am going to refill my coffee. Do you want a cup?"

"That would be nice."

He settles into the chair next to mine while I get the coffee. I am looking forward to talking to him today. We only meet once every other week now. I thought about stopping the appointments altogether, but I know I could use the support for a little bit longer.

"How are you doing? Are you getting nervous about moving?"

"I am doing pretty well. I am nervous, but excited too. I know I can take all of the memories I love about this house with me. So now, I am ready for what comes next."

"That is good to hear, but I feel like there is more to it. Is there something else you want to talk about?"

"There is. I have a situation I am trying to work through. Something is starting to happen between me and my friend, Sam. Part of me is unable to fully open my heart to him because I keep feeling guilty. I didn't leave Ian, he left me. It is hard to fully understand I am not married to him anymore. How do I get past that?" I ask and put my face into my hands.

"Nia, there is no secret answer to things like this. Everyone responds differently and needs different amounts of time to accept their new reality. You will know when it is right for you."

It's my last night in our house. Every wall is bare and drawer empty. The movers will be here at seven in the morning to move everything to the loft. For now, I am laying in our bed with the only thing I didn't pack, Ian's sweatshirt.

Sleeping tonight seems hopeless. I might as well put on some coffee. I sit up and put his sweatshirt on before getting out of bed. It's a bit too warm for it this time of year, but I just need to feel him close to me tonight.

As I walk through the living room, I am stopped dead in my tracks from the sounds coming from the door. Someone is trying to get in. Anyone trying to get in the house at one a.m. is up to no good. I tip-toe to the kitchen to pick up the house phone and call the police.

"Crap," I whisper when I realize the phone has been packed.

I will have to make it back to my cell phone in the bedroom. As I pass close to the front door, I hear what sounds like a baby crying. I put my eye up to the peephole to see what it going on. I sigh in relief when I realize my intruders are Sarah and Lucas.

"What are you doing?" I ask when I open the door.

"Sorry, did I wake you?" She asks as she walks into the house with Lucas in tow.

I quickly grab his carrier from her and set it down so I can get him out. I unstrap him as his crying gets louder and finally have him against my chest. He quiets as I rock him.

"Are you going to tell me what is going on? Why are you showing up on my door step in the middle of the night? I was on my way to call the police when I heard Lucas cry."

"I'm sorry. I couldn't sleep thinking about you being here for the last night. Lucas never sleeps at night. I decided to come over and check on you, but I couldn't find the right key in the dark." Sarah says and leans back on the couch.

"You didn't wake me. I couldn't sleep either. I was going to put on some coffee when I heard you at the door."

"Coffee sounds amazing. Can I have a cup?"

I hand Lucas back to Sarah and go to the kitchen. The powdery scent of Lucas is lingering in the air. It makes me think about the couple who is buying this house. Their offer wasn't the highest, but they have a boy who is about three and a little girl who is less than a year old. I can imagine them playing in the branches of the willow tree. That is what I always wanted for this house. It gives me joy to know it will be so full of life instead of the tomb it has been over the past sixteen months.

The sound of Lucas crying pulls me from my thoughts and I realize the coffee is ready. I make two cups and go back to join Sarah in the living room.

"Drink the coffee and let me hold him."

She hands him to me and I cradle him against my chest. After a few minutes, he falls back to sleep and I place him in his carrier.

"How are you doing?" Sarah asks and looks down at Ian's sweatshirt.

"I'm okay and I'm glad you came over. I was feeling pretty lonely."

"Things are changing quickly for you, but you have seemed so much better lately. Almost like you have a new lease on life."

"I think I do. I am enjoying the changes. There is one change I want to talk to you about. I don't want you making too much out of it, but I wanted to make sure you heard it from me."

I pause to take a breath. I am thankful I have Sarah here to talk to about this. She is level headed and usually helps to ground me.

"Well, what is it?" She asks.

"It's about Sam and me."

"Is there a 'Sam and you' to talk about?" She asks with a look of shock on her face.

"I don't know yet. There is something. He has made it clear he wants more, but he is giving me time to figure out if I am ready for whatever that might mean."

"Oh Nia, that boy has been in love with you since college. Blake has suspected something was going on because Sam has been so different lately. There has been no more talking about random women. He is also wanting to spend as much time as possible in Louisville. He said you would be the only woman Sam would change everything for."

"What do you think about it? Do you think it is wrong to go there with him?"

"If you are asking me if I think you would be betraying Ian by moving on and finding some happiness, my answer is no. I can't explain what Ian did, but I know Ian loved you. He wouldn't want your life to be lived in pain. If you are asking me if you and Sam are right for each other, I can't answer that. That is something you can only find out by giving it a chance. You have to be sure you are ready. Turning a twelve year friendship into a relationship is more than dating. It is instantly more serious than that. Are you ready for something serious with him?"

It always comes back to me. Sometimes I wish other people could make the decisions for me. If they had a magic ball to tell them all the decisions to make for me that would lead to happiness and steer clear of heartache, would make it even better. I don't know how much more devastation my heart can handle in this lifetime.

45 NIA NOW

The loft is finally ready for me to move everything in. The movers brought all of the furniture and boxes up this morning. Now I am just waiting for Sam to get here. His flight landed almost an hour ago so he should show up any minute.

I run to the bathroom and look in the mirror to make sure I look okay. As I am standing there, I laugh at myself. I think this is the first time in over a year I have worried about how I looked. I have begun to put back on some of the weight and muscle tone I lost and feel much better about how I am filling out my clothes.

When Sam left a couple of weeks ago, I couldn't wait for him to come back. We have been talking on the phone every day and he is constantly sending me funny texts to make me laugh. We haven't talked about what is happening between us. I think we both feel good with the speed of things and want to let it be.

I walk back out to the main area and look around at all the boxes. Luckily Gertie is going to unpack the kitchen tomorrow so I only have to focus on my room and decorative stuff. Russell and Chloe are creeping around the loft trying to figure out where they are. I hope they like it here. I know Russell will miss playing with the willow tree as much as I will miss looking at it.

I go to look out the window and see Sam getting out of a cab. I hurry to click the button to raise the garage door so he can come up the interior stairs. I run downstairs and pull open the door. Sam is standing there with outstretched arms and I jump into them.

He wraps me up and says, "You look happy to be in your new place."

"I am. Come up and see everything."

"Wow, Nia. It looks amazing. I guess this means I am banished to the couch when I visit since you didn't put a guest room in."

"I wouldn't do that to you. I have a cot in the storage room for you. You will like it down there," I say with a laugh.

"I think I prefer the couch," he says and then adds, "I have the wine, so let's open a bottle and get to work unpacking. I want to do something fun this weekend instead of dragging out the work. Plus promises have been made to Sarah and Blake. We are on duty Saturday night."

"I can't wait. Lucas is not as bad as they say. I think they are so sleep deprived it feels like he never stops crying. Sarah brought him over last night. He is so precious. He did wake up quite a bit and cry for a minute, but I enjoyed rocking him back to sleep for her."

I watch him carry a bag to the kitchen and I say, "You do realize, I have no idea where my bottle opener or glasses are."

"That is why I got twist top, single glass bottles," he says as he pulls two from the bag.

"Works for me," I say and grab a bottle.

"Why did Sarah come over last night? I spoke to Blake at ten and she was in bed."

"She couldn't sleep and wanted to check on me. We stayed up most of the night talking. I think we got two hours of sleep before the movers arrived."

"Do you want to take a nap or anything before we get started?" Sam asks.

"No, I want to get everything settled here especially if you have something fun planned for us to do."

"Then where should we start?"

"The bedroom."

We are in the bedroom and I watch Sam carefully put all my clothes in the drawers while I make the bed and I realize he is worth it. I wouldn't trade the eleven years I had with Ian to avoid the pain of losing him and I don't want to trade any happiness I could have with Sam out of fear.

"Sam."

He turns and says, "What's up?"

"Can you come here for a second?"

He finishes folding the shirt in his hands and places it in the drawer before walking over to me. When he gets close, I reach for his hand and pull him closer. He sees what I want in my eyes and leans in to kiss me. As he lays me back on the bed, I look into his eyes and say, "I love you."

46 A NEW BEGINNING

She finally said the words that will change our lives. I look into the eyes of this amazing woman and hate all the pain they have experienced. I vow to myself, right now, to not be the cause of anymore pain in her life, if I can help it.

Our bodies move together and every cell in my body feels like it is on fire. All the time I spent loving her from a far is lighting the passion. All I am thinking is "This woman loves me" as I bring her to the height of pleasure. As she tightens around me, my body releases and pulls her closer.

I move off of her and pull her into my arms. She looks up at me and starts giggling.

"Wow, laughter. Not the response I was hoping for," I say.

"Sorry. I'm not laughing at you. It's just a nervous reaction."

Her reaction worries me. Does she regret what she said? I feel myself griping her tighter, afraid she will pull away and I will never hold her again.

"Are you okay?" I ask.

"Yes, but you can loosen your grip. I'm not going anywhere."

"Good. That's all I needed to hear."

I loosen my arms and gently stroke my finger down her back. Three days and then I will be back in D.C. I wish I could stay here. Walk away from everything in D.C. and never look back. I know I cannot do that, but I can start making my way here.

"I leave in three days," I say.

"I know," she says and snuggles in closer to me. "When will you come back to visit or can I come visit you?"

"What if I came back to stay? How would you feel about that?"

I hold my breath as I wait for her answer. She is softly breathing next to me. The rise and fall of her chest against mine is stirring my desire. I swallow down the need in anticipation of her answer.

"What about your life in D.C.?" She asks.

"It doesn't compare to what my life here could be."

"Are you sure you want to take a chance like that?"

"I'm sure that I want to be close to you. I want to see where things go between us. I know you are scared and I am too. I don't want to replace or compete with who Ian is in your heart. I just want to know there is room for me there too. If there is, then I am sure I want to take that chance."

Her eyes begin to fill with tears and I instinctively kiss her cheek and say, "I'm sorry. I didn't mean to push."

"There is room, Sam. You are already in there."

"Then can we start this with an official date? Let me take you out tonight."

"You look so handsome," Sarah says and pinches my cheek.

"Shouldn't you be helping Nia get ready instead of acting like my mom did before prom?"

"I tried," she says with a frown. "Nia told me she wanted to get ready on her own. She takes all the fun out of these things for me."

I drink the last of my wine. I might need another glass before I leave. Sarah reads my mind.

"Do you want me to fill that up?"

I nod my head yes and she fetches the bottle from the kitchen.

"Blake, where are you?" I yell.

"Keep it down," he says as he appears from the hallway. "I was just checking on Lucas."

"Did the car service confirm they will be there to pick her up at seven?" I ask nervously.

"Yes, they did. You have known this girl for twelve years. You need to calm down a little bit. You are acting like this is a blind date." Blake says and slaps me on the back.

Sarah fills my glass and I take a drink.

"I know you ordered a car service for tonight, but I still don't think you should be drunk when she gets here," Sarah says.

"Do you think I should have picked her up instead of having her come over here first? I just thought it would relax the situation if we all hung out and had a drink first."

"No, I think it is fine. I also think it is sweet you got her a present. She will love having a new diary and I think it will be good for her to start writing in one again. Now you answer a question for me, will it be weird if I take pictures of you two before you leave?"

"Yes, mom," I say to Sarah jokingly.

"Honey, our little boy is becoming a man," Blake says and puts his arm around Sarah.

"Thanks a lot guys. Making fun of me is really helpful."

"Be thankful Hadley didn't make an emergency flight into town for this. She tried to get me to keep her on Facetime the entire evening. She is going to have a lot of fun with this."

I shake my head and thank her for saving me from that for the night.

"On a serious note, I am really happy for you two. I know the situation is weird and something we all have to get used to, but Ian loved you too, Sam. I know he would give you his blessing if he could. I hope you know that." Sarah says.

"I just don't want anyone to think I would have ever wanted it this way. I loved Ian too and I was truly happy for them all these years."

"Brother, get that out of your head. No one is thinking anything like that. I have known how you felt about her, but I also know who you are and you are not some sleazy guy jumping on an opportunity. So just be yourself." Blake says as the doorbell rings.

"Okay, she is here. No jokes," I say looking at them with the most serious face I can muster.

I take a deep breath and walk to the door. I open it and pause to take her in. She is wearing a black pencil skirt with a white and black stripped tank top. My eyes reach her feet and see the heels she is wearing. She takes my breath away. I reach for her hand and guide her inside and see the flash out of the corner of my eye. I don't even care Sarah is taking pictures. This moment deserves a picture.

"I feel so proud right now seeing you in those heels," Sarah says and we all smile.

EPILOGUE FIVE YEARS LATER

Sam and I got married under a willow tree at a local park last year with our three year old daughter, Lyla, holding both of our hands through the vows.

Sam took a job here not long after I moved into the loft and we have continued to live here. We converted the upstairs studio space into a bedroom for Lyla and built out the basement for my studio.

We don't plan on staying here much longer. We found out we are adding another baby to our family and started looking for a house right away. Here I am almost nine months pregnant and we haven't found anything. I think we can make it work here for a few more years, but Sam insists we find our forever home.

I am walking around the bedroom trying to get ready to meet the realtor while Sam drops Lyla off at Sarah and Blake's house. They added a little girl to their family a few months after Lyla was born. Sarah named her Lillie, and I about died. She said it was just a coincidence, but I think it is the first part of her plan to make them like sisters.

I hear the door open and look down at my uncovered belly.

"I hope you don't plan on going like that," Sam says as he walks in and places his hands on my belly. "My boy will get cold."

"Your boy? You keep saying boy, but this baby might just come out a girl."

"I'll be happy either way. You know I love my girls."

"Do we really have to go today? I don't think anything will fit over this belly and I can barely walk without bumping into stuff," I say with a frown.

"I love seeing you bump into stuff," he says and laughs.

"I know. You and Lyla enjoy my loss of grace with this pregnancy a little too much."

Just then Chloe pounces on Sam's foot and I smile. She has become my little protector.

"There is enough room here to add another bedroom. I think we talk about that again instead of finding a house right now," I say.

"Nope. I found a place I think you are going to love. I have searched long and hard for it."

"Okay, I give up. Let me find a shirt that can double as a blanket to put on."

He bends down and places a kiss on my belly and then pulls me into a long kiss. My face heats up. This man has made me so happy.

Thirty minutes later we are pulling up in front of a house painted a smoky blue color with grey and white accents. It is in a neighborhood, but the houses are on very large lots. Large enough you feel almost like you are in a rural area. I would guess this house sits on at least three acres. The front of the house actually has a white picket fence.

"What do you think," Sam asks as we park.

"It is very cute. I like all the land. Lyla would love having all this space to run around."

"I think we would have to get her the dog she wants if we moved here. You can't use the excuse we don't have enough space."

I see the huge smile on his face. I know he is the one who got Lyla on this dog trip. They have been ganging up against me.

"Come on. You haven't seen the best part yet."

He helps me out of the car and I waddle up to the front door where the realtor is waiting for us.

She shows us in and starts naming off all of the features of the house. I hear her say five bedrooms.

I look to Sam and ask, "Five bedrooms, really?"

"And an office," he says like it is a selling point.

"I think it's too much house for us."

"How do you figure? We need three bedrooms right now plus a guest room and office," he says.

"That still leaves an extra room."

"Of course. The next baby will need a room," he says as he wraps me in a hug.

"You are a crazy man. Let me get this one out of my stomach before we start planning another one."

"Follow me, I have something to show you."

Sam leads me to a picture window at the back of the house and a smile spreads across my face. He stands behind me with his arms wrapped around my stomach.

"I told you this house would be perfect," Sam says and kisses my neck.

In the center of the backyard, there is a beautiful willow tree.

"I think we are home."

Posted anonymously online:

Many people think a suicide attempt is a selfish move because the person just does not care about the people left behind. I can tell you that when a person gets to that point, they truly believe their loved ones will be much better off with them gone. This is mental illness, not selfishness. TRUTH: Depression is a terrible disease and seems relentless. A lot of us have been close to that edge, or dealt with family members in a crisis, and some have lost friends and loved ones. Let's look out for each other and stop sweeping mental illness under the rug.

Suicide prevention lifeline: 1-800-273-8255

ABOUT THE AUTHOR

Lina Holloway is a native Texan and proud graduate of Baylor University (sic'em Bears) where she double majored in History and Political Science. She and her husband reside in Houston, Texas along with their two dogs and two cats. In her spare time, she and her husband binge watch *The Walking Dead*, and talk about how they would survive a zombie apocalypse.